ROUGAROU III
THE DEVIL'S CHILD

JUDITH ANN MCDOWELL

This is a work of fiction. Names, characters, places, and incidents are products of the author's imagination or are used fictitiously and are not to be construed as real. Any resemblance to actual events, locations, organizations, or persons, living or dead, is entirely coincidental.

World Castle Publishing, LLC
Pensacola, Florida
Copyright © Judith Ann McDowell 2021
Paperback ISBN: 9781955086240
eBook ISBN: 9781955086257
First Edition World Castle Publishing, LLC, May 20, 2021
http://www.worldcastlepublishing.com
Licensing Notes
Cover: Karen Fuller
Editor: Brianna Robertson

DEDICATION

To my online family: Susie, Deb, Connie, Sibby, Janice, Tenn
Bev, Tash, Jackie, Queen, Bev and Kari, this one's for you.

The devil's child
Will never want
For the one who sees to its needs
Is the one who
Fed off its innocence

CHAPTER ONE

Saint Anthony Parish, Louisiana 2011

The house at the end of the gated lane was completed now. Huge, white, and ornate, its splendor making the previous house standing in that exact spot for over two hundred years before its demise pale in comparison.

After his release from a three-month stay in a mental facility followed by a six-month stay in a flea bag hotel so as not to call attention to his return to the parish, Lawrence Hindel wanted to make it clear to everyone in Saint Anthony Parish, Louisiana he was not going to cower and hide. The growing rage eating at him for the senseless murders of his grandfather and others carrying the Hindel linage could not be contained much longer.

Doctors at the mental hospital told him repeatedly that which cannot be changed must be accepted if the patient hoped to ever regain and strengthen his fragile hold on reality. However, Lawrence had a theory of his own. Wrongs, when perpetrated against the innocent, *could* not be accepted, and they most certainly *would* be avenged.

When he ran out of the house that day to see his beloved grandfather lying fatally injured on the ground at Jack Olivier"'s feet, the gun he had used to do the killing still in his hands, he had immediately fallen to his knees beside the body, only to be jerked to his feet and handcuffed. They did not see a man all but out of his mind with grief. They saw a man who had spent time in a mental hospital, and for the safety of all those present and society, that man had to be taken to jail then transported to a hospital for a mental evaluation. The long months of being watched like an animal only made him more determined than ever to show the silly doctors with their psychiatric gibberish that he was cured and ready for release back into a healthy society.

A reminder to the head of the hospital of the importance of the Hindel name and what it could mean in years ahead finally tipped the scales in his favor.

Now he was back, and his big, beautiful house allowed him to begin anew the life he had been born into as the son of Jonathan Hindel, the pillar of Saint Anthony Parish society, and at long last escape the poverty-ridden sty he had forced himself to live in for the last six months.

The buzzer on the intercom interrupted his thoughts.

"Yes?"

"We have a furniture delivery for you, Mr. Hindel." A man's voice came back to him.

A grin spread across Lawrence's face at the nervous tremor in the man's voice, and he flipped a switch to open the gate.

Dressed in a short-sleeved white shirt, over which he wore a yellow button-up sweater to keep off the early morning chill, black slacks, and black shoes, Lawrence walked out onto the front porch. He watched as four vehicles drove slowly up the cobblestoned driveway. As they drew even with the porch, he waited for them to get out of the vans. He tried to slow down his breathing as the strong scent of fear wafted into the air. Quickly, he shoved both hands in the wide pockets of his bulky sweater, stretching downward on the garment in an attempt to hide the effects the alluring aroma was having on him. "Welcome to my home, gentlemen." He extended an arm in the direction of the door. "If you will follow me, I will show you where everything goes."

A man carrying one end of a long and dark brown leather

couch smiled as he passed Lawrence standing off to the side.

Lawrence caught the smile and immediately returned the man's friendliness.

"This is quite the house you have here, Mr. Hindel. You must be very proud."

Unlike the others who were dressed in jeans, shirts, and warm jackets, the young man who spoke up was dressed in a pair of tight jeans and a sleeveless tank top. Although on a par with Lawrence's height and build, he was not as thin, and his arms showed the muscle tone of someone who lifted heavy objects on a daily basis.

Lawrence found himself becoming intrigued with the young man who looked to be in his early to middle twenties, noting his dark hair and eyes and overall good looks. Lawrence glanced at his own arms, noting their thinness and the light-skinned pallor of someone who spent a lot of time indoors.

The man's Cajun accent flowed with softness pleasing to the ear, and his quick smile drew Lawrence like a magnet.

The man on the other end of the couch smirked.

"Gaston, this isn't the time to try and…make time. Case you don't know, we have a lot of deliveries to make before the sun goes down."

Lawrence put up a hand, silencing the man.

"I will not tolerate rudeness in my home. As I am sure you are well aware, employment in the parish is hard to come by, so if you wish to keep your job, you will apologize."

Lawrence's sting, although difficult to accept, especially from one so much smaller and less manly, garnered but a slight sneer before being acknowledged. "Sorry, Gaston."

Lawrence turned, his light green eyes crinkling, and he winked at the handsome young man who moved his head so as not to be observed by the others and mouthed, "Thank you."

Placement of the furniture went smoothly until they were, at last, finished and ready to leave.

"I don't know `bout you, but I'm ready to get the hell out

of this mausoleum. Whole Goddamn place includin' its owner gives me the creeps." He turned, looking at Gaston as he walked into the room. "Bet you could stay here all night, though, couldn't you, Gaston?" Danny Roberts grinned at the other men as they cleaned up the boxes in readiness to leave.

"I think you should shut your mouth and do your job for once, Roberts. Maybe if you held up your end of the job, it might make it less stressful on the rest of us."

Roberts started forward then stopped as Lawrence walked into the room. "Looks like you are all finished here, so I guess you can be on your way."

The men grabbed up boxes, stuffing smaller ones into larger ones and tidying up the room.

"Gaston, could I speak to you out in the hall, please?"

"Run along, peter nipper," Roberts whispered as Gaston walked past him.

"Why do you always have to give him a hard time, Roberts?" one of the men breathed. "You know he can't help what he is."

The other men shook their heads, walking away.

"It sounds as though you have a very judgmental individual as a workmate. That has to make your job quite difficult."

"He's no joy, that's for sure," Gaston agreed.

"How long have you worked with him?"

"I guess I been with Vern's Furniture about a year now." He followed behind Lawrence as he walked down the circular staircase. "Like you said earlier, jobs are hard to find."

Leading the way across the front room, Lawrence walked into a spacious kitchen. "Have a seat." He directed him to one of the stools pulled up to a wide island in the middle of the floor. "I'll get us both a soda."

"I usually ignore people like Roberts, knowing they're just ill-bred and can't help how they think. But sometimes it gets pretty hard to turn a deaf ear and pretend they don't exist." He reached out, taking the soda, and as their hands touched, they both felt a warm tingle shoot up their arms.

"Does Roberts live around here?" Lawrence's voice was low and personal.

"We're roommates."

Lawrence's dark head whipped around to stare at him. "How in the world did you ever get paired up with the likes of Roberts for a roommate? I would think working with the man would be punishment enough, but to have to go home with him is asking too much of yourself, Gaston."

"I don't have any money." He looked away as a warm flush of shame crept up his throat to his face. "Danny's uncle Vern owns the furniture store, and he lets the two of us have the apartment above the shop real cheap."

"Gaston — I'm sorry, do you mind if I call you by your first name?"

"No, not at all. My last name is Laufett."

"As I was saying, if you were offered another place of employment, would you think about it?" The words shot out of his mouth before he had a chance to think about them.

For a moment, his hopes leapt forward before coming back to the real world where he was forced to live. His dark eyes moved to linger on those of the man watching him. "I can't think about changing jobs right now. In fact, it will be at least another year before I can think about change."

"Why's that?"

"When I first came to the parish from New Orleans, I was dead broke. Vern advanced me enough money to live on and was taking it out of my check each week until I had him paid. Then when Danny suggested we room together above the store, I had to get another advancement to pay my share. We both signed a two-year lease on the place, and if one of us breaks it by moving out or quitting the store, then we have to pay Vern a thousand dollars."

"And, of course, the signed lease and the promise to pay up if you default is safely tucked away at the furniture store."

"No. He keeps all his important papers in his safe at home.

He don't even need the money." Gaston threw up his hands in frustration. "He lives in a nice big house over on Magnolia Street."

"It's mostly those who have money who always want more." Lawrence reached out, placing a comforting hand on Gaston's shoulder.

"Vern Roberts would be…" He clipped his words as he saw Danny walk up to stand just inside the kitchen.

"We're ready to roll, Gaston. We still have deliveries."

Lawrence quickly removed his hand.

"Yeah, I'll be right out. Just talking with Mr. Hindel for a few moments." He got off the stool to hold out his hand to Lawrence, then followed Roberts out of the room.

Danny kept a tight lid on his thoughts, knowing his uncle would not enjoy a complaint from a customer as rich as Lawrence Hindel, so he simply walked around the van to the driver's side to get ready to leave.

Just as Gaston was bending to get in the vehicle, he felt something put into his hand. Without looking at the folded piece of paper, he simply stuck it in the pocket of his jeans to read later.

Alone now, Lawrence walked over to the portable bar and poured himself a glass of white wine, his thoughts uppermost on the young man who had just left his home. For no reason, he felt a smile move across his face, and he allowed it to grow.

Seating himself on the leather sofa, he stretched his legs out straight on the matching ottoman.

In the quiet, he brought forth the face of the man he had just been talking with. How easy it would be to start up a relationship, or at least a fling. His life was so lonely, especially now with all his people no longer on the estate. He had a beautiful house, plenty of money, but there was no one in his life to share it with. In his middle thirties, he was still young.

He smiled, thinking of the young man who had seemed interested in getting to know him better. Then the smile disappeared. He couldn't start up a relationship with someone. Not unless they were like him. Besides, just like everyone else around the parish, he had to have heard the Hindel name. Less than a year had passed since a lot of the children had disappeared, never to be found. It was in all the papers and on the news.

He sipped the wine, but it left him wanting. He knew what he needed, and with the new moon coming the next night, he knew his need would be met. His heart pounded and his mouth hungered for the wild taste of raw flesh.

Getting to his feet, he walked across the floor to the drawer where he kept the new phone book and turning the pages until he came to the names beginning with the letter R, he ran a slow finger down the list until he came to the name Roberts, Vern and the address. His heart soared, and he knew the new moon could not come soon enough.

CHAPTER TWO

Jack Olivier´ looked into the face of his son, and his heart swelled with love and pride. How could someone so small have such an effect? He laughed as he noticed Seelah had dressed their son in the same color jeans and black pullover sweatshirt as he was wearing right down to the same color and brand of tennis shoes. Jack snuggled him close, inhaling his clean soap and water smell, and dropped a gentle kiss atop his dark head.

His life was so blessed. He had a beautiful wife and now a son, not to mention a big, handsome German Shepherd named Lugar to come home to each evening. They had toyed with the idea of moving to the country, but neither really wanted the move. Their nice house, only a block away from his best friend and his family, made the decision to stay put even stronger. His job as a detective paid well, especially in these troubled times of no employment, so he had no reason to worry about his family's health and well-being.

Wrapping his arms around his son in a gentle bear hug, he whispered, "I love you, Donny." The ringing of the telephone had him reaching to answer it. "Hello."

"How's your day off going so far?" Donavan Hays asked him.

"Great. In fact, I was just gonna call and see if you and the rest of the family would like to join Seelah, Donny, Lugar, and me for a big ice cream celebration down at Spiggley's Ice

Cream Parlor? We'll eat out on the patio, so Brandy and Lugar will be welcomed too." He laughed as the big German Shepherd knocked his hand up in the air at hearing his name.

"What's the occasion?"

"Well damn, man, I thought you would have heard by now." Jack's voice filled with surprise. "We're celebratin' the fact that Donavan Matthew Olivier´ has the best daddy in the whole wide world!"

Laughing outright, Donavan replied, "I seem to remember that has been mentioned a time or trillion."

"So are you and the family in?" Jack grinned then added, "Hold on a minute, someone wants to talk to you." He put the phone up to Donny's ear. "Say hi to Uncle Donavan."

"Unca," a small voice squealed into the receiver.

"Hey, Donny!" Donavan's voice came back. "How's my favorite namesake today?"

"He's laughing and sending a sloppy kiss to you." He ran a hand over the receiver. "So find out if you all want to go and call me back. I'll go tell Seelah we're headed for the ice cream parlor."

"No need to ask. We'll be ready to fall in behind when you go by. Just beep the horn."

"We're headed where?" Seelah walked into the room.

"Spiggley's. Donny wants to celebrate having the best daddy in the whole wide world."

"And what about his mommy?" Seelah snuggled her son in her arms. "Isn't she a marvel too?"

"Of course, that's why you're invited."

Seelah laughed and quietly in her mind thanked God for all the blessings He had bestowed on not only her but her son and husband as well. She knew that if not for the grace of God and the Holy Ones, this day may not have been possible. Unwilling to allow dark intrusions to take hold of this moment of happiness, she held their son out to his father.

"If we're going to celebrate, then I better get ready. Males have it so easy. A comb through the hair, a quick wipe with a warm washrag, and they're ready to go. I'll bring the comb and the washrag to you in a moment," she told him, walking off down the hall to the bath.

* * *

Seated in chairs on the far side of the patio in case any of the other customers might be afraid of the two large German Shepherds lying beside the table, Donavan looked around at all the parents and their small children and felt a slight pang of envy. Then he glanced down at Donny as he sat playing with Brandy and Lugar, and he laughed out loud.

"I was feeling a little old there for a moment seeing all the little ones here, but now that we have Master Donavan here to share, I'm back to enjoying my youth again." He smoothed a hand down over the all-but-flat stomach he had acquired from working out at the gym and laughed. "Looks like we're all in a jeans, sweatshirt, and tenny runners wearing mood today."

"Okay, so there's a slight chill in the air, but you know as well as me, it wouldn't be a family outing without Brandy and Lugar along to share in the fun. Yep, just one big happy family!" Jack said, trying not to get emotional. He knew how easily all their lives could have taken a different direction than the ones they were enjoying now.

Seelah reached out, squeezing Jack's hand as it lay on the table, and smiled.

A waitress walked up to the table, her bright, young face taking in the closeness of the two families, and she grinned. "I'm a little surprised to see so many out on the patio today. It's been a little breezy," she said, bending down to ruffle the head of each dog.

"Aren't you two a couple of beauties!" she laughed. "I love Shepherds! I want one so bad, but I live in an apartment, and the super wouldn't hear of it."

"If we couldn't have ours, we would be looking for another place to live," Barbara spoke up.

"I get so upset when you hear people put them down.

Saying they're dangerous. I don't believe that for a moment." She watched the little boy climb onto the back of the female to bounce up and down, and all the dog did was enjoy the attention.

"It isn't the fault of the animal; it's the fault of the owner," Donavan told her. "If an animal is treated right, then that animal will go out of its way to treat those living in its environment with love and loyalty."

With a final pat, she took their orders then left to go and prepare them.

"She seemed like a nice person," Jenny said, glancing around the area. "I wish everyone felt the way she does about German Shepherds. Some people even compare them with wolves. Saying they will turn on people they've been with for years."

"Some people are full of..." Jack broke off his words as Seelah nudged him.

A deep rumbling growl sounded in the throat of both dogs, spurring Jack to pick Donny up in his arms as the dogs lunged to their feet.

"What's the matter with you two?"Jack pushed back his chair.

"They smell danger, Jack," Seelah told him, taking Donny from him in case he needed to have his hands free.

"What kind of danger?" Barbara pulled Jenny's chair over closer.

"That kind of danger," Donavan breathed, getting to his feet to stand beside Jack as two men walked toward their table.

Jack's hand fondled the .38 he had stuffed in the back of his belt. His dark eyes watching each step the men took as they neared their table.

"Oh my God!" Seelah breathed. "It's Lawrence Hindel."

"Yeah, I heard the puke was tuned loose," Donavan said, his eyes never leaving the pair.

As though a hand had been placed in front of him, Lawrence stopped. "My goodness, it's Detective Hays and Jack.

Good day to you," he greeted them in his soft, girlish voice, holding out his hand then dropping it back to his side as neither man acknowledged his greeting. He stepped back as Brandy and Lugar walked forward.

"Those dogs look dangerous," Gaston murmured, backing away only to feel a protective arm slide around his shoulders.

"It's all right, Gaston," Lawrence assured him, removing his arm and looking around. "These two men are detectives, so I am sure they have trained their dogs to listen when they are told it is all right that no danger lurks nearby."

"Depends on which side of the fence you're on, Hindel," Jack said, his eyes never leaving those of the man in front of him.

"Yes…well…I can see you are having a pleasant day with your families, so my friend and I will get out of your way and allow you to continue." He had taken but a few steps when he stopped and, turning, stood looking at Donny. "You have a very handsome boy, Jack." A bitter tone crept into his voice as he recalled what part this child could have played in transporting his father's spirit back to this plane. "You and your wife are to be congratulated."

Without warning, Jack jumped, grabbing Lawrence up by his throat and squeezing. "You evil son of a bitch, you know better than to look at my son."

Quickly, Gaston moved to help Lawrence get loose from the irate man trying to strangle him. "Are you out of your mind? Turn him loose!"

Jack shoved Lawrence away from him.

"I'm all right, Gaston, please, just…I'm all right," he said, gently removing his hands from his shoulders. "This is simply an old feud between the authorities and the Hindels. I was wrong to stop and speak."

"You're damn right you were, you whinin' little slug. Now crawl the hell outta here 'fore I beat the shit outta you in front of your bitch!" Jack's eyes skimmed over Gaston, letting him know he knew what was going on.

"Hey, man, I don't even know you. But I think you're

bein' way too hard on my friend here." Gaston stepped in front of Lawrence.

"You know what?" Jack walked forward, poking a finger in Gaston's chest. "If you're smart, you will simply turn around and walk away from here and this piece of puke you think you need to stand up for."

"Guess I'm not smart then." Gaston swung, catching Jack on the side of his jaw to send him reeling backward.

Coming forward, Jack removed the .38 from the back of his belt, laying it on the table in front of Donavan. "You just made a big mistake, Pimple Dick!"

"Jack, let it go for now," Donavan told him. "We both have family here."

"Let it go? Are you serious? This little prick just threw a punch."

"I know, and if we weren't with our families, I'd tell you to wipe up the floor with him, but this isn't the time or the place to take care of it."

"I'm glad to see you are able to contain your partner, Detective Hays. You may recall the advice my grandfather offered some time back and think about getting Jack some professional help for his temper."

"Get the fuck out of here, Hindel, before I shoot you myself," Donavan warned, uncaring of his language in front of the females present.

At Hays' words, Lawrence placed a hand on Gaston's shoulder. "I think it is time we left, my friend. I have already experienced the unfairness when it comes to the Hindel family."

As the two walked away, Donavan looked around the now empty patio. "One thing you can say for us, we sure know how to empty a room."

* * *

Walking into the house, Lawrence tossed the car keys on the island in the kitchen.

"Let's go in the living room, Gaston, and I'll pour us both

a drink."

"I can't believe the police in the parish are allowed to behave this way. That detective was ready to fight us both."

"The vendetta between the Hindel family and Detectives Donavan Hays and Jack Olivier´ goes back a long way." He finished pouring them both a glass of Brandy. "What you saw earlier is nothing compared to what has happened to my family and to me."

Gaston reached out, taking the drink to set it on the table in front of him.

Instead of sitting on the couch, Lawrence opted to seat himself in the chair beside the hearth. He wanted to keep a clear head, and he knew if he sat near Gaston, he would not be able to do that.

"If you don't mind my asking, what started this feud?"

"My father, Jonathan Hindel, was a very important man in the parish. Any time there was a need for a donation, he was the first one they came to. If something needed to be added, such as a new wing on the hospital, my father was the one who put up the money for the project." Lawrence lifted his glass to his mouth, taking a deep swallow.

"Your father sounds like a very giving man. I'm surprised the parish don't show your family more respect knowing how much donations help in these matters."

"Gaston, how long have you lived in the parish?"

"I was born in New Orleans, and as I told you earlier, I have only come to the parish recently. Why?"

"Have you ever heard the Hindel name?"

"Just when Vern got your order to fill your new house up with furniture from his store. He told us you were very rich and to treat you nice, so if you were ever in need of more furniture, you would come back to his store."

"Hmmm, living in New Orleans, I'm surprised you never heard the name. A lot of our family lived there, and I am pretty sure some still do. Did Vern mention any trouble in the parish attributed to the Hindel name?"

"He did say there were a lot of rumors flyin' around about the Hindel estate. That it was supposed to be haunted and…oh yeah, somethin' about disappearin' kids awhile back." He threw back a large swallow of his drink. "I don't listen to that bullshit. Stories like that are made up to scare the weak-minded."

"The disappearance of the parish children is what started the feud. The detectives and a lot of the people in the parish believe those rumors are true."

"I don't believe them, Lawrence. I would bet my life you could never hurt children."

At the mention of the missing children, Lawrence felt his hunger rise up, and he briefly closed his eyes to better bring the smells and tastes of those unforgettable nights to the forefront of his mind. He could hear again the frightened screams and knew their fear would add to the richness of their blood and give the raw flesh of their bodies that wild taste he knew he could never get enough of no matter how long he stayed on this plane. Also, he knew what these memories would have on his own personal needs and desires. Opening his eyes, he stood and holding out his hand, he waited as Gaston finished his drink, then left the couch to join the man offering to still and satisfy the hot cravings burning within their loins.

Much later, as Gaston slept, Lawrence left their bed to ready himself for what he had been yearning for all day.

Walking across the room, he pulled the cord to open the heavy drapery. The full moon shone down on him, and he reveled in its touch. He turned to make sure Gaston still slept, and seeing his body motionless in the large king-sized bed, he smiled, knowing he had at last found a mate he could stay with.

Walking out into the night, he allowed the shower of moonlight to fall over him, bringing forth the changes his body needed to make him whole.

The ground beneath his feet felt good as he covered the miles between his house and that of the man he was going in search of. He was young, and his body rippled with taut muscles as he moved ahead with little effort.

The house was in his sights now, and his heart picked up speed at the thought of feasting at last on what he craved most. It had been so long. Now he didn't have to wait any longer. He could enjoy himself at his leisure.

Slowing his steps, he moved to the back door and, to his delight, found the door unlocked. He moved into the house and, sniffing the air, followed the smell up the stairs until he came to the room where he detected the smell the strongest. He moved quietly to the bed and was glad to see only one body stretched out in a deep sleep.

He reached out, nudging the body. He didn't move but inhaled a loud snore into the quiet. With one sharp nail protruding from his claw-like hand, he sliced open a bare arm. The man in the bed woke, but before he could draw in breath to scream, his throat was sliced open, allowing a gush of warm, red blood to spurt out into the waiting mouth covering the wound.

At last, he was enjoying the warm, sweet taste he had been craving. He continued to satisfy his thirst until he had his fill, then knew it was time to feast. The lanky body before him would fulfill his need, and the only other thing that would make this night complete was having Gaston there to enjoy the feast with him.

Lawrence knew he must hurry now and get back to the estate, so when the first rays of dawn brought about the rotting change from werewolf back to a normal human man, he could shower and try to get rid of the sickening smell of decomposition clinging to his body.

Lawrence was already in the kitchen, brewing a pot of coffee and taking a pan of homemade cinnamon rolls out of the oven. He remembered how much his grandfather had enjoyed his rolls after a night of debauchery, and he smiled into the silence.

"Good morning," Gaston breathed, coming forward.

"Good morning to you, Gaston. You're looking well-rested," Lawrence told him, pouring him a cup of coffee. "I will have a sweet roll ready for you in just a moment."

As Lawrence set the cup of coffee in front of him on the table, Gaston covered his hand. "Thank you."

Lawrence drew the back of his hand down the side of Gaston's face. "So what do you want to do today? It's Sunday, and we have the entire day free." He moved over to the coffee pot.

"My time is yours. Whatever *you* choose to do, then that is what we will do," he said, reaching into this pocket to withdraw his ringing cell phone.

"Uh-oh, there goes our day."

"It's Danny. What the hell could he want on a Sunday?"

"Don't answer it. His uncle might want you to come in and work in the store," Lawrence said.

"Naw, it has to be something else. We never work on the weekend." He flipped the button on the phone. "What's up, Danny?"

Lawrence acted as though he wasn't listening to the conversation going on around him.

"What the fuck...are you serious...I mean, what the hell happened?"

"What's wrong, Gaston? Is something wrong with Danny?"

Gaston put the phone against his chest. "Danny's uncle Vern was murdered during the night. Someone killed him while he slept."

"Oh my. That's not good," Lawrence offered, getting to his feet. Suddenly, he was very hungry, and he pulled open the door to the fridge to take out bacon and eggs and hash browns and a bottle of orange juice.

"Yeah, Danny, I'll be right there," Gaston told him before turning off the phone.

"I will have us a nice big breakfast ready in no time."

"Uh, nothing for me, Lawrence, thanks. I told Danny I would come home and help him deal with what's going on. He's already called the police."

"Oh, okay. I guess you know best about what you should do." His voice echoed his disappointment, but not wanting to force his opinions on such a new relationship, he pasted a smile on his face and started putting away what he had taken out of the refrigerator. "Who found the uncle?"

"His wife. She spent the night with one of their kids and had just come back early this morning and found him dead in their bed."

"That had to be a shock. Did Danny say how he was killed?" Lawrence kept his face turned away so Gaston would not see the pleasure he was deriving from hearing all about the murder.

"Danny said it looked like a wild dog got into the house somehow and attacked him, although that doesn't make sense. No dog could get into a house with the door shut. Vern had more sense than to leave his door open all night."

"Well, I'm sure the police will find out what happened." He turned as Gaston made ready to leave. "Gaston, I don't mean to make light of such an obviously terrible tragedy, but now that you are no longer bound to the lease Vern had you and Danny sign, what would you say to coming to live here with me? You could help me keep up the house and grounds, and for doing so, you would be paid and have this house to live in." He was afraid to turn around in case his answer turned out to be less than he hoped it would be.

"That's a very nice offer, Lawrence, and I will certainly give it some thought, but right now, I need to concentrate on helping Danny deal with what he has going on."

"Of course, Gaston, of course." He tried to swallow his disappointment. "I was simply trying to lighten your load of not having to worry in case you find yourself out of a job now."

"I doubt that will happen. Danny's Aunt Shirley will make sure the furniture business is not interrupted. She likes money too much to allow that. She keeps the books, so she knows what is what concerning the financial end of the business."

"And she will be sure and uphold the lease you had to

sign too," he murmured almost to himself.

"I can guarantee you she will do that." Gaston grinned. "She knows about every penny that goes out of that place. So if someone killed poor old Vern because of a debt owed, they can forget about it not being upheld. All they would do is find themselves going to court and believe me, she would be the winner when it was all said and done."

"I wouldn't bet on that if I was you, my newly found friend," Lawrence said beneath his breath.

"I'm going to be taking off now, Lawrence," he told him, walking across the floor to give the other man a big hug. "If you're going to be home later, I'll give you a call and let you know what's what. Maybe we can get together later this evening if you would like."

"I would like that very much, Gaston. I don't know about your feelings, however, to me, last night meant something."

"It meant something to me too, Lawrence. For the first time in a long time, I was with someone who made me feel whole again."

Lawrence turned, his face lighting up at Gaston's words. "I feel the same way. So many times, I wished for someone to come into my life who would want to be with just me. Not for my money or what I could give them or do for them, but someone who wanted to be with me."

"It was a lucky day for me the day you walked into Vern's store. A lucky day for him too since his wife is going to need all the money she can get now to lay him to rest in the style he would want."

"I will be waiting for your return," he told him as Gaston walked from the house.

Alone now, Lawrence tried not to let his newfound happiness take him over. There was a chance Gaston would not want to move in with him and be the mate he longed for.

Another thought crept into his mind, interrupting his fantasies of a perfect life. The way Vern was killed would most likely lead Hays and Olivier´ straight to *his* doorstep.

CHAPTER THREE

"I feel bad about showing my ass in public like that." Jack berated himself. "Real great example to set for Jenny. Donny had no idea what was going on, but he still shouldn't have been subjected to such an ugly scene."

"You know, it's funny, but I was just as angry and forthright as you this time involving a confrontation with a Hindel. You know how careful I was before about making sure we acted like professionals. After what happened to Jenny, all bets are off. Now, if they get in my line of fire, they're fair game."

"I know, Donavan. Still, though, now that I have a son, I need to get a tighter hold on my temper. Maybe Hindel has a point on my getting some counselin' for anger management."

"I would like to see one of those know-it-all counselors deal with a Hindel. Hell, they'd be sitting in the corner pulling their pud, sucking their thumb, and playing switch within a week!"

"I don't doubt you're right."

The jingle of his cell phone interrupted their thoughts on the ongoing dispute with the Hindels.

"Now, what the hell's going on?" Donavan breathed, seeing the call was from the station. "Detective Hays."

Jack got to his feet to go see what the rest of the family was up to on the patio. As he pulled open the glass door, he heard

Seelah's laughter.

"Poor Brandy, she looks like me about nine months ago."

"I know what you mean." Barbara grinned. "The last month is the hardest. You feel like you need a tourniquet tied around your belly to keep it up off the floor."

"Oh, come on now, you couldn't have been that big."

"I wasn't, but it felt like any minute everything was going to fall out."

"I think a woman is at her most beautiful when she's pregnant," Jack spoke up, sitting down on the end of the lounge Seelah was relaxing on.

"Is that a hint, Jack Olivier´?" Seelah glanced over at Barbara, whose eyebrows, too, were raised in question.

"No, sweetheart, it wasn't. Well, not at this time it wasn't. Maybe in a few years, we can bring up the subject again."

"Jack," Donavan called out, standing in the doorway, "could I talk to you for a minute inside?"

"Uh-oh, sounds like police business," Barbara said. "I have a feeling we'll be cooking dinner inside instead of on the barbeque."

Her words were no sooner spoken than both men stepped out onto the patio.

"The station just called. We have to go to work, hon." Donavan leaned over, dropping a quick kiss on Barbara's head.

As Jack lifted Seelah to her feet, she felt a jolt of complete evil slam into her mind. Pictures of a man lying in a blood-soaked bed, his dead and horror-filled eyes staring out into the room as police searched for evidence. "I don't believe this is all starting over again." She shook her head and started to reach for her son but dropped her hands, not wanting him to be near the evil assaulting her mind. "I can't go through this again, Jack."

"We're going to find out what happened. Maybe Hindel isn't even involved with this one, sweetheart." Jack tried to calm her fears.

Seelah stood, her eyes staring straight ahead as she looked inward to see what she needed to know. Within moments, the face of Lawrence Hindel floated into her mind.

"Hindel did it. He went over to the man's house and slaughtered him while he slept."

"Come on, Jack, we need to get going. The police are already at the scene."

"Have to go, baby. I would prefer that you stay here with Barb and Jenny. I don't want you and Donny to be by yourselves if it turns out Hindel *is* on another rampage."

"We'll be all right," Barbara spoke up, coming forward. "You two get going before you get in trouble with the brass."

Donavan stopped in the bedroom to get his loaded .44 from the drawer in the nightstand. Usually, he kept the gun out in the open, but since Donny had arrived in their lives, he wanted to keep it out of the way.

"I guess we can stop wondering if Hindel's on the prowl again. Seelah wouldn't see him if he wasn't the one at the heart of this." He pulled his .38 from his belt to double-check the chamber. Seeing a bullet resting in all the slots, although he already knew they would be, he stuffed it back in his belt. "Saying Hindel's at the heart of this one too's probably a poor choice of words. I doubt if the poor bastard he took out has a heart or most of his body left."

"Let's just go see what we find. I'm not doubting Seelah has it straight. I just want to see it for myself." Jack pulled the seatbelt across his chest and clicked it into place.

As Donavan turned the key, he hesitated a moment, turning in the seat. "Why the hell didn't you have the forethought to take out Lawrence at the same time you took out Rafael? Could have saved us having to go to work on our day off."

"You don't think I wish the same damn thing?" Jack flicked Donavan's seat belt. "Don't want you to get a ticket."

Donavan pulled the seatbelt into place and gave Jack a sideways glance.

"When I shot Rafael that day for knockin' the hell out of Christina Crawford, all I could think 'bout is destroyin' the son-of-a-bitch once and for all. His hittin' her was the last thread holdin' my sanity intact. Evil fucker was right up there with Jonathan when it came to needin' to be taken out."

"That was always a regret of mine. I wanted to be the one to end Jonathan. So just in case we get the chance, remember Lawrence is mine."

"Tell you the truth, I wouldn't get my hopes up on that one blossomin' out. At the rate the Hindels are fallin', somebody might just beat you to the punch. Wonder how long he's gonna wait before he turns his little fuck buddy into the same evil piece of piss he is? That is if he hasn't done it already."

They pulled up in front of a three-story brick then waited a moment before getting out of the car. "This is going to bring back some bad memories, Jack, so steel yourself."

"Let's just get on with it. The sooner we know what we're up against, the sooner you can go over and shoot the shit outta Hindel."

The house was beautifully furnished: thick rugs on the floor, fresh flowers in a vase on the dining room table and gracing each end-table in the immaculate living room. Everything in the house bespoke pride and good taste.

"Mrs. Roberts." Donavan walked into the front room. "I'm Detective Donavan Hays. I'm sorry to hear about your husband."

She barely nodded and didn't lift her head.

"I understand you are the one who found him?"

Another nod, but this time her head lifted, and she looked squarely into Donavan's dark brown eyes. "I walked into the bedroom and saw him…lying in bed…his throat…" She fell into a fit of sobbing, and Donavan knew he had lost any chance to get any more information from her at that moment.

"Come on, Jack, we can let Mrs. Roberts try and calm down while we go and see what we're dealing with."

The smell of blood was heavy in the air as they climbed the stairs. That strong metallic smell that couldn't be mistaken.

"Been here, done this," Jack breathed, stepping into the room.

"Hey, Jack, Donavan," one of the deputies spoke upon seeing them enter. "Is this a familiar sight or what?"

"Looks like the cockroach crawled out of his hole again," Jack said, trying not to look at the man on the bed, but knew he had to.

"You sayin' you know who did this killin', Jack?"

"We have a pretty good idea, but of course we won't know for sure `til we do some more investigatin'."

"Has the coroner been called?" Donavan asked, standing near the bed to get a closer look.

The same deputy nodded in the affirmative as he walked around the bed, snapping pictures and trying to still his jumpy nerves.

"I guess we've seen enough." Donavan turned, walking out into the hall. "I guess our next stop is the Hindel Mansion."

As they walked to the front door, Jack chanced a quick glance at the dead man's wife, and what he saw surprised him. No longer the grieving widow, she lifted her head and, looking straight at him…smiled.

Jack stopped, pulling his hand back from the knob. "I'm sorry," he said as he strolled across the hall and into the room, "but maybe I missed somethin' here."

She glanced up at him, the smile still fixed on her lovely face. "When I walked into that room and saw Vern lying there in the bed, his blood splattered all over the room, I thought I was going to start screaming. I didn't know if the killer was still hiding in the house and planned to kill me too if I should get the hell out of the house, or just what I was supposed to do other than get on the phone and dial nine-one-one. Now that you're both here and the deputies are upstairs, I know I'm safe."

Donavan retraced his steps upon hearing the conversation going on in the room. "Are you sure you aren't simply overcome with emotion, Mrs. Roberts?"

Her laughter was shrill and loud, filling a room that upon the circumstances called for whispers.

"Hell no, I'm not overcome with emotion, or grief, or sorrow." She threw up her hands. "What I am filled with is relief. I've been tied to that no life, limp dick son-of-a-bitch for almost forty-five God damn years, but not anymore!"

Both men stood looking at her, their mouths ajar, their eyes wide and staring.

"And before you ask." She pointed a finger straight at them. "As I can already see, you're gonna ask…if there were any problems in our marriage, the answer to your question will be *hell* yes, there were problems! Friction problems! Money problems!" She got to her feet and, walking to the portable bar off in the corner of the room, pulled forth a tall glass, dropped in two ice cubes, then filled up the glass with a goodly amount of brandy. "Would you boys care to join me?"

Both men shook their heads. "No, thank you, Mrs. Roberts. And if you could, I would prefer that you try and keep a clear head until we're ready to leave in case we need to ask you some more questions."

Deliberately, she lifted the glass to her mouth and, watching Donavan over the rim, took a long swallow of the liquor. "Let's see, what could you possibly ask me that I haven't already told you? Oh yes." She drank, laughed. "Do I have a lover? And if I do, is he the reason I killed my husband in such an obviously rage-killing way?"

"Did you?" Jack moved closer to her.

She walked back across the room to drop unceremoniously into her chair, bouncing and spilling her drink down the front of her top. "If I was going to get rid of my husband after all these years of abuse, bad sex, and shame for filthy, nonexistent hygiene and unbelievable boredom" — she plopped her glass down on the end table by her chair — "I would have simply taken my trusty .38 in my hand and shot his fuckin' brains out!"

"You forgot to mention if you have a lover," Jack breathed with a roguish wink.

"I did, didn't I?" She rose to her feet a little unsteadily. As she reached over on the end table to retrieve her empty glass, she swayed then giggled as Jack caught her and, with an arm around her trim waist, walked with her across the room to the bar.

"If I remember right, it was two ice cubes and a glass filled with brandy."

She snickered. "If you ever get fired from your job as a detective, you can come here, and I'll hire you as my bartender." She added on a flirtatious giggle. "Damn, I bet you'd be good at about anything you tackled."

"I've enjoyed hearin' that complement a time or two." He walked her back to the chair, and as she plopped herself down on the soft leather, totally unmindful of the pink satin robe covering a matching nitey, she reached for her drink.

"Mrs. Roberts, I see you're dressed for bed. Did you get changed before or after you found your husband dead?"

"We don't share the same room. I got in late, showered, and after dressing in this robe and nitey," — she flipped open her robe — "I went to bed. I didn't find Vern until late this morning when I glanced in his room on my way downstairs."

"You still haven't answered the all-invasive question yet." Jack gave her a playful slap on the arm. "Do you have a lover?"

"Yes, I have a lover. I've had a lover for the past six years now. And I'm not ashamed of it." Her playfulness disappeared, and she was all seriousness again.

"Do you have any idea who might have wanted to kill your husband…Mrs.…what is your first name? I feel silly calling you Mrs. when you can't be much more than my age," Jack teased.

"My name is Shirley," she said, her voice little more than a whisper. "And to answer your question, I don't have any idea who would want to kill Vern. At least not in the manner he was killed."

"Do you know if he has ever cheated anyone? Was he a gambler who needed money?" Donavan took a seat in the chair closest to hers.

"Vern had a terrible temper, but he never cheated anyone as far as I know. And no, he wasn't a gambler. As far as his needing money, up until yesterday, he was making the bills all right and the mortgage on this house."

"Then what happened?" Jack spoke up.

"He had a windfall. A man called the store and gave him an order that had Vern dancing in the aisles. Didn't even come to the store to pick out what he wanted, just ordered an entire house full of furniture sight unseen."

"That had to have brought in a pretty penny."

"It sure did. Vern only carries top of the line furniture. We're talking close to forty thousand in furniture. Fridge, stove, not to mention a washer and dryer. I mean, the works. He stopped by the store and gave Vern a check for the entire amount."

"I hope you checked his bank to see if he was good for the money before all that was delivered." Jack grinned.

"Didn't need to. When he saw the name on the check, he knew the man was good for the money."

"Let me guess." Donavan felt his stomach start to churn. "The man's name was Lawrence Hindel. Am I right?"

"That's right, and I'm here to tell you right now, if he *ever* wants to order any more stuff from the store, all he has to do is ring my phone and tell me what he wants because thanks to old Vern leaving this earth, it all belongs to little miss Shirley Roberts now!"

"Thank you, Shirley, you've been very helpful," Donavan told her, getting to his feet and holding out his hand.

With a playful wink, Jack walked with Donavan to the door.

"I think we have enough to at least go and ask a few questions of our old friend Lawrence Hindel," Donavan said.

"I'm right behind you, partner."

* * *

Driving up the long lane leading to a house set back and secured by a wrought iron gate, both men felt like it was nine months ago all over again.

"I'll tell you something right now, Donavan, if Hindel starts runnin' his mouth or threatens us or our families in any way, I'm just gonna shoot the evil fucker and get it over with."

"I hear you, but you have to be realistic in this. We both have families, and Lawrence Hindel is not worth our taking a chance on losing them." Donavan stopped the Jeep outside the gate.

"Do you want to do the honors, or do you want me to?"

"Go ahead. I remember how much you always enjoyed it."

They both got out of the Jeep to walk over to the intercom.

"Doesn't look like it sustained any damage from the blast."

"I don't think the blast reached this far." He laughed, recalling how the dynamite destroyed the entire mansion. "Simms only wanted to take out the mansion. As you know, Quigley's cottage was already a pile of ashes mixed with a bunch of well-done werewolves before everything was set up to destroy the mansion."

"Damn! That had to be a sight to see! I still wish I could have been here to see the mansion blow. All those years we would come here to speak to those evil assholes!"

"You already had your hands full with Seelah giving birth to Donny. You were exactly where you needed to be, my friend."

Jack walked up to the intercom and pressed the button.

"Can I help you?" Hindel's voice came back to them.

"Yeah, we need to come in and talk with you, Hindel. And this time, you don't even need to ask which Hindel because thanks to Donavon and me, you're the only Hindel left."

"Don't antagonize the little prick, Jack. I want to ask him some questions."

To their surprise, the gates swung open, giving them access to the long driveway leading to the house.

"Would you get a load of this fuckin' place? It's even bigger and gaudier than the old one," Jack breathed.

"He's flaunting his wealth, Jack. He wants to make sure everyone in the parish knows he's back and he's not going to hide."

"He might want to flaunt his wealth, but he's already made a big mistake by killing Roberts. And we do know Hindel's the killer in this one too."

As Donavan braked in front of the large front porch with big stone pillars gracing each side, Lawrence walked outside to greet them. He wasn't alone. His newfound lover was by his side.

"I swear this is like déjà-vu all over again, Lawrence." Jack sauntered over to the porch. "First it was your daddy, Jonathan, we would come to see and question 'bout murders. Then it was grandpa's turn to be questioned 'bout murders. Now here we are again, and this time it's you we're here to question 'bout a murder. Is this a fuckin' coincidence or what?"

Lawrence could feel his hands begin to shake, and he couldn't make himself look over at Gaston to see how he was handling Jack's words about his family. Swallowing deeply, he tried to calm himself, knowing he had to keep a clear head if he was going to convince Gaston what the detective was saying was all a lie.

"Are you going to invite us in so we can talk about this in comfort, or do we sit ourselves on this fine porch of yours?" Donavan breathed.

"Who is it Lawrence is supposed to have killed, detective?"

"Not that it's any of your business, but the man we're talking about was named Vern Roberts," Jack told him.

"Vern Roberts is very much my business, detective. He was my boss, and his nephew is my roommate." The look he gave Jack dared him to disrespect him.

Donavan walked forward. "If that's so, then I think we should be getting you down to the station for questioning."

"There's no need for that, Detective Hays. We can do our talking inside," Lawrence spoke up.

Following behind Donavan, Jack couldn't help but admire the beautiful craftsmanship and pride the architects had invested in when building the house. "Easy to see you spared no expense in getting a new one put up, Lawrence." Jack looked at him, noting the pure look of hatred staring back at him. "You hate me, don't you?" Jack didn't bother to stop the laugh spilling forth.

"There are no words to describe the hatred I feel for the two of you. You have all but destroyed my world."

"We did our damndest," Donavan informed him. "But, like the resilient little piss ant you are, you just keep bouncing back."

"You said you wanted to ask me some questions, Detective Hays. I suggest we get to it," Gaston spoke up, earning him a touching smile from Lawrence.

"Sounds like you got a real he-man at *your* disposal, Hindel. That has to brighten your days since you sure as hell can't defend yourself in a rough situation," Jack scoffed, doing his best to bring out the anger to a more potent degree and bring on an attack.

To the surprise of all three men standing just inside the front room, Gaston stepped up and, putting his arm around Lawrence's thin shoulders, pulled him close. "He don't need to take up for himself, detective. He has me to do that for him."

"Before I puke on the new carpet, let's go have a seat and get to the reason why we're here," Donavan said, walking across the floor to seat himself in a chair beside an elaborately decorated hearth.

Keeping a protective hand on the small of Lawrence's back, Gaston ushered Lawrence forward to take a seat beside him on the couch. Without a word, he placed his arm around Lawrence's shoulders.

"We're ready to begin when you are, detectives."

Jack remained standing. "This ain't gonna work, Donavan. Either we go to the station and question these two ass-stuffers one at a time, or we split them up here." Jack made no bones about his unease in being in the company of two men being so obvious about their attraction to one another.

"Or, we can just run a background check on the two and see what comes up." Donavan watched to see what effect this idea would have on Gaston.

"All right." He quickly removed his arm from around Lawrence's shoulder. "We can do the questionin' here. There's no need to make everyone uncomfortable."

"Glad to see you finally see it my way," Jack murmured.

"Gaston, can you tell me where you were last night and most of today?" Donavan took out a pad and pen.

"I was right here."

Donavan glanced over at Lawrence, who nodded in agreement.

"Gaston spent the entire evening and night with me." Lawrence smiled over at Gaston.

"Oh, Christ," Jack breathed, dropping down in a nearby chair.

"Lawrence, where were you last night?"

"We just told you, Detective Hays, Gaston and I were together all yesterday and all last night."

"Did you get any sleep during the night?" Jack snickered.

Before Lawrence could respond, Gaston waded into the conversation. "Any time a body's totally drained by a rigorous workout, the only thing you want to do is take a hot shower to unkink the muscles, then fall into a relaxing sleep. And that's what we both did."

"Then since you say you were both exhausted from the aftereffects of working the muscle..." — Donavan tried not to snicker — "you can't alibi each other. If you were that bombed-out, one of you could have left without the other one knowing about it."

"Fuck, man!" Gaston jumped up off the couch. "Are you this addlebrained that you have to invent shit so you can try and pin somethin' on someone who didn't do nothin'? No fuckin' wonder the Hindel name has such a bad rep in this parish!"

"You need to simmer down there, Skippy," Jack told him, getting to his feet. "In the first place, since you ain't from around here, you probably ain't heard what all the Hindels have been involved with in this parish, so let me ask you something, do you believe in rougarous, Gaston?"

* * *

Seelah tried to calm herself by staying close to Barbara and Jenny and by holding Donny close to her even though he wiggled, wanting to get down and play with his best playmates Brandy and Lugar.

"Aunt Seelah, if you want, I can take Donny and Brandy and Lugar out on the patio so they can get some fresh air," Jenny offered as she watched Donny squirm, trying to get loose.

"Oh no, Jenny, he's fine here on my lap," Seelah told her.

"Seelah," Barbara spoke up, "you need to stop worrying. Donny is fine. We are all fine. Just because Lawrence Hindel is back in the parish doesn't mean the whole fiasco is going to start up again."

Seelah turned away, not wanting to voice what she had seen earlier. Being psychic had its drawbacks. When the face of Lawrence Hindel had crept into her mind, she simply waited to see what else the other side was trying to show her. She didn't have to wait long before the grotesque body of a werewolf leaning over a man in a bed that was covered with blood slammed into her mind. She covered her mouth, trying to stifle the hot tears threatening to fall.

Donny put a hand on each side of his mother's face and, opening his mouth, wide gave her a wet kiss on her cheek followed by a gentle pat.

"Donny knows you're upset, Aunt Seelah," Jenny said.

"I can't help it." She handed the little boy over to Jenny and tried to still her words until they had already closed the patio door. "It's all starting up again, Barb. I just don't know if I can go through it all again."

Barbara felt an uncomfortable knot beginning to form in the pit of her stomach. "What is starting up again?"

"Lawrence Hindel's evil. He is a werewolf, and he killed a man in the night. That is why Jack and Donavan left earlier. They are investigating the murder, and right this minute, they are at the Hindel mansion talking to Lawrence Hindel and another man."

"Oh good God no," she cried, rubbing a brisk hand over her forehead. "I swear I wish someone would just shoot that son-of-a-bitch and put him out of the parish's misery."

"I thought when we were rid of Jonathan and Rafael that our worries were over, but now that I see Lawrence was also made into a monster, the entire mess is starting all over again."

"You would think that God in his tender mercy would come and destroy each and every Hindel on this earth. Because if they have the last name of Hindel, then they are evil." Barbara got up from the couch to begin pacing the floor, her eyes going to the patio to check on Jenny and Donny.

"When Jonathan tried to return to this earth by replacing Donny's soul with his, I thought I was going to go out of my mind. I can't stand having to worry that the same thing might happen all over again."

"You know the other side won't let that happen. They stopped it the last time, and they will stop it again."

"Yes, they stopped it, and for that, I am eternally grateful, but in the meantime, we have to be alert every moment of the day and night in case evil comes crawling upon us again."

"Seelah." She walked over to sit down beside her and, putting a reassuring arm around her shoulders, leaned close. "In no way do I want to tell you how to raise your son, but one thing I do know and that is we can't smother our children by keeping too tight a rein on them. When Jenny was almost killed by Roland Lybbert, who turned out to really be another member of the Hindel family, I thought I would never be able to allow her out of my sight. But as the days passed, I was able to let up a little, and now, although I still keep a close eye on her, I don't let her know it."

"If you think I'm bad, you should see how Jack watches Donny's every move. This is why I am so afraid of this pressure starting up again. It is unhealthy for all of us."

"We aren't alone in this, though. You have your psychic powers that allow you to tune into all of us, and we have Brandy and Lugar to alert us of any danger here in the real world. I would say we're pretty well covered."

To her surprise, Seelah laughed and then hopped to her feet. "Let's go make us something to soothe our frazzled nerves, something all chocolate."

* * *

"Rougarous? You're askin' me if I believe in fuckin' werewolves? Man," — he turned, laughing, to look at Lawrence — "is this the kinda shit you been puttin' up with here?"

Lawrence simply looked away.

"Wait a minute, why are you lookin' away? These two are pullin' shit out of fairy tales, and you're lettin' them get away with it?"

"Kinda boggles the mind, wouldn't you agree?" Jack said.

"Lawrence, I'm waitin' to hear what you have to say about this." Gaston knelt down in front of him. "I don't like to think that the man I just spent a heavenly night with could believe in somethin' that goes around killin' people on every full moon."

"Did you happen to notice the beautiful full moon last night, Donavan? It was a sight to behold. Too bad you were so drained, Gaston, it really was worth seein'," Jack asked.

"Why are you just sittin' here ignorin' me?" Gaston's voice took on a desperate plea.

"If you would like to take a seat, I will be glad to explain why Lawrence is keeping his silence," Donavan said in a calm voice.

Without warning, Lawrence leapt to his feet. "Gaston doesn't need you to explain anything to him, Detective Hays. We have both answered your questions about where we were last night. We were together in my bed! All night! When we woke this morning, we were still together in my bed. No one left the other during the night to go out and prowl on the full moon you are so fucking anxious to talk about! Now, if you will both be so kind as to leave my house, I will appreciate it!"

"I think we're bein' asked to vacate the premises, partner,"

Jack chuckled, getting to his feet.

"I think you're right, Detective Olivier´," Donavan said, lurching to his feet. "I guess I will join you in leaving."

"Speakin' of leavin', don't either of you leave town. We're not through investigatin' a murder."

"I don't think you need to worry, detective." Gaston swung an arm around Lawrence to pull him against his hip. "I would say we're both quite content to stay right where we are."

Back in the Jeep, both men sat still, trying to wrap their minds around what they had just witnessed.

"Remember some time back when we were trying to figure out why a young black girl would be walking alone on the Hindel Estate, and you threw out the theory that she was a hooker there to service Quigly?" Donavan said.

"I do, and you responded with, if Quigly ordered up a piece of ass, it sure wouldn't be a split tail. Right?"

"Right. I think Seelah must be rubbin' off on me because to me, that was a given."

"Now Quigly was a messed up individual," Donavan said. "I bet he's still roasting in hell."

"Yeah, thanks to me. Son-of-a-bitch tried to run me through with that pig sticker he carried. Little bastard wound up feedin' the gators that night after I slit his throat and sent him to the bottom of the swamp."

"I thought for sure all this was over and done with. Now it looks like we're going to have to contend with one more before we can call it good."

"Good thing, though?" Jack turned in his seat. "With Lawrence bein' a tail-blazer, we won't have to worry 'bout him renewin' the Hindel bloodline."

CHAPTER FOUR

"You've suffered a lot of pain, Lawrence. Pain that you didn't deserve."

Lawrence shrugged his hand from his shoulder and walked a few steps away to put some much needed distance between them.

Confused, Gaston simply stood where he was, staring at Lawrence's stiff back. "Did I say something to upset you?" The hurt in his voice was palpable.

Without saying anything, Lawrence walked to the bar and, lifting two glasses into the air, waited for Gaston to accept or decline. At his slight nod, Lawrence filled the glasses.

"Do you always need a drink before you can do what you want? Last night you needed a drink to relax before you could let yourself go with me, and now it's obvious you have something important to talk with me about."

Lawrence threw the drink down his throat and reached for the decanter of Brandy, only to have his hand stilled. "You don't need to drink your courage, Lawrence. Just say what you want to say. I'm sure whatever it is you have to say to me, I've heard it before." His voice was filled with pain and defeat.

Lawrence set the decanter down on the bar and squeezed Gaston's hand. "Let's go sit down." He indicated a chair across from him, not allowing the pain on Gaston's face to deter where he wanted him to sit. "The detectives brought up a subject that sooner or later is going to have a strong bearing on our relationship. If we still have a relationship after I finish telling you what you need to know."

Gaston's hand trembled slightly as he lifted the glass to his lips. This time, he didn't interrupt when Lawrence was ready to talk.

"The Hindel name is old and very revered. If anyone has the name, you can be sure they are in the Hindel lineage."

"You must be very proud of such a heritage."

Lawrence simply nodded. "When my father Jonathan was still alive, no one dared to disrespect the Hindel name. Not only because of the vast wealth our family amassed throughout the years, but also for another reason." Lawrence could feel the hot tears dripping down his face, and he did nothing to stop them.

"Please continue, Lawrence. I'm here, and I won't let anything hurt you. Not even you," Gaston promised, a stronger tone in his voice now."

"You will be leaving here after I tell you what I must, and it breaks my heart to know this," he cried, trying to gain control over his emotions.

As Gaston got to his feet, Lawrence held up a hand. "Please don't come near me until I have said what I need to, or I will never be able to get it all out. And, yes, Gaston, you deserve to hear it all."

"Then please continue." He walked across the floor to the portable bar. "I've changed my mind. I think we both need a refill. Not for courage." He looked over at Lawrence. "But to steady our nerves."

It was quiet in the big house as Lawrence and Gaston sat nursing their drinks. The chiming of the big clock in the corner announced the dinner hour, and still, they remained sitting quietly, each in his own chair.

"Some years ago when my father, Jonathan Hindel, was still a young man and after his mother and father had parted, he left England to come to New Orleans to stay in the home of his father, Rafael. At that time in New Orleans, Grandfather carried the same power and respect my father was to earn in this parish." His hand, resting on the arm of the chair, clenched into a hard fist before relaxing once more.

"Together, they ruled the city, and to this day, you can still mention the name of Hindel, and almost everyone will have heard it." He chanced a quick glance at Gaston and was glad to see a reassuring smile. He continued with what he had to share, anxious to get it all out and know for sure if what they had shared last night would be repeated.

"Beautiful homes, beautiful women, all that money could buy, and believe me, money can buy a lot, Gaston. However, as with anything else, there was a price to pay for all this power and riches."

"And now we've arrived at the part you don't want to share with me," Gaston whispered, his voice tender and caring.

"It would seem so. I am going to tell you something that will make you walk out that door and never return, but you have to know."

"What are you going to tell me that all those spooky stories I heard about you and your family are true?" Gaston laughed slightly, wanting to ease Lawrence's fears of him walking away.

"That's part of it," he whispered, "but the most important thing you need to know is that I didn't remain by your side all night last night."

Gaston's head snapped up. "What are you sayin', Lawrence? That you have someone besides me that you take to your bed?"

For the first time since he sat down to share his darkest secrets, Lawrence laughed, and he didn't stop until he got to his feet. "If only it were that simple, my newfound friend. If only it were that simple."

"Lawrence, for Christ's sake, will you stop draggin' this out and come to the point?"

Knowing the time had come to risk losing everything he

now wanted with the man watching him from across the room, he took a deep breath and continued with what he knew must be said.

"The one thing the Hindels have always had to have in their lives is money and power. And they achieved both but at a high price."

"And what was the price they had to pay to achieve their goal?"

"The price they paid was the giving of their souls."

"I don't understand your words, Lawrence. How can someone pay for something with their soul? And who did they pay their soul to?"

"The dark side of this plane, Gaston. They traded their souls to the master himself, and for this, they were given a life that anyone would yearn for."

Gaston simply sat looking at him, unable to speak for fear he might start screaming and bolt from the house.

"When a person gives their soul to the dark side, they achieve powers that many only dream of. Riches, a strong and healthier body that can live on this plane for hundreds of years without having to die and come back to begin life all over."

"And for all this giving, what did you have to become in return?"

"I became a creature of the night, Gaston. I became a rougarou, as did all of my family."

CHAPTER FIVE

Donavan looked over at Jack. "I don't know about you, but I don't think Lawrence's new fuck-buddy has the slightest inkling about what's going on with him."

"I have to agree. But he will," Jack chuckled. "I mean, you can't keep a secret like that for very long. Someone's bound to notice how much you enjoy hikin' your leg and pissin' on people at every full moon."

"So, since we already know about Lawrence being a werewolf slash rougarou, I think we can safely surmise he is the one we are after for this murder of Vern Roberts."

"What I want to know is why did Lawrence go after a man he just bought a houseful of furniture from? I'd say it has more to do with the victim's nephew bein' Gaston's roommate."

"Maybe Gaston suggested a threesome, and Lawrence got all bent out of shape and went after Roberts," Donavan said, laughing at his own suggestion.

Jack sat looking over at him. "Have you noticed how much I'm rubbin' off on you? Hell, a few months ago, you woulda been bitchin' and spittin' if I'd made a remark like that. Now you're makin' them yourself."

"A few months ago, I was a different man, Jack. Stressed to the max with no letup until I had a fucking heart attack that damn near killed me. I'm not going to play that game again. I am going to enjoy life if it kills me, even if that life entails the presence of Hindels. And if I should luck out and put another one of those bastards in a hole, that will just make my day all the brighter."

"Just so you know, I like the new you a lot better. It's almost like havin' two of me."

"I can guarantee you one damn thing; soon as we get rid of this last pain in our ass, I'll be laughing a lot more."

"Guess we can't put off going to the autopsy to check out the latest of Hindel's victims."

"All part of the job, Jack," Donavan told him, turning onto the street that would take them to the hospital.

* * *

"Lawrence," —he stood up—"since I don't find anything even halfway amusing here, I think you are on the brink of going into hysterics." Gaston cast a concerned look his way.

"Don't let it worry you, Gaston." Lawrence breathed deeply against the wild and out of control laughter that seemed to erupt out of nowhere. "I guess I just find it ironic that when I find someone I want to be with, something always comes along to ruin it for me."

"You were going to tell me where you went while I was sleepin'." Gaston refused to let Lawrence veer from the subject at hand.

At last, he was able to get back his control and quiet the maniacal frenzy that had overpowered him. "I went to visit Vern Roberts," Lawrence told him, watching him to get his reaction.

Gaston drew in his breath. "Why the hell would you do that? You don't even know the man."

"No, but you did. I wanted to get rid of the man who holds a debt on you."

"Did you offer to pay him my part of the lease?" The tight fist squeezing his gut was starting to relax a little knowing there could be a plausible explanation for the late-night visit.

"He wasn't in a talking mood, Gaston. In fact, he didn't even wake up until…right at the end."

"What the fuck...are you sayin'...you're the one who killed Vern Roberts?" The fist tightened its hold as Gaston backed away from the man watching him.

"Yes, Gaston, I'm saying I killed Vern Roberts," Lawrence told him. "Not only did I kill him, but I drank his blood and then took my time feasting on his body."

"Ah, for Christ's sake, man...you gotta be nuts." Gaston stumbled over the ottoman, and before he could get to his feet, Lawrence was standing over him.

"You said you wanted to be with me, Gaston. Are you saying now that you've changed your mind?"

Kicking out, Gaston struck Lawrence in the stomach, making him lose his balance. Seeing his chance to escape, he jumped to his feet to run out of the house.

Within moments, Lawrence was after him. Without warning, extreme pain moved up his body, stopping his steps in midstride.

Chancing a quick glance behind him, Gaston froze, staring at what his mind told him could not be happening.

Lawrence reared up on his hind legs, a high-pitched scream shattering the night's silence as his body continued to change.

As though his legs had lost all feeling, Gaston simply stood where he was, his mind splintering off in a hundred different directions as the thing that moments earlier had been Lawrence Hindel moved closer.

Lawrence reached out and, with one swift jerk, yanked Gaston into his arms and, without stopping, sank his teeth into his neck. As the warm blood filled his mouth, he forced himself to stop. It was not his intention to kill Gaston but to make him one with him. Shoving him away, he ran off into the swamp in search of a warm body to appease his hunger.

Gaston staggered to his feet, and as much as he disliked going back inside the house, he knew he had to stop the blood running down his neck. Grabbing a washrag from the bathroom, he wet the rag to hold it tightly against the wound. When he was sure the bleeding had stopped, he poured peroxide over the wound then bandaged it.

Going to the phone, he punched in numbers to summon help, then immediately slammed down the receiver. Who was he going to call? Danny? And tell him what, that his lover is the one who killed his dad? Not likely. The police and let them know that what they suspected about Lawrence Hindel was true? That he was the one who'd killed Vern Roberts?

He needed a drink badly. Going to the bar, he filled a glass from the first bottle he pulled forth. What the hell was he going to do? Then a thought slammed into his mind that almost stopped his heart in his chest. Lawrence had bitten him. He was a fuckin' werewolf, and he had bitten him. Didn't the legend say if a person was bitten by a werewolf, they would become a werewolf?

"What the fuck am I goin' to do?" He stood, slapping a hand on the bar, trying to collect his thoughts. "I can't call anyone. I can't stay here'n be attacked again…I am just fucked."

A noise from outside made him whirl around. "Oh fuck almighty! He's back." Without stopping to think, he took off running up the stairs to the bedroom. He had to get to the gun he had left lying on the bed stand.

The cold steel in his hands made him feel some better, but the sound of the front door being slammed back against the wall brought the terror back.

With the gun as his protector, he walked silently out into the hall to peer over the banister. All was quiet. Then, as he stood there, a shadow moved into the room. The shadow outlined the figure of a large wolf that walked upright.

As he watched, the huge head lifted, sniffing the air, then turned toward the upstairs hall to look straight at him.

Gaston tried to keep his senses alert, but the blood pounding in his ears was making it difficult to hear. He could see the monster moving toward the stairs now, and he started to shake so badly he was afraid he might drop his gun.

When he turned, he could see the rougarou standing only

inches from him. He tried to cock the gun, but his hands were shaking too badly to get it done.

Without warning, the gun was knocked from his hand, and before he could make a move to retrieve it, he felt himself being grabbed by his shoulders.

Lawrence looked at him. And knowing he did not wish harm to Gaston, his grip on the man's shoulders became gentle as he waited for Gaston to look at him.

Gaston could smell the foul odor of wet hair and blood, and he tried not to retch, but he couldn't help himself. He began to struggle until, at last, he felt the grip on his shoulders loosen then withdraw their hold all together.

Gaston took off running down the hall to the bathroom just in time to empty out the contents of his stomach. Turning the spigot on full blast, he doused his face with warm water and rinsed his mouth. Knowing he had no choice, he flushed the commode then walked out of the bathroom and up the hall. He could see the monster sitting on the landing waiting for him.

"If you're gonna finish killin' me, then do it. I can't run no more. I'm too tired, too scared, and too fuckin' sick." Unable to remain standing, he slumped to the floor. "Lawrence, I don't know where we go from here, but I guess since you bit me, before long, I'm gonna look just like you. So please do me a favor and kill me now `cause I can't go through life lookin' like you every full moon and drinkin' other people's blood." He knew he was rambling, but he couldn't seem to stop himself.

* * *

Walking into the morgue of Parish General, both men felt their stomachs begin to churn.

"I swear to Christ," breathed a man with a full head of thick, white hair. He was standing beside a stainless steel table with a body outlined beneath a sheet. "Every time I get a body brought in that looks like it's been thrown to the dogs, I know I can expect to see your ugly mugs."

"Hey, Perkins, let's go easy on the ugly if you don't mind,"

Donavan laughed, coming forward.

"Jack." Perkins nodded.

"Ain't he a pretty sight?" Jack flung out a hand in the direction of the body on the table.

"Jack, I've been workin' here for a lotta years, and one thing I can tell you is I never get used to working on a mangled body. And this one is one of the worst I've ever seen."

"We got a quick glance at this one while he was still at the crime scene. His throat had been pretty well ripped open, but I didn't think it was all that bad." Donavan walked over closer as Perkins whipped off the sheet.

"One thing that I'm glad to see is at least the victims are getting older. Before, they were young kids or in the case of that one hooker, a young woman." Jack kept his eyes turned away from the body.

"Yeah, that one came from The Gentlemen's Elite Club. She was beat to shit, but this," — he cleared his throat — "this takes the prize." He pointed to the other side of the corpse.

"Jesus Christ, half his body's been torn away," Jack whispered, trying not to throw up. Quickly, he covered his mouth and stepped back away from the table.

"If you're gonna puke, go in the bathroom back there." He nodded behind him. "I got enough to deal with without having to clean up after you," Perkins told him.

Donavan motioned for Jack to stay back.

"Not to add to your discomfort, but his body wasn't torn away. Something or someone had themselves a little feast."

"Are you serious?" Donavan walked around the table to get a better look. "Holy shit, you're right." Donavan motioned Jack forward. "Come here and look at this, Jack. The whole damn side of his body is gone."

"I'll take your word for it, Donavan." Jack headed for the swinging doors of the morgue, knowing if he didn't get some fresh air and fast, he was going to be sick.

"Perkins, I probably don't need to say this, but after the last time a body came in here in somewhat this shape, I told you to test for human saliva. I am saying it again." Donavan gave the other man his full attention. "I want a complete work up done on this body. I want a DNA test done. I want him tested for human saliva. I want fingernail scrapings. I want the works. Do I make myself clear this time?" He could feel himself getting a little on edge as Perkins stood for a moment staring at the ceiling as though the words leaving his mouth were wasting his valuable time. "And come to think of it, you never did let me know what you found on the Stewart girl after you found conflicting results and sent them off to be tested again."

"Guess you got a right to know, Hays. When I found the results showed human saliva, I didn't believe they could be right, and instead of sending them off again like I told you I was going to do, I just threw the samples away."

Donavan couldn't believe he was hearing the man right. "Do I need to tell you how Goddamn inept that was? You're supposed to be a professional, not some first-year medical student!"

"All right!" Perkins held up his hands. "You're not telling me anything I don't already know. I'll be sure and test this time for saliva, and I'll be sending off another test that I hope comes back negative. If I was a betting man, though, I would put my money on a positive return."

"What test is that?"

"This poor bastard not only had his throat ripped out and his body dined on, but he was also raped. And again, unless I miss my bet, he was raped after death."

"How the hell can you determine that? And I'd appreciate your making it brief so I don't have to join Jack in needing a breath of fresh air."

"The rectum showed tearing and bruising consistent with force, and since there was no blood pooled..." He stopped talking as Donavan turned to hurry his steps from the room. "Hmm, guess he wasn't as interested as he thought."

* * *

Gaston waited where he was, trying to get up his courage to look over at Lawrence.

Suddenly, Lawrence jumped up to run down the stairs and out of the house.

Thinking himself safe, Gaston remained sitting in the hallway as the first rays of dawn crept into the house.

All that day, he waited for Lawrence to return. Finally, early that evening, he heard the back door open and close. When he looked up, he saw Lawrence standing in the archway of the living room.

"You're still here." Lawrence couldn't believe what he was seeing. "I thought you would have packed up and be gone by now...after...after."

"I can't leave until you tell me where we go from here, Lawrence. I told you last night that I can't live like you do. I can't be a monster that kills people." He got to his feet but stayed standing in front of the couch.

"You have no choice, Gaston. But if you want to enjoy all that this life can offer you, you need to give your soul to the master of your own free will. You're going to be a rougarou no matter what." He spread his hands wide. "So why not go all the way and make it worth your while to enjoy all the perks...if you will?"

"This is not a fuckin' joke, Lawrence. You have destroyed my life, and all you can think to do is stand there makin' jokes?"

"Giving one's soul to the master is not a joke, Gaston. I am trying to help you." He walked across the room to take the other man into his arms, then stepped back at the sick look crossing his face.

"What the fuck is that smell? I smelled it yesterday too. It smells like something dead," he whispered.

"When the change transforms me back to human form from that of the rougarou, the rougarou form literally decomposes."

"Can't you shower and get rid of it? You reek." Gaston was trying to keep from being sick, and the closer Lawrence moved to be near him, the closer he came to having to leave.

"I already bathed in the swamp, but in a while, I'll go and take a shower."

Gaston sat back down on the couch, unsure how long his legs could be trusted to hold him upright.

Lawrence moved closer, but instead of sitting on the couch, he seated himself in the chair across from him. "I want you to know all that you have to look forward to as you change from man to rougarou the first time."

"When will this happen? I mean, how long do I have to be normal before I have to kill myself?"

"Instead of thinking about killing yourself, why don't you give this new life a chance? You may find that you have never been more alive in your life."

"You call killing people and drinking their blood and eating their flesh a great life? Not to mention smellin' like a dead body?" He looked away as disgust again replaced anger.

"Those are only some of the things that will happen. After your first change, you will look forward to the taste of warm blood and raw flesh." His eyes closed as they always did when he recalled the exotic tastes and smells.

"You look like you're enjoyin' these things right now as we speak," he said as he jumped to his feet, ready to run out of the house if he needed to.

"Yes, the smells and tastes have become a part of me, just as they will become a part of you, Gaston. Please sit down. You have nothing to fear. I am not going to change again until the next full moon. I could if I chose, or I could stay my human self on the full moon. It is my choice."

"How do you rectify this…killing of others with God? Are you sayin' you no longer want to be a child of God?"

"I can serve but one master, Gaston. And that master is Satan ruler of all that is worthy."

"You sick son-of-a-bitch! I curse the day I met you! I am a Catholic, and I denounce Satan and all that that evil bastard stands for."

"You will change your mind when you see what you can achieve by giving your soul over to the one who can do you some good. Would you like me to show you what you can expect as a child of Satan?"

"Yeah, sure, go ahead. Then I'll tell you what you can have if you give your soul back to God," Gaston told him, sure that when he was reminded of all the riches the Heavenly Father offered, he would choose to return to God.

Getting up from his chair, Lawrence moved over to kneel in front of the couch. "Look at me, Gaston, and continue to look at me. You have nothing to fear."

Gaston did as he was told, and within moments, he felt himself becoming very relaxed.

"Now, you will see what you can have if you give your soul over to the dark side of this plane."

Gaston saw himself living in the mansion with Lawrence, his every whim catered to, and he felt as though for the first time in his life, he was alive. No longer did he feel the shame he always felt at knowing he was not like other men because he preferred to be with those of his own sex. He wore clothes he had always yearned for but could never afford. He opened his wallet, and instead of seeing only a few ones, he saw hundred dollar bills. He found himself laughing instead of crying as the deep, dark depression that had plagued him all his life lifted to completely disappear. He watched himself walking down a street, his head lifted in pride instead of hanging in shame. Men and women spoke to him and patted him on the shoulder instead of shying away and laughing.

"Do I need to show you what you have now, Gaston? Do you need to feel the dark depression creeping over you again, as you know it will?"

As he sat there, he heard the voice of Father Dowdy telling the congregation how this earth was not where any would find riches; that riches awaited in heaven. But he needed to feel a change from his present life. He needed to know that he could wake up and have something new to look forward to instead of the same heart-wrenching sadness day in and day out like he had all of his life.

Lawrence watched him, listened to his thoughts as they sped through his mind at breakneck speed, telling him what he already knew. Letting him know he had nothing to look forward to except more of the same.

"I can't continue to live like this! I can't! I want to laugh and love and enjoy my life. I can't keep fighting and crying and begging for my life to be over and not have to be tortured anymore with trying to figure out ways to kill myself without having to feel the pain."

"Then join with us on the dark side, Gaston. Give your soul over to the master of all and of your own free will denounce your God." Lawrence whispered his words.

"I do," Gaston breathed. "I embrace the dark side and all it has to offer me."

"Open your eyes, Gaston, for the first time in your life, and greet your master."

Lawrence stood up and looked around, then drew in his breath as a figure dressed in a thick, long black robe with a cowl covering its head materialized before him. As the figure held out his arms, Lawrence walked unsteadily forward until he was completely enfolded.

"Now you are one of us, Gaston. Now you will be able to live hundreds of years and enjoy a life you have only dreamed of."

CHAPTER SIX

Donavan hung up the phone. "That was Sheriff Daniels. He wants to know what is being done on the Roberts murder. I guess Perkins and Daniels are good friends, and while having a drink last night at the local hangout, Perkins informed him on what all went on during Roberts' murder."

"He was attacked and eaten by our local Hindel werewolf."

"That isn't all that the poor bastard suffered…well, I can't really say he suffered since, according to Perkins, he was already dead when Hindel raped him." Donavan pulled an ashtray closer as he lit up.

The soda Jack had been drinking shot out of his mouth and nose, making him head for the paper towel dispenser. "What the fuck did you just say?"

"I wish you would get over that habit of spewing what you drink." Donavan ran a hand over the side of his face then reached for his handkerchief.

"Well, I probably would if you'd stop throwin' out shit that shocks the hell outta me while I'm drinkin' somethin'. Now, what were you sayin' 'bout Perkins?"

"I said Perkins was saying that Roberts was raped, and apparently, due to the signs showing around the rectum, it was after he was already dead. If you hadn't run out of the morgue on the pretense of needing a breath of fresh air, you would already know all this."

Jack blew his nose and tossed the soiled towels into the wastepaper basket sitting beside Donavan's desk. "Do we need to wonder now if Hindel's an ass popper?"

"I didn't doubt it after the show at the mansion. I'm just curious to know how long it's going to take Hindel to initiate Gaston into the fold."

"I remember that day sitting at the table talkin' with Jonathan Hindel about the dark side and how a person comes to be a werewolf. I gotta tell you that gave me the Goddamn creeps."

"I thought you were going to draw your .38 at any moment and start filling him full of holes the way you kept fingering it behind your back." Donavan had to laugh in spite of himself.

"Evil asshole came real close," Jack said, nodding to give emphasis to his words.

"I been thinking about something I want to run by you," Donavan breathed, stubbing out his cigarette.

"What's that?"

"I'd like to start watching the mansion. When the old mansion was blown to hell, that took care of the cave leading from the basement out to the lake, so I doubt if any rituals are going to be held there. But it would be interesting to see who comes and goes."

"Uh, Donavan, did you forget that when the mansion and cottage were blown that all the Hindels were blown along with them?"

"Too bad Lawrence couldn't have been home to enjoy the festivities with the rest of the family. I can guaran-Goddamn-tee you that would have been one blowjob he would never forget!"

"That was my fault he couldn't be home. He was needed at the nut farm for some more tests."

"All jokes aside, though, I do want to start watching the mansion. We could park a little ways from the gate and still be able to see the front door."

"Who we gonna get to cover the back? They do have a back door, you know."

"I don't think we need to worry about the back of the house. If you remember, when Chandra held her voodoo rituals, she always held them in the swamp not too far from the mansion. I'd like to have a look around that area too."

At the mention of Chandra, the beautiful quadroon Jack had lost his heart to and almost his mind over, he became quiet and wistful.

Donavan glanced over at him. "Sorry, Jack. That was thoughtless of me to bring her up."

He glanced over at Donavan then waved his apology away. "It ain't that. I guess I'm still not over feelin' guilty 'bout the terrible way I treated her when none of what she put me through was her fault. It was all thanks to Jonathan's threats of what he would tell Lawrence and what he would do to me if she didn't do as she was told."

"You need to let go of all that. I'm sure Chandra has. In fact, since we now know how easily a spirit can come and go between this plane and the other side, it might be a good idea for you to call on her and tell her you're sorry. Maybe if you actually hear her say she holds no ill feelings toward you, you'll be able to put it all behind you and go on with your life the way you're meant to."

"Do you think Seelah would mind bein' the go-between for us? She's the psychic, not me."

Donavan smiled. "I think she would be very happy to be a go-between for you and Chandra."

* * *

Seelah had just turned from putting Donny down for his afternoon nap when she felt the presence of someone in the room with them.

"Seelah."

Seelah saw Chandra sitting in the chair beside Donny's crib, smiling at her.

"Chandra." Seelah rushed forward to enfold the other woman in her arms. "I am so happy to see you." She grabbed her hand. "Come and see our son and tell me if you think he's the best looking little boy in the whole wide world!"

"Chandra caught her breath as she stared down at the handsome dark-haired boy sleeping quietly on his stomach. "He looks just like Jack," she whispered, twining her arms around her body in her old familiar way.

"Yes, he does." She glanced over at her, hearing the sadness in her voice. "Even though you've gone home to the other side, you still have love in your heart for him, don't you?"

"I always will, Seelah," she told her, unashamed of the tears falling down her face. "Simply because we go home doesn't mean we stop loving those closest to our heart." Placing a kiss on her fingertips, she touched them gently to Donny's forehead. "Sleep peacefully, my darling child. I will be watching over you."

Seelah held out her hand. "Come visit with me, Chandra. I have a lot to tell you." She turned and walked out into the hall. In the living room, she plopped down on the couch.

Chandra took the chair next to the couch.

"I feel like I should offer you something to drink, but since you're a spirit, I guess you won't care for anything."

Chandra only smiled. "I felt that I was needed, so I came."

"You still keep yourself attuned to all of us, don't you?"

"I always will. You still have danger around you. Now that Lawrence Hindel is back, the danger is even greater."

Seelah's head snapped up. "Are you saying that Lawrence means to do us harm? Still? When is this going to end?"

"It will not end until every Hindel is dead and removed to the dark side where they will be kept until they return their souls willingly to God."

"Can't they see they've been beaten on this plane? That no matter what they do, they can't win against the Holy Light of God?"

"A dark soul can only see what they want to see. They have been led to believe that Satan is all-powerful and, in the end, will win out against our Holy Father. We, who live in the light, know this can never happen. But it does no good to try and tell this to a dark soul. They have traded all they are for the luxuries and riches and longevity they have been given. If they could see what awaits them after they leave this plane, unless they are reborn into a new fetus, they would see that all they have to look forward to because of all the evil they have done to their fellow man is suffering in the darkness of the dark side. If only they could be shown this instead of the lies they *are* being fed when making their choice to go with good or evil, they would run back to God and forsake the evil of Satan."

"One thing I have never understood is if they can't leave the dark side to give their soul back to God, how do they ever achieve the chance to do so?"

"God's legion goes into the dark side to talk with them and try and get them to see how they can change all that they are suffering now."

"That has to be scary even for God's legion," Seelah said as a creepy feeling crawled over her.

"They are not afraid. They know God has them surrounded with the white light of the Holy Spirit. God never turns His back on us. We are the ones who have the choice to turn our back on Him."

"God sheds so many tears over his children, and we still continue to hurt Him," Seelah said.

Chandra nodded then replied, "Jack is going to ask something of you, Seelah. This is one of the reasons I came here."

"What is it he needs? You know I will do anything for Jack."

"He wants you to be a go-between for him and me. He can't see me right now unless I raise his psychic energy, and I was not really comfortable with doing that before as I know how Jack feels about seeing ghosts and all. But if you think it would be all right, then I would like to raise his energy enough so he can see and talk with me himself. It would make things a lot easier."

"I will do whatever the two of you want. I think it would be better if you and Jack could talk face to face. He has a lot of old guilt he needs to get rid of."

"I know this, Seelah, and I feel once he says what he wants to say and is able to hear what he needs to hear, he will let go of a lot of stress. He needs a clear head right now. He and Donavan both are going to be having a lot of stress in their lives now that they will be dealing with Lawrence Hindel again."

"Donavan's heart can't take a lot of stress. His doctor warned against it. Jonathan was sending him terrible dreams like he was doing with Matt Paulson. The one he made into a werewolf. Jack is still carrying guilt for his part in Paulson's death."

"This is only a small part of the makeup of a werewolf, Seelah. Most, but not all depending on how much love they hold in their hearts for the Heavenly Father, feel once they have given their souls over to the dark side, they no longer need to feel any regrets. They are like the human psychopath. They feel no remorse for anything they do. Matthew Paulson was not a true werewolf. He had only been forced into what he was by Jonathan Hindel, and he never gave his soul over to the dark side. He knew what he was doing when he forced Jack's hand into killing him that night."

"Jack needs to hear all of this. I don't know what I would do if I ever had to go through with Jack what Barbara had to go through with Donavan." Hearing a car pull into the driveway brought Seelah to her feet. "That will be Jack now." Without thinking, she raised a hand to her hair. She wanted to look her best for her husband.

Jack scooped her into his arms as soon as he walked through the door. Placing a sound kiss on her full mouth, he held her close to him. "Have I told you how very much I love you, my beautiful wife?"

She returned his passion and answered his question with one of her own. "Could your love for me and our son be any stronger than my love for the two of you?"

"Never in a million years," Jack told her, setting her back on her feet. Walking across the floor, he opened the fridge to pull a bottle of beer forward from the six-pack. Twisting off the cap, he flipped it into the wastepaper basket.

"I am going to go check on Donny real quick. There is someone here to see you. She's in the living room."

Jack continued walking into the living room to greet his visitor. "Well, if you're here, you must be invisible `cause I sure as hell can't see you," Jack said into the silence.

Seelah walked into the room and heard what Jack had just said. "Chandra is here to see you, Jack. Being attuned to all of us as she continues to be, she knew you wanted to talk with her."

"I mentioned that I wanted to talk with her while talkin' to Donavan earlier, yeah. I didn't expect to come home and find her waitin' on me, though."

"Chandra has something she would like to try on you, darling. She would like to try and raise your awareness, your energy high enough so you could see and hear her on your own without my having to be a go-between. Would that be all right with you?"

"Yeah, I guess so. I mean, you know I'm not really into seeing ghosts and all."

"Would you like me to stay here, or would you like to talk with Chandra in private?"

"No! Stay! I don't want to be here alone with a ghost," he told her, taking a long pull off his bottle of beer. Jack sat down on the couch and pulled Seelah down beside him. "Okay, so what do we do now?"

"Just be patient and let Chandra do what she wants to do."

Within moments, Chandra began to emerge in the chair she was sitting in.

"Oh fuck! It's workin'! I can see you, Chandra," he said, taking another drink from his bottle of beer. "Uh, honey, before we get started on all this, could you do me a favor, please?"

"Of course, what is it?"

"Could you throw this empty bottle in the trash, and on the way back, stop at the bar and fix me a triple scotch with ice?"

"Why are you nervous being around me, Jack?" You never

were before," Chandra told him, a wide smile spreading across her beautiful face.

"You were not a ghost then, Chandra. I just don't feel comfortable around ghosts."

"Maybe it would help if instead of thinking of me as a ghost, you could think of me as a spirit. Which, by the way, I am. A ghost is someone who has not transcended to the other side while a spirit is someone who has."

"You're still just as beautiful as you were when you were here, Chandra. I have to give you that."

"Thank you, Jack. That is nice coming from you."

Seelah walked over to hand Jack his drink and to set her glass of orange juice and ice down on the coffee table in front of her.

"One of the reasons I have come here today is, as I told Seelah, there is a lot of danger around you and Donavan and your families now that Lawrence Hindel is back in the parish. I don't think I have to tell you that he is here to do all of you harm because of the destruction you and Donavan did to almost all of the Hindels."

At her words, Jack lowered his drink. "What the hell do you mean 'almost'? Didn't we get rid of all the Hindels when Donavan had the mansion and Quigly's cottage blown up?"

"The Hindels go back centuries. A lot of their family, including Rafael and Rolan Hindel, once lived in Romania many years before they came to live in Louisiana. They didn't all come to stay at the mansion when Rafael was there. So to answer your question, no, not all of the Hindels have been destroyed. They will be coming to the parish very soon to stay with Lawrence. He is not aware of this yet, though."

"My God, will we ever be rid of them in this life?"

"Like I told you years ago, Jack, evil doesn't die. It only lies dormant. Waiting."

"How soon can we expect the rest of the vermin to show up? You may not be able to give me an exact date, but can you at least scale it down to where we can have a pretty good idea?"

"They will be here within a month from now. And they will be coming with vengeance in mind."

"Just so we have an idea when to be ready for them. It'll give us a chance to get some more dynamite ready. I'll be interested to see how many times Lawrence intends to rebuild the mansion. That is if he makes it this time `round."

"Lawrence is a man who is bent on your destruction, Jack, and he will not rest until he sees you lying dead at his feet. You and Donavan Hays both."

"If that's so, then he better get ready for an all-out fight because I don't lie down easy."

"The ones who are coming this time are like Jonathan and Rafael. And by this, I mean they have lived on this plane for over two centuries. They are steeped in evil, and they are very strong."

"What is it that makes them so strong? Did they come from hell itself or just raise a lot of it?" Jack laughed at his own joke.

"They are not someone you will wish to take on, Jack. They can be killed by a bullet just like anyone else when they are in human form, but when they have made the change into the form of a werewolf, they are all but indestructible."

"I know that, Chandra. A werewolf can only be killed by a silver bullet or by fire."

"What you don't know is they are what your horror writers like to refer to as The Devil's Children. Satan himself smiles on them."

"Then he better get ready to bake up another batch `cause the ones he's sendin' to do his dirty work now are fixin' to meet their redneck ancestors in hell!"

"Jack, don't go getting all cocky and think you can take on the Hindels all by yourself. Chandra just told you they are evil and not to be messed with."

"Honey, I am not about to do this all by myself. I will let Donavan share in the fun too. And this time, when the shit hits the fan, I will be front row, center seat to enjoy all the action!"

"In fact," — he held up a hand after taking a strong swallow of his drink—"I need to let my partner and best friend in on all the info." He punched in some numbers then waited for Donavan to pick up on the other end of the line. "Hey man, I need for you to get over here if you can. I got some shit to tell you that you are not going to believe."

"What's coming down, Jack? Did you get a call from the department?"

"Nope, not from the department, partner. The information center I have is sitting right here in my own living room."

"I'll be there in a few minutes. Is it all right if I bring the family?"

"You can bring anyone you want. They can all join Seelah out on the patio. Don't forget Brandy or Lugar will send you right back home to get her."

Donavan breathed. "I try not to make the same mistake twice. See you in a few," Donavan told him, hanging up the phone.

* * *

"Let me guess," Barbara laughed, "we're headed over to see the rest of the family, right?"

"Yeah, Jack said he's talking with someone who has some information. I'm guessing it has to do with Lawrence Hindel or, if not him, then at least about his new boyfriend."

"Jenny," Barbara called out. "Come on, we're headed over to see Aunt Seelah and Uncle Jack. Grab Brandy, and let's go."

"Is Jenny coming with us?" Donavan finished tying his shoes.

"I don't know. Jenny? Are you getting ready to go?" Barbara walked down the hall to tap on her door. "Jenny, are you comin' with us to see your Aunt Seelah and Uncle Jack? Your dad has his shoes on, so shake a leg, honey."

"Mom, I really have other plans. I'm going to go to the mall with some of my friends." She zipped her jeans and pulled a long-sleeved sweater down into place.

"Did you ask your dad if it's all right with him?"

"No." She slipped her feet into her high-topped tennis shoes and picked up her jacket from off the bed. "I was hoping you would. He gets so paranoid whenever I want to go anywhere with my friends."

"I know, and I am going to have a talk with him about it. You're thirteen years old, and it's normal to want to be with kids your own age."

"It isn't that I don't want to be with Aunt Seelah, Donny, and Uncle Jack, but…"

"You don't have to convince me, sweetheart. You just have to convince your dad. After all, we almost lost you, Jenny…" She knew Jenny had heard it all before, and she couldn't blame her for not wanting to hear it all again."

"I'll go ask him," she said, then turned, "but can you come with me and try and help me talk him into letting me be a normal teen?"

"Lead the way." She shooed her forward.

"Oh good, you're ready, hon. Is Brandy out on the patio or out back?"

"Dad, I don't want to go with you this time. Some of my friends are meeting me at the mall, so I'm going to pick up Shandi, and we're going to take the bus downtown. Is it all right with you?" She had kept her eyes downcast, not trusting herself not to burst into tears if he said no, again.

"Jenny, I think that will be fine if you go and be with your friends. Do you need any money?"

Jenny's head snapped up, and without another thought, she threw her arms around her father's neck. "Thank you, Daddy. And no, I don't need any money. I have my allowance, and, like Mom says, I need to start living within my budget."

"We shouldn't be gone too long, but if you get home before we do, you know where to find us."

As Donavan turned to go out back to get Brandy, Barbara pulled him back to slip her arms around his waist. "I know that had to be difficult for you. I just want you to know I'm proud of you."

Donavan kissed the top of her head. "I've been thinking, and I know it isn't fair to Jenny to leash her to my belt. She has her own life to live, and we have to trust that she thinks before she makes a move like we've taught her and does the right thing."

"You don't know how glad I am to hear you say all this, darling." She drew back, looking at him and smiling.

At the feel of her soft body held close against him, he leaned back, gazing into her upturned face. "You know, I could call Jack and tell him we decided to stay home. Jenny's leaving to be with her friends, which means we would have the house all to ourselves," he murmured, inhaling her clean soap and water fragrance as he reached up under her sweater to unhook her bra.

Barbara drew in her breath. It had been so long since they had really been together. "And since we're both fast strippers, it wouldn't take us long to get out of these clothes."

"Okay, I'm leaving now, you two. I'll be back before dark."

"Have fun, and if we're not here when you get back, come down to our second house down the street."

As soon as they heard the door close behind her, they started pulling off clothes as they raced down the hall to the bedroom.

Donavan stopped long enough to unplug the phone before crawling his way up to Barbara from the foot of the bed. For the first time in all the years they had been married, they didn't spend time on getting each other ready. They knew they didn't have to.

Barbara threw her long legs wide as Donavan reached her, a wide smile spreading across his face at her total abandonment.

"We'll need to take it slow, sweetheart. It's been a long time, and I don't want to disappoint you by not being able to stay up with you."

Wrapping her strong legs around his waist, she yanked him inside, feeling, at last, his hot, pulsating cock rubbing her slick walls the way she so needed to be rubbed.

Donavan felt his breath rush out of his lungs as she enclosed him in her soft, slick vault. Everything flew right out of his mind except the beautiful woman lying beneath him urging him on. He started to buck and, to his utter surprise, felt himself being rolled to one side as Barbara climbed on top to ride him without mercy.

She threw back her head, gasping as Donavan kneaded her firm breasts, then pulled her forward to suckle them one at a time in his hot mouth.

At the same time, they both moaned as Barbara felt their hot juices explode and mix, and she screamed aloud her pleasure.

Rolling from his body, she laid panting and smiling, then sat up. "Oh my God, Donavan, we forgot to check your pulse before we made love. I could have killed you!"

"Could have, but it would have been one hell of a way to go," he laughed, kissing the tips of his fingertips to place them on her full mouth, too tired to do anything else.

* * *

"What in the hell could be keepin' him? He said he would be here in a few minutes." Jack went once more to the front door to look outside. "Maybe I should jump in the truck and go check on him."

At the same moment, both women smiled and glanced at each other.

"I don't think you need to check on Donavan, Jack," Seelah told him. "Barb is making sure he is in very good hands."

Her meaning, coupled with the slight wink she aimed at him, had him rethinking his options. "The least he could have done is call and let me know he was gonna be busy for a few."

"Jack, I doubt if you even entered his mind." Seelah laughed.

"Seelah, would you mind if I talk privately with Jack out on the patio? Since Donavan is being taken care of, I think this would be a good time for me to talk with Jack about one of the reasons I came here today."

"Of course, I don't mind," she said, then turning to Jack, she told him, "Were you able to hear what Chandra just said, Jack?"

"Yes, she said that she wants to talk with me privately. I have been wanting to get a few things off my chest too. So this is a good thing."

"I'll go and check on Donny while the two of you are talking, sweetheart." Seelah gave him a quick peck on his cheek before moving down the hall.

When Jack was sitting comfortably in one of the chairs, Chandra asked him to tell her what had been bothering him that concerned her.

"The biggest thing is how bad I treated you. I'm sorry, Chandra."

"You didn't know what was going on, and I couldn't tell you," she told him, wanting so much to take him in her arms and hold him to her.

"Jonathan Hindel had you locked in on not tellin' anyone about anythin' that was goin' on. That had to war with your morals."

At his words, she got to her feet. She so hated to tell him what he needed to know. "Jack, this may be the hardest thing I have ever had to do, but I can't hide any longer."

"I'm here, Chandra," he said, taking her hands in his, surprised they felt no different than if she had been a living, breathing woman.

"Jack, I loved you with all the love a heart can hold for someone, and to tell you the truth, I still love you."

Jack caught his breath, wishing he could tell her the same thing, but he couldn't. "Chandra, there was a time I felt the same way about you. When you dumped me, I thought my heart had been ripped from my chest. It hurt that fuckin' bad. I lost my job on the police force because I couldn't sleep; hell, I couldn't even focus. I crawled into a bottle of pills and alcohol. If it hadn't been for Donavan and Barb, I would have killed myself at the rate I was goin'. I wound up in the hospital more dead than alive. And it was all because of you. You kept it from me about your bein' into voodoo. My mind would conjure up all kinds of reasons why you would be out all night instead of with me. I would sit for hours with a loaded gun in my hands, wanting to find out who it was you were with, so I could kill him and you too. No, Chandra, what love I had for you is long dead. And whether it was your fault or not, the feelings I had for you are still dead. I do regret the way I treated you, though. Now that I know none of what happened was your fault."

Suddenly, he felt completely drained. He sank down in one of the chairs to try and regain his strength and clear his mind.

"I wish I could lie and say that you are right in thinking that none of what happened between me and Jonathan was through no fault of mine, but I can't. When Jonathan first found me when I was still a young girl of sixteen, I thought there was no man on this plane who could compare with him. I know now it was because of my tender age and innocence that I felt this way, but at the time, he was all I could think of. Then little by little, he introduced me to the darker side of his life."

"I don't need to hear all this, Chandra." Jack held up a hand to silence her.

"Yes, Jack, you do. To make me do what he wanted, he began lacing my food and drink with a strong desire-inducing powder called Cantharis that would make me want to have sex with him all the time. Later, he did not stop with just him having sex with me. He would bring others. He would force me to have sex when he was not in human form. One of the other men he brought for me to have sex with later on in our days together is the man who fathered my one and only child."

"You had a child? That had to be difficult what with the life you were livin' with Jonathan." His voice softened, knowing she had lived such a terrible life, and even though he hadn't known all the ins and outs at the time, he had contributed to it.

"It was, but I loved him with all my heart, and I still do. He has been blamed for so much he didn't do."

"Where is your son now, Chandra?" Jack shook a cigarette out of the pack then threw the pack on the patio table. "I mean, is he still alive?"

"Yes, Jack, my son is very much alive and living in the mansion he had rebuilt on the Hindel estate."

Jack drew the nicotine deep into his lungs, needing to relax. At Chandra's words, he could only sit and stare at her. Then as though her words had finally sunk into his mind, he leaned forward. "Are you tellin' me that Lawrence Hindel is your biological son?"

"Yes, I am Lawrence's mother. Jonathan would always threaten me with telling Lawrence I was his mother if I didn't do everything he told me to do. When Lawrence was still quite young, he was sent away to England. A nanny was hired to raise him. Three or so times a year, Jonathan would make the trip to England to visit with him."

"Wait a minute." Jack sat forward in his chair. "Didn't you just say that a man that Jonathan brought to you was the man who impregnated you? If that's so, then Lawrence is not Jonathan's son. Holy shit! Did Jonathan know this?"

"No, that is one secret I was able to keep hidden from Jonathan. If he had known Lawrence was not his son, he would have thrown him into the street. However, since no one but I knew of this, Lawrence is heir to the vast Hindel fortune."

"So no one in the Hindel family knows about Lawrence bein' the son of someone other than Jonathan Hindel?"

"One person in the Hindel family knew. But I only told him when it was too late for him to do anything about it or bring Lawrence any harm."

"Who did you tell?"

"Rafael Hindel. He said he could not leave this plane as long as his grandson needed him. I told him he was free to leave since Lawrence was not of his blood."

"Wish I could have been there to see his face when he heard that little bombshell," Jack laughed. "What made Jonathan decide to bring Lawrence back here to live?"

"He wanted Lawrence to know about the Hindel secret and to later be like him in giving his soul to the dark side, except he didn't live long enough to see that wish come to fruition."

"Did Rafael see to Lawrence becoming a werewolf?"

"Rafael started the process of Lawrence becoming a werewolf right in the kitchen of the Hindel mansion. Then later, he took Lawrence to a ritual in the cave where he gave his soul over to the dark side and was welcomed into the cult by Satan."

"What the fuck?" Jack jumped to his feet. "Are you sayin' you saw Satan with your own eyes come and welcome Lawrence to the dark side? I can hardly believe that!"

"What you choose to believe or not believe is up to you, Jack. I know what I saw. Rafael and others of his kind were sacrificing children. The sacrificing of the innocent is always done in a high ritual. It makes everything more binding. Or so those of the damned believe."

"So much goes on in this world that no one knows about or would believe even when they are told, just like me now. My mind can't accept shit like this."

Chandra rose to her feet. "I must leave you now, Jack. I am glad that we were able to get everything that needed to be said out in the open. I know you feel better knowing I do not hold a grudge for anything you did. I will say it now, so there is no misunderstanding." She walked forward to embrace him. "I forgive you, Jack. I will never stop loving you, and for this, I do not apologize." Leaning forward, she took his face in her hands and, without another word, kissed him softly on his open mouth. "Do you forgive me?"

"I forgive you, Chandra, and I was wrong when I said I feel no more love for you. I guess in some strange way, I will always feel some love for you," he told her, hugging her to him for just a moment, then watched as she disappeared.

"Jack, sorry it took us so long to get here," Donavan said, coming through the sliding glass door leading to the patio, a wide smile spreading across his handsome face. "Hope you're not too upset. Had something come up at the last minute."

In spite of what had just happened, Jack couldn't help but laugh at Donavan's choice of words. "Naw, in fact, it turned out better this way. I had some things I needed to get cleared up."

"So, who was the person you were talking with?"

"Believe it or not, I was talking with Chandra. She raised my energy level so I could both see her and talk with her. We were able to get rid of a lot of pent-up feelings and anger we had both been harboring toward each other."

"You said that's what you wanted to do. It always helps to clear the air."

"You may want to have a seat because she told me something that is going to shock the shit outta you."

Barbara and Seelah walked outside carrying drinks and bowls filled with chips and salsa. After everything was set on the patio table, everyone took a seat to hear the shocking news.

"Okay, Jack, we're ready to hear what it was Chandra wanted you to know," Donavan said.

"Lawrence is not a Hindel. Jonathan Hindel was not his father. He doesn't know it, though. Chandra said the only one she told was Rafael."

"Then he has no right to the Hindel fortune." Barbara laughed.

"No, he doesn't, but no one knows this. Rafael is roasting in hell, so he can't blow the whistle," Jack said.

"I'll tell you something, though. As much of a surprise as this is, I would have loved to have seen the look on Rafael's face when he heard the news." Donavan pulled forth the drink sitting in front of him.

"That's what I told Chandra. God, that would have been priceless. I bet old man Hindel `bout shit when he heard that the irritatin' little nitwit who was always drivin' him up a wall was not even his blood and that he could have eaten him at any moment without havin' to feel guilty." Jack threw back his head, allowing himself to get all the tension and stress he had been feeling for too long to drain from his body in one long burst of laughter.

Then he stopped as he remembered what else Chandra

had told him.

"What's wrong, Jack?" Seelah looked over at him, noticing the look of sadness on his face.

"Chandra told me that she was Lawrence's mother. I guess Jonathan used that fact to blackmail her into doing whatever he wanted her to do, or else he would tell Lawrence who his mother was."

"What an evil son-of-a-bitch," Donavan said.

"Thank God he is no longer here to wreak havoc," Seelah chimed in on the conversation.

"I'll drink to that," Jack said, nodding as everyone at the table raised their drinks in a toast.

CHAPTER SEVEN

Danny Roberts let himself into the house in search of his aunt. Spying her sitting in the kitchen with a cup of coffee in front of her, he walked into the room.

"Good morning, Aunt Shirley. How are you holding up today?" He dropped a kiss on the side of her face then moved to the sink to grab a cup from the drain-board.

"I'm doin' all right, Danny. Thanks for asking. I'm going to be going to the mortuary later this morning to pick out an urn for Vern's ashes. Would you like to go along?"

Danny set the cup on the table and picked up the coffee pot. "You're plannin on havin' Uncle Vern cremated? When did you make this decision…by yourself?"

Shirley looked over at him. "Vern was my husband. Who the hell else would I ask about what needed to be done?"

"He was my uncle. Maybe I would like to have a funeral for him where the people who cared about him could come and pay their respects." The disgusted look he gave her was not missed.

"We can have a memorial service for him if you'd like. I just don't think we need to have him laid out in a casket. Hell, there ain't enough left of him to even fill up a casket, and for damn sure, we can't have an open casket. We'd have people pukin' on the floor."

"Was there ever a time that you had even the smallest bit of feelin's for him?"

"Don't start, Danny. I'm not in the mood to hear about poor Vern this morning."

"For Christ's sake, the man was eaten alive in his fuckin' bed!" Danny jumped to his feet. "I would think you could pull some feelin's of sympathy out of that cold heart of yours!"

"Listen to me, you whinin' little fuck!" Shirley reached out and grabbed hold of his arm. "I was the one married to him, not you. I'm the one who had to smell his rotten breath in the bed at night and listen to him complain about every penny I spent! So don't you be tellin' me what a worthless bitch I am. I already know that!"

"I suppose you're still gonna keep that lease over Gaston's and my head too."

"You're damn right I am. Vern might have been a lot of things, but a bad businessman he wasn't. You two can still live over the store, long as you keep your rent current."

"I don't think Gaston's gonna be roomin' with me anymore. Seems he's dropped into a nicely cushioned nest."

Shirley got up from the table. "Whatever are you ramblin' about, Danny?" She leaned into the fridge to pull out a jar of fruit. "He knows he can't move out unless he pays me two thousand bucks. You did both read the lease." She came back to the table. "It states if either of you moves out before the two years is up, you have to pay up."

"I don't have a thousand dollars to pay you. I'm your nephew, for Christ's sake. Have a little heart."

"I have a heart, and if I want this heart to keep beatin', I need money to see to its welfare. So my advice to you is, find out if Gaston has moved out, and if he has, you can kiss your apartment and your car goodbye. I'm sure I can sell the car for at least half of what you will owe."

"You're not takin' my car, bitch! That I can promise you! I'll be payin' Gaston and his lover a visit today. If he don't want his ass kicked all over the Hindel estate, then he better shit two thousand bucks!"

"Are you tellin' me he's moved in with Lawrence Hindel?"

Her eyes grew wide, and she snickered. "Where the hell did you get that idea?"

"They were makin' cozy while we were there at the estate deliverin' his furniture."

"The man who paid the store over forty thousand for furniture is queer?" She forked peaches out of the jar and into her bowl. "Oh my God. That's priceless. Why the hell couldn't I find someone with that much money? I would give my soul to be rich!"

"Yeah, well, keep that thought, Aunt Shirley. Maybe someday some rich ole fart will come beatin' on your door, and if you're real nice, she'll make you her bitch."

"I could live with that. Long as I have money to buy enough mouthwash." Shirley giggled, knowing how much she was irritating Danny.

"You make me sick," he told her, pulling his car keys from his pocket. "I'm gonna go pay Gaston a visit and see what the story is. I'll just tell him either his boyfriend's gonna fork over expenses for his nightly ride, or I'm takin' the entire two thousand out of his ass! Either way looks like my ole buddy Gaston's gonna have to eat his meals standin' up!"

* * *

Lawrence filled a bowl with his favorite cereal then reached out to pull the milk pitcher over closer. He glanced up as Gaston walked into the room amid a strong scent of aftershave and sporting a towel draped over his head.

"I hope you don't mind. I availed myself of your aftershave." He shot a cocky grin across the table.

"You are welcome to use anything I have, Gaston." He motioned him to be seated. "We're having cereal and toast this morning. I hope you don't mind."

Although it wasn't one of his favorites, he sat down and poured some into a bowl.

"Have you decided what you're going to do about moving in here with me? As you can see, there is plenty of room. And, too, by living here, you will not only be paid a monthly salary for your help on the estate, but anything you need, you have only to ask."

"I already told you, Lawrence, I have to pay off the lease Danny and I signed or pay two thousand. I don't have that kinda money. And I don't want you paying it for me. I don't think the lease is fair, and I will not pay for something if I don't agree with it."

"I would have no problem paying off the lease if it would free you to move in here with me. I will be honest with you. I can't afford to have strangers coming and going on the estate. I am sure you can understand this."

"Yeah, I can see why you don't want people here, but I still can't move in until the debt is paid. It's a matter of principle with me."

"If I can free you from this debt without paying the money, would that satisfy you?"

Gaston drew back, staring at Lawrence as he sat calmly enjoying his breakfast. "You're talkin' 'bout doin' another murder, ain't you?"

"Does that bother you, Gaston?" Lawrence buttered his slice of toast, adding a small dab of jelly from one of the decorative jars sitting in a round wooden basket. "You yourself said the debt is unfair. So why not simply remove the obstacle?"

"I can't do that. I can't just murder someone. Especially someone I know and who hasn't done anything to me."

"Danny's aunt will call in the debt, and that will be doing something to you. It will make you worry about paying a debt that you feel you don't rightly owe. I agree with you. It is a matter of principle."

"No, to answer your question, no...I can't move in with you at this time."

"I can get the lease agreement without doing anyone any harm, Gaston if that is what you prefer I do. You said it was kept in the safe at the Roberts' home."

Gaston thought for a moment, then nodded. "All right,

if you can get the lease without anyone getting hurt, then I will accept that."

"Then it's settled. Now enjoy your breakfast. We have a big day ahead of us."

Gaston laughed outright. "It seems that no matter what problem pops up, you always have an easy solution on how to fix it."

Lawrence ran a hand down the side of Gaston's freshly shaven face. "Like the old saying goes, where there's a will, there *is* a way. And when you're as rich as we are, I can promise you, there will always *be* a way."

The buzzer on the intercom told them a visitor had arrived on the estate.

"Are you expecting company this morning, Gaston?"

"No." He shook his head. "I would never assume you would be all right with my inviting someone to your home unannounced."

"Thank you, Gaston, that is very thoughtful of you and much appreciated. I don't take kindly to unannounced visitors."

Lawrence walked to the intercom. "Yes?"

"Yeah, this is Danny Roberts. I need to come in and talk with Gaston if he's there, and I am bettin' he is."

"Do you want to talk with him, Gaston?"

"Yeah, I have no problem with talkin' to Danny."

Lawrence flipped the button to open the gate.

They both walked out onto the front porch to wait for Danny to tell them what he wanted so early in the day.

* * *

Danny drove up the driveway, admiring the many trees and flowers lining it.

This is one hell of a place, no gettin' around that, but I'd have to decline. He snickered to himself as he drove up and parked in front of the mansion.

Gaston remained standing on the porch, letting Danny get out of the car.

"Hey there, Gaston." Danny slammed the car door. "I've missed seein' you. Thought you'd come home by now."

"Been busy, Danny. So what brings you all the way out here?"

"Like I said, been missin' you around the apartment and the store. You are still workin' there, right?" He walked up on the wide, shiny porch and, without waiting for an invitation, sat down in one of the many rockers.

"Don't be rude, Danny. You can see Mr. Hindel standing here. After all, this is his house."

"Hey there, Lawrence," Danny said, not holding out his hand. "So anyway, Gaston, as I was sayin', are you still workin' at the store and sharin' the apartment or not?"

"And like I told you, I've been busy."

"Yeah, I just bet you have." He snickered, giving Lawrence a scathing glance. "You do recall that we got a signed lease with my uncle. And now with my Aunt Shirley. I sure hope you intend to hold up your part of that lease, 'cause it states very clearly that if even one of us moves out before the two years is up, we each owe a thousand dollars."

"The lease is not fair, Danny. You know that as well as I do. We neither one should have signed it."

"That don't make a shit, my friend. Fact is we did sign it, so you need to tell me right here and now what you plan on doin' 'bout your part." He glanced over to see Lawrence standing off to the side, watching him. "You ain't actin' like much of a host there, Lawrence. I could do with a glass of orange juice or a cup of coffee."

"Shut the fuck up, Danny. You don't need to come here and start runnin' your mouth. Mr. Hindel hasn't done anything to deserve your disrespect." Gaston walked over to stand beside Lawrence.

"That's true, Gaston, but I bet he sure has been doin' a lot to you," Danny breathed, getting to his feet. "Now, I have two options to offer you in this matter. Your first option is to pay me a thousand dollars, which I will give to my Aunt Shirley and tell her I will have to have some time to come up with my money."

"And the second option?"

"I can kick your ass and the ass of your little fuck-buddy here until you come up with my money."

Lawrence walked a short way down the porch, motioning Gaston to follow. When they were sure Danny couldn't hear what was being said, Lawrence offered a proposal. "I will tell Danny that I will not give him the money but that I will go to his aunt's house later today and pay her the full amount."

"I don't want you to do this, Lawrence. This is not your place to pay money that I was stupid enough to sign a lease on."

"You had no money at the time, Gaston, and Danny's uncle knew this. He took advantage of your situation, just as Danny is trying to take advantage of you now. Only he thinks the way to go about it is to use brute force."

"What's it gonna be, boys? I ain't got all day."

"Do whatever you think is best, Lawrence. He's gonna make an ass of himself no matter what."

"Then leave it to me, Gaston."

Lawrence turned, walking back across the porch to where Danny stood waiting, a nasty look on his face that made it clear to Lawrence and Gaston that what he really wanted to do was fight.

"I will not be paying *you* any money, Danny. However, I will pay money to your aunt later today. I think this should take care of the matter at hand. And now, I would like you to leave my home."

"You smug little bitch," Danny told him, his hands balling into fists at his sides. "You think you're so much better'n me just cause you got money."

"Danny, you need to do what Mr. Hindel said and leave. You came here to get this matter settled, and now thanks to the kind heart of Mr. Hindel, it is. You have no more reason to remain here after you've been told to leave."

"You think you're man enough to make me leave, pencil dick?"

"Come on, Danny, let's get off the porch and go out back. Then we'll see whose gonna do what." Gaston grabbed him by the arm to sling him off the porch.

"You French mother fucker! You been askin' to get your ass kicked for a long time. It's time we got to it!"

Gaston lashed out with a kick that sent Danny reeling backwards onto the ground. Before he could react, Gaston was yanking him to his feet to land a fist square in his mouth.

Danny rolled onto his stomach and, seeing his own blood spurting from his split lip, jumped to his feet. "You filthy son-of-a-bitch, I'll kill ya for that!"

"I'm right here, Danny."

Like a charging bull, Danny plowed into the man taunting him.

Gaston grabbed his head and, with the quickness of a striking cobra, latched onto Danny's ear with his teeth.

He screamed as he saw Gaston holding part of his ear in his mouth. "You rat bastard, you bit off part of my ear!"

Something was happening to Gaston that he couldn't understand. The taste of blood in his mouth did not taste like it had in the past. It tasted sweet, and although the desire made him sick to his stomach, he wanted more. He grabbed Danny and sank his teeth into his neck, sucking hard on the blood seeping to the surface.

With all his might, Danny yanked away. He put a hand up to his ear and ran for his car.

Gaston stood where he was, letting him go and still tasting the sweet nectar filling his mouth.

Lawrence stood watching him. When Gaston turned in his direction, he walked over.

"What is wrong with me, Lawrence? I bit part of his ear off, and when the blood ran into my mouth, I didn't feel bad but wanted more. It tastes like sweet wine."

"You are becoming what I made you, Gaston. You are becoming a rougarou."

"But why ain't I changin'? I saw what you looked like, and

I am not like that."

"Trust me, Gaston, you will change, and when you do, you will experience a whole new way of life. A life you never imagined."

"I feel like I have to have more blood. I'm like an addict."

"It will only get worse until you find yourself hardly able to wait for the full moon."

"Do we have to wait for the full moon? Can't I begin my change now?"

Lawrence laughed, enjoying his eagerness. "Yes, we can hold the ritual this very night, and as we will need a sacrifice, I know just the person to invite for your ritual into the dark side."

"What do we need to get ready?"

"We will need to go into town and get a few things since everything was destroyed when the other mansion was blown up." His head came up at the memory, and he tried to leash his anger, knowing now was not the time.

Gaston watched him, knowing what was going through his mind. "We *will* be callin' in the debt for that, I hope."

"Oh yes, it will just be you and me, but if we go about it one by one, we will get the job done quite nicely, I am sure."

"You will not be alone in the destruction of those who have slighted the master," a deep and familiar voice spoke into the silence.

Lawrence looked around until he saw the figure of a man begin to materialize.

"I am not alone, Lawrence. Those of our family who were not bound in chains and transported into the darkness are with me."

"The master has sent you here to help me?"

"You know he would never desert you in your time of need."

"But I always thought that once a child of Satan passed from this realm, he only had a short time to be reborn before he was taken into the darkness to suffer for his deeds on this plane."

"You were not right in your assumptions, Lawrence. A dark soul must be bound on this plane and taken to the darkness by a white spirit. We who were killed here have only been biding our time until your return to the estate. You will be happy to know that there are more of our family coming here from New Orleans to stay with you."

The look of complete surprise spreading across Lawrence's face brought a chuckle from the one standing before him.

"I thought all our people died that day in the mansion."

"There are many Hindels on this plane, Lawrence. And to be sure we will always live on, we do not all stay in one place."

"Now I know why I was being pushed to build this house so big and to have a basement with a large room built on the other side of one wall. It was for our people to come and help me in my continuing fight for the master."

Gaston tried to stay brave as he watched Lawrence talk to someone he couldn't see. But he could feel his nerves begin to fray.

"Lawrence, who are you talking with, and why can't I see them?"

"I am talking with one of my family who was killed in the blast and who has since moved on to the dark side. His name is Rolan Hindel, and he has come to help us in our fight against those who wish to destroy us."

CHAPTER EIGHT

Shopping with Lawrence was a whole new experience for Gaston, who always had to count his money to make sure he had enough to buy what he needed, and he had to be sure he was getting only the essentials. It had been that way all of his life. No sweets or good food, only the same old thing day in and day out. Clothes from the hand-me-down store and shoes that may or may not have someone's fungus still lingering inside.

Walking into the most expensive men's store in the parish, Lawrence turned Gaston in the direction of a person busy hanging clothes on a rack. "We will get this man to help you. He will need to measure you for the correct size and all. I want you to pick out whatever you want to get, Gaston. You will need to try on all the clothes to make sure they fit still as I don't really trust the word or mind of a clerk." Lawrence smiled, watching the disbelief turn to joy as Gaston walked over to tap the man on his shoulder.

"Yes, can I be of help?" His haughty gaze slid over Gaston, taking in his faded jeans and sleeveless, tight-fitting shirt that showed off well-toned biceps to perfection.

"Yeah, I need to get some clothes, but I'm really not sure of my size anymore...you see, I've been workin' out and..." His words were abruptly cut short as the clerk rudely interrupted him.

"That is all unimportant," he told him, one hand fluttering

in the air. "If you will just follow me, I will have your size figured out in a few short moments."

Lawrence followed at a discreet distance behind, wanting Gaston to have his privacy as the clerk walked behind a counter to pick up a tape measure, then impatiently motioned Gaston forward.

"Now, do you need to know shirt size too, or are we simply getting rid of the mishmash you have seen fit to clothe yourself in today?"

Getting irritated with the man's uncalled for attitude, Lawrence stepped forward. "He will need all of his measurements taken as he will be buying a complete wardrobe," Lawrence spoke up, the testy tone in his voice daring the man to argue.

The clerk glanced up, and seeing the well-dressed man standing at Gaston's side, he became instantly more pleasant. "My, your daddy must be a very wealthy man." He stooped down to begin getting the measurements. "This is the best clothing store for the up and coming in all of Saint Anthony Parish. I am sure you will be pleased with our selections as we have the very latest in apparel."

"What is your name?"

"George," the frail man who looked to be in his middle sixties answered.

"Do you enjoy your job here as a clerk?"

"Yes, very much. I've been here for…" His words came to a halt as Lawrence stepped closer.

"I could not care less about your years of employment in this menial job, George. What I do care about is your disrespect for my friend. I am not his father or his…daddy, as you referred to me. However, I am the man who will be paying for the clothes purchased here today, so if you want to keep your employment in this store, you will show some respect. Do I make myself clear?"

"Perfectly, sir, and I am sorry. I meant no disrespect to the young man."

"Then tell him you meant no disrespect."

"I am sorry, sir, I meant no disrespect."

No one had called him sir in his life, and Gaston knew he could get used to this treatment quickly.

* * *

Shirley Roberts stood holding the fur-lined gloves she had just picked out for her boyfriend and smiled. Without stopping to think, she followed behind Gaston and his benefactor.

When they stopped at a large array of socks, she saw her chance to be noticed. "Hello, Gaston." She held out a hand to him. "I see you are doing a little shopping too."

"Gaston turned, and taking her hand in his, he squeezed it briefly. "Shirley, you remember Mr. Hindel. He's helping me get some clothes for my new job," he told her, wishing she would simply go away and let him shop in peace.

"I do wish you had called and let me know you were no longer an employee of Roberts Furniture, Gaston. That was very rude of you."

"Yes, well, shit happens, Shirley." Gaston turned away.

"Listen, you, we have a little matter of two thousand dollars to discuss in case you've forgotten."

"Ms. Roberts, if you will excuse my intervening here since I am the one who lured Gaston from your employment and as a former renter, I feel I should be the one to pay for his half of the monies owed you. I am sure you will agree." Lawrence reached into his wallet and withdrew ten one hundred dollar bills and a receipt made out to her for the exact amount. "If you will be so kind as to sign this receipt showing that you have been paid in full, you can be on your way a richer and much happier lady, and we can get on with our day as well."

She thought about trying to collect the entire $2,000, knowing that it would be very unlikely that Danny could come up with his half, but as she looked into the face of Lawrence Hindel, she changed her mind. Something warned her to be happy with what she had already been able to collect and call it good.

"Thank you, Mr. Hindel, and I know you will be satisfied with Gaston's services. He is a very hard worker." She scrawled her name across the bottom of the receipt then accepted the bills Lawrence laid in her hand.

"I am sure I will be satisfied with Gaston. In fact, I already am," he told her, following his words with a slight wink.

"You be sure to stop by the store if you find yourself in need of more furniture and especially now that Gaston is moving in with you. He might want to decorate his room with furniture of his own choosing."

"You know," — Lawrence placed a hand on the crook of his arm and raised a finger to his chin — "I never thought of that." He turned, glancing over at Gaston as he continued to stand still while George measured him. "*Did* you wish to change the furniture in your room, Gaston?"

Gaston could feel a hot flush creeping up his face as everyone stopped what they were doing to look at him. "I'm all right with what's there already, Lawrence." He moved his leg as the clerk went back to checking his inseam. As he brushed the inside of his leg, Gaston jumped. "Is this gonna take much longer?"

"No, I think I have all I need to help you pick out what apparel you will need in your size," he said, getting to his feet. "If you will follow me," — he motioned them forward — "we can begin with your choice of underwear."

"Are you comin' with us, Lawrence?" Gaston glanced behind him.

"It was nice seeing you again, Ms. Roberts, and I would like to offer my condolences on the passing of your husband. By the way, if it would be all right, I would like for Gaston and myself to come to the funeral if you would let me know where and when it will be."

"I am having Vern cremated. I think under the circumstances of his death, that would be best."

"Yes, I believe Danny did mention something about his being attacked by a wild dog that had somehow gotten into the house. Terrible, just terrible," he mused.

"I will have it posted in the paper when the memorial will

be, Mr. Hindel, and I would like very much for you and Gaston to come. You made Vern a very happy man with your large purchase."

"Like my father and grandfather before me, we Hindels do our best to bring joy and prosperity to our little parish," he told her, walking away to follow Gaston, then stopped. "Oh dear, I almost forgot. We had a most unpleasant visitor earlier today. Your nephew, Danny, stopped by begging for money from Gaston. I'm afraid a fight erupted in which your nephew was the loser. You may want to give him a call and check on him. Have a pleasant day, Ms. Roberts." He waved a hand in the air as he walked away.

The clerk left Gaston, who was busy looking at shirts to take the many packages of underwear, to go to the counter, then hurried back to help Gaston try on some of the shirts, noting that his taste ran in pastel.

The material was smooth and felt good against his skin. Seeing Lawrence walking his way, he posed, smiling to get his opinion.

"You have very good taste in clothing, Gaston. I will do my best not to rip these nice shirts from your body in a fit of passion," he whispered.

"I would appreciate that. Maybe we could pick up a few from a cheaper store just for that purpose, though."

George cleared his throat, letting them know he was close enough to overhear their intimate conversation.

"If you work on commission, George, this is going to be one lucky day for you financially," Gaston told him.

"Yes, we all work on commission here at The Parish Emporium. We have a very select clientele, though, so I make a good living." His bleached blond head came up, and a prideful smile spread across his middle-aged face.

"Happy to hear it, George," Gaston told him. "It's always nice to know where the next meal is comin' from and for damn sure if it's comin' at all."

"I didn't mean to eavesdrop on your conversation with the lady, but I heard her call you Mr. Hindel?"

"Yes, I am Lawrence Hindel."

"Were you any relation to Jonathan and Rafael Hindel?"

"Yes, Jonathan was my father, and Rafael was my grandfather."

"I had the pleasure of serving both of them in choosing a new wardrobe each year before the store began catering to the younger crowd. I am so sorry to hear of their passing, your grandfather's passing being less than a year ago."

"Thank you, George, your kind words are music to my heart. Now you will have the pleasure of serving Mr. Laufett and me from now on."

"It will be my pleasure, I assure you. I always enjoyed the company of both men when they would come into the store."

"Some people in the parish forget how much they have been helped by the Hindels and choose to instead listen to idle gossip. Hearing you speak so kindly of my family makes me feel bad about the way I treated you earlier."

"You have no need to feel bad, my friend. The Hindel name will always be spoken with much respect by me and others who matter in this parish."

CHAPTER NINE

"You know, I was thinkin' it might be a good idea to get a copy of the blueprints on the Hindel Estate. We need to know what's goin' on out there. The prints should show if he had a tunnel dug from the house back out to the lake."

"Oh Christ, tell me we don't have to go through all this shit again," Donavan said as he veered off the lane and into some trees. Stepping from the Jeep, they stood for a moment getting their bearings, then headed out to see if they could circle round and come in behind the mansion. "Damn moss is so long it keeps smacking me in the face."

"Aw, quit your bitchin'. Remember, this was all your idea."

"Sounded like a good one when I made it." Donavan laughed as he noticed Jack keep checking the ground. "What are you looking for, Jack? Afraid one of them nice, fat Water Moccasins is going to come calling?"

He knew Jack's phobia with snakes, and he couldn't keep himself from teasing him every chance he got.

"What the hell are you afraid of, Donavan? I know you gotta be scared of somethin', everybody is. So what's your cold sweat maker?"

"My phobia is drowning or being buried alive. I can't watch movies when they show that shit. Scares the hell out of me to tell you the truth," he said, turning and heading back the way they had just come. "The grounds end just inside the fence, so we can't get any closer."

"Don't have to ask me twice to get the hell outta here."

"Since we can't do any good here, we might as well get on getting a copy of the blueprints of the mansion. I'll tell you right now if I find he has put in another secret room, I am going to be hard put not to come over here and just shoot the son-of-a-bitch."

"Do you want to bet he has? I'll put a twenty dollar bill on it, you in?"

"No, I'm not in. I think he has too. They have to make everything so all about the master." He held up his hands, curling his fingers into talons. "Too bad 'the master' wasn't visiting the mansion and got his black ass blown back to hell when it blew."

From where they were, they could see Lawrence's Land Rover parked in front of the mansion. As they watched, they could see them taking bags out of the vehicle.

"Looks like somebody's been shoppin'," Jack laughed.

"Wonder who does the cooking and cleaning? Bet they share them. But if you still want to lay out that twenty dollar bill, I'll bet a twenty that Lawrence is the little woman," Donavan said, trying to keep his voice down since he knew how it carried, especially with the wind blowing as it was.

"Another bet that won't be taken," Jack said, laughing again. "He probably trembles every time he feels those tight-muscled arms slippin' round him to lift him and carry him off to bed."

Donavan stopped walking to look at him. "Do you mind? I would like to keep my breakfast where it is."

"Sorry. I guess I shouldn't be makin' jokes at other people's expense. I hear they can't help bein' fucked up."

At that moment, a car came flying through the open gate and right up to the front of the house.

"What the hell?" Donavan said, hoping they didn't need to blow their cover and lend a hand.

Two men got out of the car, slamming the doors and

stalking up to the front porch.

"Aw fuck," Jack murmured, "this doesn't bode well. Guess we better go see what the hell's goin' on."

"So much for keeping them under surveillance without them being aware we're here."

Donavan backed out of their hiding place and then drove up the driveway. He parked close behind the car to deter it from taking off in case they needed to be detained. They both got out to check and see if they were going to be needed.

The two men were so busy pounding on the front door they didn't see the two detectives walk up onto the porch.

"Can we help you fellows with something?" Donavan asked.

When the men turned around, Donavan and Jack could see the one man was Danny Roberts. "Nobody called you two so you can be about your business," Danny snarled.

Noting the bandage attached to the side of Danny's head, Jack walked closer. "Looks like you already been in one tussle today, and hell, the day ain't even half over."

"Fuck you," Danny told him, turning to begin banging on the door again.

Without warning, the door was jerked open, and both Lawrence and Gaston stepped outside. Gaston was holding a .38 in his hands.

"What'd you do, prick, call for backup?" He eyed the detectives standing off to the side now.

"We're here to make sure no one is going to go off their nut and end up spending the rest of their lives in a cell," Donavan said.

Jack reached behind him to lift his own .38 from his belt. "I suggest you all just calm down, and I need you to put away your gun, Gaston."

"I gotta permit to carry, detective." He continued to point the gun at Robert and the other man standing on the porch.

"That may be so, but at the moment, you are endangering

another life," Donavan spoke up.

"They are trespassing. This is private property, and we have a right to protect ourselves," Lawrence told them.

A slight look between the detectives had Jack returning his gun to his belt and Donavan drawing his .44 from his holster.

In a flash, Jack grabbed Gaston's gun arm and removed the weapon, tossing it over to Donavan. Then before Gaston could respond, Jack had his arms behind his back in handcuffs.

"What are you doing? Gaston was only protecting us and our property. You will remove those handcuffs instantly!"

"Shut the fuck up, Lawrence or you're next," Donavan told him, bringing a surprised look to Lawrence's face.

"Now, what the hell's this all about?" Jack said.

"This little cocksucker" — he nodded to Gaston — "bit part of my ear off earlier today," Danny told them.

Donavan pulled a pad and pen from his blue shirt pocket and started taking down information.

Quickly, he jotted down Gaston's true name before he was tempted to use Danny's slur. "Is this true, Gaston? Did you bite part of his ear off in an altercation?"

"Yes, it's true. He came out here trying to get two thousand dollars off me."

"Why were you trying to get money from him, Danny? Does he owe you money?"

"Hell yes, he owes me money. We signed a lease with my uncle when we rented the apartment over the furniture store, and in the lease, it states that if either of us moves out before two years is up, we have to fork over two thousand bucks. This little bitch moved in with his boyfriend here and stuck me with owin' all the fuckin' money."

"Danny, the best you could do, if the money were really owed you, would be to take your complaint to small claims court." Lawrence entered into the conversation. "This is not something that would concern the detectives."

"You're right, Lawrence, the money wouldn't be of concern, but assault is very much a concern," Donavan told him.

Then turning to Danny, he said, "Danny, do you wish to press charges on Gaston?"

"I sure as hell do. Little fucker's gonna owe a doctor bill too."

"If I was you, Roberts," — Jack leaned over close to Danny — "I'd make sure and get a rabies shot. Although I doubt it's gonna do you any good. A bite from a Hindel or those they are known to run with is usually lethal."

"What the fuck are you sayin'?" His hand went automatically to his injured ear. "Aw shit! You ain't tellin' me this son-of-a-bitch has AIDS!"

"Not that I'm aware of. But from all my dealings with the Hindels, and I'm counting you two and all their kin," — his eyes widened as his brows lifted — "I'd say AIDS is the least of your worries if one of them bit you," Donavan informed him.

"You know, Detective Hays," Lawrence spoke up, "defamation of character is not a good thing either, and you are defaming my character in front of witnesses."

"Lawrence, may I remind you that I have seen Jonathan Hindel in full makeup running out of my own yard? As did Detective Olivier' and our wives, so don't stand here and tell me I don't know what the hell I am talking about."

"If we were to go into court, would you be willing to stand up and relate this sighting to all present? I think you would be heralded as a lunatic who believes in horror movies. Not a good person to have as Chief Detective on the Saint Anthony Parish Sheriff's Department." Lawrence smothered a laugh with his hand.

"A person should never cast aspersions when they can be made to look worse than the person they are calling out," Donavan told him, moving closer. "I wouldn't be threatening someone who can have you sent back to the psych ward with simply a phone call. You may want to keep that in mind before you start running your mouth next time."

"You will not threaten me, Detective Hays." Lawrence

looked him right in his eyes. "If you do believe I am a rougarou, then you may want to keep that fact in mind before threatening me. Only a cautionary measure you may wish to heed."

Without a word, Donavan lifted his .44 Magnum from where it had been placed after Jack had secured Gaston in cuffs and put the barrel squarely against Lawrence's temple. "If you even think about coming after me or any of my family, and I am including Detective Olivier´ and his family here, I will blow your fuckin' head clean off your shoulders so I know you can't come back again." He smiled as he saw Lawrence swallow deeply. "Then I will have Seelah call on the Holy Ones to come forth to bind you in chains and cast you into the fires of hell with your daddy and grandpa, so these are a few things *you* may want to think about before deciding to come creeping up on me or mine."

Lawrence wisely backed away, rubbing his temple where Donavan's gun had left a prominent groove.

The man who had come with Danny spoke up with a noticeable tremor in his voice. "Danny, I think we need to get the hell out of here and get you to someone who can do you some good."

Danny turned to leave then turned back. "Gaston, if I find out you've given me somethin' that's gonna fuck with my life, I will make sure I take you out before I die. This is not a threat, Gaston. This is a promise I am making right here in front of two officers of the law and anyone else who wants to listen."

"Danny, if you know of anyone…voodoo…shaman…witch, you best be payin' them a call `cause I can tell you right now, if Gaston's sharin' pushups with our friend Lawrence here," — he gave Lawrence a mighty slap on the back — "you can bet your ass he's sharin' more than a little slap and tickle. There's gonna come a night when you find yourself barkin' at the moon and lopin' `round the countryside on all fours!"

"So what's it going to be, Danny? Are you going to come down to the station to press charges against your former roommate here?" Donavan laid a hand on Gaston's shoulder.

"Fuck Gaston. His time'll come," he yelled. The two took

off running then stopped. "You wanna move your vehicle so we can get the hell outta here?"

"I'll get it, Donavan," Jack told him, moving off the porch. "The keys are still in the ignition."

As Donavan removed the handcuffs, Gaston threw back his head, laughing loudly. "You're too late, Danny, you stupid asshole. You're too damn late!"

"For two cents, I would shoot both of you where you stand," Donavan told them.

"We haven't done anything, though, Detective Hays," Lawrence spoke up, joining Gaston in his humor.

"I can wait, Lawrence. Just remember when the time is right, just like Jack took care of Rafael and Chandra took care of Jonathan, I'll be here to take care of you and any others of your species that need to be wiped from this earth."

And when the time is right, we'll be here to take care of you, Lawrence thought to himself, taking great pleasure in the visual.

CHAPTER TEN

The night was waning fast, and Lawrence knew they must be getting ready for the ritual to introduce Gaston to the dark side.

The room on the other side of the wall in the basement was all but set for the ceremony.

Lawrence wished they still had the cave with all the tables and couches used so often by his father, Jonathan. He knew he would never stop missing the man who was such an important part of his life.

Gaston walked over as he saw Lawrence standing just inside the door of the room.

Slipping his arms around Lawrence's slim waist, he pulled him back against him. "What has you so sad? This is an important night for me. You should be happy."

"I was thinking about my father, Jonathan, wishing he was here with us this night. He always enjoyed the rituals so much."

"I heard the one detective say Jonathan was in hell along with your grandfather, Rafael. Was that only a figure of speech, or is it true?"

Lawrence swiped a hand beneath his eyes unashamedly. "No, it is true. He was supposed to have come back to this plane to be reborn."

"How do they do that? I've heard about the protestant religions talkin' 'bout bein' reborn, but I think they have a whole different meanin'."

"Yes, the Protestants believe if you give your soul to God and follow the path of Jesus, your soul is reborn into a new life. However, we believe that to be reborn after living on this plane for centuries, the spirit who is ready to be reborn onto this plane must find a woman who is about to give birth, and after pushing the soul of the fetus aside, the spirit enters the fetus with its own soul to be born and grow up to live life all over again."

For a moment, the thought of an innocent child being pushed to the side for another's needs pulled at him until that strange numbing of his feelings moved over him again, and the feeling went away. "But where does the soul of the fetus who has been pushed aside go?"

"The soul goes into limbo to await another time to be born, and if that time never comes, then so be it. The fetus the new mother births will love her little child thinking all is well until he or she begins showing its true self, killing and eating the family pet, or suddenly small children around the neighborhood will begin to disappear one at a time."

A cold chill passed over Gaston as Lawrence's words crept over him. Is this what he was becoming? He had never had any desire to harm a child or an animal. He withdrew his arms from around Lawrence's waist. He loved animals, and he had always cared about the safety of small children. Then the taste of sweet wine filled his mouth as it had when he had bitten off part of Danny's ear, and he forgot all about the horrors of animals and small children as the craving for that sweet taste filled him with an overpowering need to enjoy that taste again.

"The room is ready, but we still need to have our sacrifice for the ritual."

"Where are we going to find a sacrifice?"

"For your introduction into the dark side, you will need the offering of a young person. Preferably a child or at least a teen. Innocence is what will bring the master forth to welcome you into the fold."

"Where do we find such a person?" He was getting that backing away feeling again.

"Leave that to me, Gaston. I know since you have not given fully of your soul, you still have the feelings of the weak. This will pass quickly, though, once you know what lies ahead for you," Lawrence told him, noting the sick look crossing Gaston's handsome face.

"What should I be doin' to get ready?"

"Relaxing. You will need all your strength for the ceremony," Lawrence told him, then walked into the living room and seating himself in a chair and, closing his eyes, breathed deep to relax his mind.

Within moments, he was joined by the presence of Rolan. "How kind of you to invite me for this evening's ritual, Lawrence. I will be bringing all the souls of the ones who lost their lives here on the estate and others still in body if that is all right with you."

Lawrence spoke his thoughts aloud, wanting to get Gaston ready to accept spirit presence. "That will be fine, Rolan." Then turning to look at Gaston as he stood watching him from the doorway, he said, "We have an important visitor, Gaston. Rolan is here to let me know he will be bringing many of the souls killed here on the estate and others who are still in body to your initiation into the dark side."

"Will all those comin' be rougarous, too?"

"Yes, Gaston, why, were there others you wished to invite?"

"No." Gaston turned and walked out of the house.

Undeterred, Lawrence rose to his feet to follow Gaston outside. "Gaston." He looked at him, noting how different he looked in the soft pastel blue long-sleeved shirt rolled up to the elbows and name-brand jeans instead of the faded and time-worn attire he had been wearing before. He felt a rush of pride, knowing this handsome man was his. He walked up to him now as he stood on the porch looking out across the yard. "I understand your hesitancy to enter into all this. It is all new and strange to you. But this will all change once you have finished all that is needed to become a rougarou. When my grandfather wanted me to come forth and become one with the rest of my lineage, I didn't think I could do it. I will not lie to you, Gaston. At the onset of the ceremony, you will probably be very frightened with what you see and hear. This will pass. Will you trust me on what I am telling you?" Lawrence took him by the shoulders to turn him around. "I will never lie to you, Gaston. I love you. A relationship built on lies cannot last. I want our relationship to last. I want this very much."

Without a word, Gaston moved into Lawrence's arms, holding him close against him until he felt Lawrence pull away.

"I must get ready to go out and see to our offerings for this night, my love. While I am gone, I want you to enjoy some white wine and try to relax your mind. I caution you against anything stronger than wine until after the ceremony has ended. I want you to have a clear mind and a relaxed body."

Dressed in a pair of black slacks, a pale yellow long-sleeved shirt topped with a yellow v-neck sweater, and a pair of black leather shoes, he waved a hand in the air on his way to the Land Rover parked in front of the mansion.

Lawrence knew he should have already found the offering for this evening's ritual and slapped one hand against the steering wheel in his anger. So much unfairness had invaded his life this past year. He wondered when the cycle of bad luck would reverse and begin to benefit him. Since he had done nothing to call forth these bad happenings, he was at a loss as to how he could change them. First his father, then his grandfather, and many of the family had been taken from him, then as if that wasn't enough, his own freedom had been ripped away with his stay in the mental hospital and all through no fault of his own.

At that moment, a face drifted into his mind, and he knew without a doubt in his mind whose life he would be offering up for the ritual.

* * *

Donavan drew a comb through his dark brown hair on

each side and down the back of his head, wishing he had the full head of hair he had when he and Barbara first met a little over sixteen years ago. Then he laughed, being glad there was any hair at all with the stressful job he had. It wasn't easy being the lead detective in the Saint Anthony Parish Sheriff's Department.

After splashing aftershave over his freshly shaven face, he pulled open the wooden door on his bathroom cabinet to take out the cologne Barb liked for him to wear when they were going out on the town. Pouring a small amount into each palm, he rubbed his hands briskly together then drew them down the front of his dark blue long-sleeved shirt, making sure not to get any on his pale blue silk tie. Walking over, he stood in front of the floor-to-ceiling mirror and, turning this way and that, admired his slimmer body with the all but flat stomach. He smiled with pride that his hard work at the gym was paying off nicely. His weight loss allowed him to feel comfortable wearing the cream-colored slacks he had donned for this evening that made him feel better about himself.

"Admiring yourself in the mirror again, are we?" Barbara walked into the bathroom wearing a soft pastel green dress that clung to her ripe curves and showed off her dark tan to her advantage. A few hours each week was all that was needed to keep her skin the honey color she liked and Donavan admired. She had recently had her blond hair cut short and layered, and the dark green studs peeking out from the bouncy curls accented the dress to perfection.

Without warning, Barbara grabbed him in a bear hug to sniff up and down his shirt front. "Yummy, I could rip this shirt off your body and kiss my way up to your lips," she purred, bringing a pleased laugh from Donavan

"Or better yet, I could kick off these slacks and shorts and let you feast your way in the other direction."

"Gettin' to ya, am I?"

"You got to me when you shucked your clothes and jumped in the shower. If I'd been smart, I would have jumped your bones right then," he whispered against her throat. "Now

I'll have to lug this heavy boner around all night."

Jenny cleared her throat loudly before walking into the bedroom. "Not interrupting anything, I hope," she giggled, moving to the bathroom door.

"No, sweetheart, you're not interrupting anything," he said, turning so his back was facing her. "Mom and I are just finishing up getting ready to go out this evening. Are you all dressed to babysit Donny?"

"Yep." She posed in the doorway. "Wearin' my favorite outfit of jeans and t-shirt and tenny runners."

"You know you are more than welcome to come with us this evening if you don't feel like babysitting. Aunt Seelah and Uncle Jack can always call on the teenager across the street to watch Donny," Barbara told her.

"Donny is my responsibility. He will not stay with anyone but me." She looked at her mother as though she should have already known this. "He will cry his little eyes out if I'm not there to watch over him when his mom and dad are gone. I am his Jen Jen."

"He does seem to love you a lot. Just as we all do." Her dad dropped a quick kiss atop her dark brown head.

"You have both of our cell numbers, and also here is the telephone number of where we'll be this evening. If you have any problems, no matter how small, just call this number, and we will be home before you can hang up the phone probably," her mom told her, handing Jenny a folded piece of paper that she quickly stuffed into the pocket of her jeans.

"You guys worry too much," Jenny laughed, turning and heading down the hall to get Brandy, who was sleeping in her room.

"I wouldn't worry half as much if Lawrence had stayed his ass gone like I hoped he would," Donavan whispered, smiling as he felt his arm thrown in the air as Brandy came up to him. "You and Lugar be sure and take good care of the kids tonight," he murmured.

"I feel the same way," Barbara said, bending down to give the big dog a brief hug. "It's like having a poisonous snake living under the house, and you never know when it will crawl through a crack and come inside to get you," Barbara told him.

Donavan glanced at her, nodding. "That's a damn good description of him. A slithering little fuck you want to beware of." He grabbed a light jacket off the back of a kitchen chair. "Just in case it turns chilly," he laughed as Barbara stood looking at him.

* * *

It was a merry foursome who piled into the family car to head out for their favorite restaurant, leaving Jenny, Donny, Brandy, and Lugar behind to enjoy a fun-filled evening on their own.

He watched the car pull away from the curb, and his adrenaline climbed to its highest, making him want to get in the house and enjoy what awaited him. Quietly, he crept forward to hide in some trees bordering the side of the house to watch and wait for his chance.

* * *

With their orders taken, they pushed back their chairs to take advantage of the great band playing some of the latest music.

"Have you noticed how much lighter I am on my feet now?" Donavan asked, snapping his hips first to the right then to the left to bring a loud twitter from Barbara.

"You don't have as much to move as you did before."

"Now, if I could get a hair transplant, I think I'd be looking pretty damn good."

"You already look pretty damn good to me, and I'm the only one you need to worry about looking good for," she told him, leaning forward to plant a kiss on his puckered lips.

"All right, you two, no gettin' down on the dance floor," Jack snickered, "they have places called a motel for urges like that."

"They also have a place called home to take care of those urges," Seelah spoke up then giggled as Jack leaned her into a dip. "Aw, you are so groovy, Detective Olivier´."

"I have moves you ain't even seen yet, baby." He pulled her upright, then burst out laughing as she leapt into the air to throw her long legs around his waist.

"What were you saying about moves, old man?"

Jack was still laughing as he stood her on her feet.

Seelah drew both hands down her slim hips, smoothing her mini black and white dress into place, then bowed to the applause ringing out around the dance floor.

Jack, enjoying the attention, flipped up the collar of his black long-sleeved shirt, clicked his black boots together and with a leering grin, threw a surprised Seelah over his shoulder to stride back to their table.

Seelah was still laughing as she looked around, catching all the admiring glances coming their way, especially from the ladies. At first, seeing their hungry eyes moving down Jack's slim physique encased in tight jeans and catching their whispered comments about his devil-may-care good looks, she felt a stab of jealousy, but as she looked at him, her jealous feelings changed to pride that the man they were secretly wishing belonged to them already belonged to her.

"I love you, ole' man," she told him, pulling him over for a long, passionate kiss that left them both shaken and panting.

"I can tell right now this is gonna be a short night out," Jack snickered, glancing around the table.

"Oh, come on, you guys," Barbara said, "you have all night to work off your needs. Let's enjoy this great time we're having together."

For a moment, Seelah started to protest but then gave in, knowing how much they all needed a night out on the town. Most of all, Barbara and Donavan. Too much stress was not a good thing, and it had been less than a year since Donavan had had his heart attack. With a real smile, she grabbed onto Jack's arm to pull him up and out of his chair and back onto the dance floor.

* * *

He worked his way around to the back of the house to quietly try the door, cursing under his breath when he found it locked. Not to be deterred, he kept moving around the house until he came to a window that had the curtains only partially drawn. He could see her now, sitting on the couch with the baby cuddled up beside her watching a show on TV. His breath caught in his throat as his hungry eyes slid down over her budding breasts that he knew would be firm and taste so good in his dry mouth. He slid a hand down his body until he came to the pulsating bulge demanding to be satisfied. Pulling open the snap on his jeans, he pulled the zipper all the way down to slide his hand inside. Feasting his eyes on the beautiful young girl inside the house, he began to fondle his swollen cock, all the while wishing he had the nerve to go inside and work off his needs like the men did to the women in his dad's porno movies he was so fond of watching when no one was around. His favorites were the ones showing bondage and the spilling of blood.

Jenny felt Donny's small hand pulling at her arm, and she glanced over at him to see his little face staring at the window where a slight movement caught her eye.

Without being obvious, she slid from the couch and, picking Donny up in her arms, she walked down the hall to the back of the house to where Brandy and Lugar lay sleeping in the doorway of the guest room.

She smacked her leg to get their attention, and slipping quietly to the glass door leading out onto the patio, she pulled the door open to whisper, "Hold, Lugar!" The huge shepherd took off with Brandy right behind him.

A scream split the air as she was dialing 9-1-1.

CHAPTER ELEVEN

Gaston donned the blood-red robe with an attached cowl. He stood before the long mirror, admiring himself and trying not to think of the coming events, telling himself Lawrence would not lead him into anything he knew would cause problems in their blossoming relationship.

"It is almost time to go, Gaston," Lawrence murmured his pride at seeing Gaston dressed in the red robe that only enhanced his dark good looks.

Gaston looked at Lawrence's reflection in the mirror and felt a shiver of unease at how ominous he looked dressed in a black robe with the attached cowl covering his head and hiding part of his face.

Lawrence put a hand up to touch Gaston's shoulder, then drew back as he felt him pull away. "What is wrong?"

"I'm not sure this is what I want to do. It just all seems so unreal. Like something I would see in a horror movie, not in real life."

"This is a very normal feeling, Gaston. You don't know what to expect, and until you do, until you have gone through the ceremony, you will continue to feel as you do now."

"What if I said I want to leave and forget the ceremony?"

"Is that what you want? Even knowing it is you, everyone has come to the estate to meet and welcome into a new life?"

"Can I trust you, Lawrence? I mean, really trust you not to bring me any harm?"

His voice was like that of a child, and Lawrence moved closer to take him into his arms. "I will never hurt you, my darling. You have become much too important to me."

"Then let's go and join the others. I know how hard you have worked to make this night a success. I don't want to shame you by not being ready to accept what you have planned."

Slipping an arm around Gaston's waist, they left the room to make their way down the basement stairs and to the room on the other side of the wall.

* * *

Both Donavan and Barbara were out of the car and running to the front of the house, their hearts in their throats as they saw all the police cars lining the driveway and the street.

Jenny ran outside to meet them halfway in the yard.

"Jenny, are you all right, sweetheart?" Donavan wrapped her and Barbara in his arms. "I almost went into cardiac arrest when you called."

"I'm fine, Daddy," she told him before bursting into laughter.

"What did that son-of-a-bitch do, Jenny?" Jack ran up to pull her out of Donavan and Barbara's arms and into his.

"I can't believe I didn't get a heads up that you were in danger," Seelah moaned, standing in the yard wringing her hands. "Especially since you were in our own house with our son."

"Don't go blaming yourself for this, Seelah," Barbara told her, walking over to put her arms around her.

"It was Hindel, wasn't it?" Jack's anger exploded. "I'll kill that son-of-a-bitch if he laid one finger on you or Donny!" Jack looked around. "Speakin' of Donny, where the hell is he?"

"A policewoman is holding him. He's fine. But the sick little twit across the street ain't. He's the one who was peeking in the window." She burst into laughter again.

"What the hell are you finding funny about this, Jenny?

Are you sure you're all right and not going into hysterics?"

"When you see him, Dad, you'll understand." Reaching an arm around her parents' waists, she walked with them into the house.

One of the officers walked over to begin filling them in on what was going on. "The boy across the street has been peeking into windows around the neighborhood for months now, and even though the police have had a lot of calls about him, until tonight, they were never able to catch him in action."

"How was it they were able to catch him this time?" Donavan asked.

"They didn't," Jenny told them. "When I felt Donny pulling on my arm, I looked at him to see what was wrong, and that's when I saw a movement at the window. So I went and woke up Lugar and Brandy, and after giving Lugar the command to hold, I eased open the glass door onto the patio. Then I called nine-one-one."

"That sick little bastard. When I get to the station, I'm gonna beat the ever-lovin' piss outta him. Comin' on to my property to get his thrills watchin' my babies!" Jack raged, smacking a closed fist repeatedly in the palm of his hand.

"You don't need to go to the station, detective," the officer spoke up. "The perp is still on the patio."

At the officer's words, they all trooped outside to find a young male lying on the floor of the patio, a puddle of urine spreading out around him, his jeans unsnapped with the zipper pulled all the way down. Still standing over him were Brandy and Lugar, daring him to move.

"This is the young man, detectives. His name is Bobby Denton, and he lives across the street from you," the same young officer told them.

"Looks like you got yourself in quite a pickle, Bobby, my boy." Jack walked over to him and, drawing back his leg, kicked the teenager square in the seat of his pants as he stared up at them. "What do you have to say for yourself, fuck tard?"

"Could you call off your dogs?" He tried to sound brave, but the tremor in his young voice let him know he was failing miserably. "I ain't goin' nowhere."

Donavan leaned over and, with one hand, yanked the boy upright to his feet. "That's for Goddamn sure, prick!" Motioning one of the officers forward, he told him, "Cuff this deviant little bastard and book him."

Standing with his hands behind his back, waiting to be cuffed, he drew back as he saw the pretty young girl he had been watching walk over to him. For a long moment, she stood there. Then, drawing back her hand, smacked him as hard as she could across his pimply face. "I hope this teaches you something, you sick, pathetic little creep, but I doubt it." She laughed in his face before turning to walk away.

Reaching down, she hugged both dogs, telling them how brave and needed they were.

"Yeah, now if they can stay awake, they might turn out to be pretty good watchdogs," Jack laughed as they all walked inside, and he felt some of the tension loosen its hold on the back of his neck.

"So, are you all going back to finish your evening out?" Jenny asked, walking to the fridge to get herself a soda.

"After the scare I just had, you couldn't pay me to leave you and Donny alone again," Barbara spoke up, her voice still trembling.

"You thought we were dealin' with another Hindel attack, didn't you, Mom?" Jenny put her arms around her mother's neck to pull her close.

"Yes, Jenny, I did."

"Oh no," she cried, "does this mean you're all gonna start watchin' me like a hawk again?"

Seelah stepped forward to pull them both close against her. "From my perspective, I would say you handled this so well that you don't need to be watched like a little girl who can't take care of herself and our son."

"Donny was the brave one, Aunt Seelah. When he saw we

were bein' watched, all he did was pull on my arm to show me what was happenin'."

"That's my big brave boy," Jack told him, lifting Donny into the air to make him laugh.

"I think there's a little more to it than Donny just being brave," Seelah told them.

Lowering his son back down in his arms, Jack turned to look at her. "Please tell me he don't have...the gift."

"I'm not real sure how strongly he has the gift since at Donny's age, all children are psychic, but if I were to guess, I would say I don't think our son is going to outgrow his psychic abilities."

"Well." Jack looked at her. "Although I don't like the thought of my son bein' able to see spirits and talk to the dead, I know there ain't a damn thing I can do about it. I'll just put my trust in you as his mama to make sure this part of his life is safe and as normal as it can be under the circumstances. Right now, I just thank God that none of what happened here tonight had anything to do with a Hindel."

* * *

The ritual was about to begin, and Lawrence could see the shimmering spirits gathered around in the large room. He was glad to see his people had not disappointed him when Rolan had summoned them. Upstairs, he could still hear the ringing of the doorbell heralding more and more people coming once more to the Hindel estate to join in on the festivities. He had sent Gaston upstairs to welcome their guests, knowing he needed something to take his mind off the coming ceremony and knowing the guests would all still be in human form, he knew Gaston would be all right.

He tried to close his mind to the fact he had been unable to secure Olivier"s young son for the ceremony, knowing the master would not be pleased. When he had given his soul over to the dark side, he thought all his failures to be over, but it was not to be. He continued to be a disappointment in so many ways.

Gaston walked up to stand beside him. "I was told that all the ones who are coming have arrived, so I came down to be with you," he breathed, pulling a surprised Lawrence into his arms for a big hug and a deep kiss.

"Good." Lawrence stepped back. "The ritual is about to begin." He pulled the cowl into place over Gaston's head before leaving him to walk to a black, silk-draped altar. Holding up his hands as he had seen his father and grandfather do many times, he smiled as those in the room became silent.

"I would like to welcome you all here this evening to join in on the giving of yet another soul to the master. I also have to tell you that as heir to the Hindel Monarchy, at least here in the parish, I have failed in a very important part of the coming ritual." He broke off his words as he heard a scream coming from the back of the room. In an instant, he saw a black-robed man dragging something forward toward him.

"Am I right in assuming you have brought what I, in my ineptness, failed to bring forth?"

"I have brought an offering for you, Lawrence. I think he will do quite nicely for what we have in mind for him."

A teenager was laid out on the floor, and as he looked around the filled room, he knew he was not going to like what was about to happen to him this night.

"What is your name, young man?" Lawrence helped the teen to his feet.

"My name is Bobby Denton." His frightened eyes looked around. "Why have I been brought here?" He looked over at the cop who had brought him there. "I heard that detective tell you to take me to jail."

"Yes," the young officer who had just left the Olivier´ house responded, "seems I did hear Detective Donavan Hays say something like that. But knowing what was coming down this night, I thought since you didn't get to finish what you started at the Olivier´ house with Hays' young daughter, you might like to join in on the festivities here."

The officer stepped back as Lawrence came forward.

"Perhaps this night will work out well after all," he said, watching the teenager closely. "Tell me, Bobby, have you ever thought of what you would give to have all your wishes on this earth granted the rest of your life with simply the snap of your fingers?"

CHAPTER TWELVE

"Donavan, don't tell me you're calling to make sure everything is all right with Jack, Seelah, and Donny?" Barbara laughed, bringing her glass of scotch and water with a lime twist with her to the couch.

"No." He picked up her drink from the end table to take a sip. "I just want to make sure that our peeping tom got booked all right."

Barbara tapped her thumb on the arm of the couch in time to the music she had put on to listen to, still in the mood to be out on a dance floor laughing and having a good time.

"Detective Hays here, Sonya," he spoke into the phone, "connect me to central booking, please." He winked at Barbara, knowing she was still in a partying mood. "This will only take a moment, babe, then we can get back to enjoying that good music… hey, this is Hays. I just wanted to find out how that peeping tom I had sent in for booking is handling being behind bars?" He put his other hand on his chest to dance in place while he waited to hear from the man at central booking. "Denton. Bobby Denton. The teenager we caught window peeking earlier at Detective Olivier"'s residence."

"No one by that name has been brought in yet, Detective Hays. Do you have the name of the transporting officer?"

Donavan tried to bring the name of the young officer to mind but gave up. "No, tell you the truth, I don't think I even heard his name."

"Without his name, I'm afraid I can't help you, Detective Hays."

"What the fuck is going on here?" He hung up with central to punch in some more numbers.

The call was answered on the second ring. "This better be important," Jack said.

"Sorry to bother you, Jack. I didn't think you'd be asleep yet."

"I wasn't if you get my drift, so I would appreciate your making this quick." He sat up, pulling a grinning Seelah up close.

"I'm workin' my way up to that myself." He laughed, then grew serious. "The reason I'm calling, and I'll make this brief, is, did you happen to catch the name of that young officer who took Denton to the station? I just called central booking to see how things were going and was told the little asshole hasn't arrived yet."

"No, I didn't catch his name, and I don't recall even seein' his nameplate. This don't make any sense, though." Jack sat up straighter now, his curiosity piqued. "Little fucker should have been there an hour or so ago."

"I'll call and see who the department sent out on the call. No big deal. Maybe he got another call in the meantime and just took the perp along with him. Although, that is for damn sure against the rules. Anyway, carry on, Jack, and I'll catch up with you about all this tomorrow." He smiled as he heard a distinct click.

Barbara got up from the couch to dance her way across the floor to where Donavan stood, his arms outstretched, waiting.

"I don't want to turn the music up too loud since I'm sure by now Jenny is safe in her bed with Brandy fast asleep beside her." She nuzzled his ear, enjoying the manly smell of him mixed with her favorite aftershave and cologne he wore just for her.

"Sorry your evening was cut short, sweetheart. We can do it again tomorrow night if you'd like." He moved in time to the music, pulling her slender body in close.

"When Jenny called telling us to get home, that the cops were on the way, I thought I was going to pass out right there at the table."

"I know me too. I don't know what gets into some kids. TV programs have been thrown out as part of the cause, but I can't accept that. Why in the hell hasn't that little bastard been taken to booking yet?" He stopped moving as his mind continued to whirl around the question.

"Your heart is not in this, darling, so I suggest we just sit down and enjoy our drink."

"I still want to call the station and find out who they sent out on the call." He sat down in the chair and reached for the phone.

Barbara finished her drink and, grabbing both empty glasses, carried them to the kitchen for a refill.

"Hays here. I need you to check out the name of the officer sent out on that peeping tom complaint at Detective Olivier´'s residence."

"Here you go," Barbara said, setting a fresh drink on the table for him.

"Thanks, hon," he told her and then held up a hand for silence. "Officer Ronald Balfur. All right, thanks a lot, Jensen," he told the dispatcher. "Oh, by the way, what is his location?"

"Out of vehicle. That was over an hour ago. We still don't know his location."

Donavan felt his heart speed up. "What the fuck are you, a rookie? You know the rules. If an officer doesn't check in with his location every half hour or so after being out of vehicle, you go and find him!" With that said, he hung up the phone.

"What's going on, Donavan?"

"Seems the officer who transported our peeping tom hasn't been heard from. He gave his status as being out of vehicle over an hour ago, and he's not answering his page."

"That doesn't make any sense. He was transporting a prisoner. You don't take a joy ride with a prisoner in the car."

"You would think," Donavan agreed as he grabbed up the phone again.

"Who are you calling now? It is getting pretty late, you know."

"I know, and this phone call is not going to be happily received, so you might want to stand back out of the way of the bitching that's going to come flying through my ear and out the other side."

Without a word, Barbara took a sip of her drink and walked over to seat herself once more on the sofa. "Could I make a suggestion? If you know what you're going to do is going to get you in trouble, then why don't you come to sit down for a moment and enjoy your drink? That way, maybe the person you're trying to talk with won't be busy anymore."

Donavan hung up the phone and, grabbing his drink off the end table, walked across the floor to take a seat beside Barbara on the couch. "How did I luck out and get such a smart wife?" He pulled her into his arms and, taking a deep breath, felt himself relaxing.

* * *

Pulling Seelah's long legs from around his waist, he rolled to one side, taking her with him. He looked over at her now lying in his arms, the moonlight shining on her face, and drew her against his chest. Then leaning forward, he dropped a gentle kiss on her forehead.

For a moment, she lay still, relishing the love shining from his dark eyes. For the second time in her young life, she now had the overwhelming love of a man who made her feel like the most cherished woman in the world. However, at the moment, she was not in the mood for moonbeams and flowery words. One of the great things she had learned in the time she had been married to Jack Olivier´ was when it came to the art of making love, he was a master, and he was not afraid to share the lead with his woman.

Without a word, she moved atop his relaxing body and, leaning forward, began nipping and suckling his hard nipples, making him moan deep in his throat, all the while rubbing her warm, wet clit against his flaccid manhood until she felt his damp cock begin to stir then harden. She moved back and, with a snap of her hips, rammed him inside her hungry vault where she so wanted him to be.

A delighted grin dispelled the utter shock, and he gladly moved beneath her small body, all the while guiding her hips in a steady up and down rhythm, hoping he could keep up with her as he had just finished this same dance minutes earlier.

Seelah looked down at him and, seeing the grin spreading across his handsome face, pumped her body faster and faster, determined to wipe the teasing grin away.

"Baby, you need to slow down, or you're gonna be left wantin'. I can't keep up this pace since you already ravaged me once tonight!"

Seelah ignored his cries for mercy and pumped her body all the faster until she felt the telling chills begin to rack her body. Only then did she slow her pace and allow Jack to catch up and explode inside her velvet tunnel for the second time that night.

She rolled to the side, panting, "You have just been conquered, old man."

* * *

"I don't want anything but out of here." Bobbie Denton looked up at the young officer staring at him, a large grin covering his face. "You need to do your job and take me out of here and to jail."

"I will ask you again, my young friend, would you like to have everything life has to offer, or would you rather leave with this officer of the law and go to jail?" Lawrence interrupted, trying to keep his patience. "What was it you did to call attention to yourself from the law?"

Bobbie simply glanced at him then away.

Seeing as how Lawrence wasn't going to get anything from Bobbie, the officer, Balfur, told him, "He was caught peeking in the window at the home of Detective Olivier"'s residence. He was watching the young daughter of Detective Hays while she was babysitting the Olivier´'s' young son."

At the mention of the young boy whose body was to be the vehicle for his father's return to this plane, he could feel his anger spinning out of control.

"Jack Olivier´ and Donavan Hays have both been a thorn in my side for far too long. They must be made to realize a Hindel is not to be made a fool. There will come a time when they will beg me to end their worthless lives."

Rolan stepped forth from the shadows. "Lawrence, the ceremony is ready to begin." He turned, looking to the young man still laid out on the floor. "Is he to be a sacrifice to the master, or will he be one more conquest to the dark side?"

"What will you choose, Bobbie, life on this plane for hundreds of years? Or the most horrible death you can imagine?"

Bobbie scrambled to his feet as those standing around the room began to change into creatures he had only seen in horror movies. "Oh my God! What are you? You ain't real!" He tried to run, but the young officer grabbed him to hold him in place.

"You can forego all this ugliness, Bobbie. Simply say aloud that you give your soul of your own free will to the master."

"Fuck you! Get away from me! You are all freaks!"

"Strip him and clothe him in the white robe. He will be our sacrifice this night," Lawrence said, then walked to the altar.

Holding up his hands, he waited as those in the room became silent. "This is a night of both happiness and sadness. This night of offering up in sacrifice to our beloved master the soul of Gaston Laufett so he can live for centuries without having to die and return after only a few years will bring much pleasure to the master who always enjoys welcoming another child into his fold." Lawrence spoke his words quietly as he looked to the end of the room, where he could see Gaston waiting to be summoned forward.

"However, there is also sadness felt this night for those in the Hindel family who are missing. My father and grandfather will not be able to join us in spirit as they have both been bound and thrown into the darkness to await the turning of their souls over to the God of light."

At Lawrence's words, a great clamor of moans and stomping of feet rose up around the room.

"They will never do this!" he continued, his voice growing in strength as he looked out over the room. "They were two of our greatest leaders! No more will we be able to call on their spirits to come to the rituals to join in on the souls being offered up to the master! The two men responsible for this atrocity are our sworn enemies, Donavan Hays and Jack Olivier´!"

"Kill them! Kill them"! Became the chant heard around the room.

"All in good time, my loved ones," Lawrence promised, raising his hands in the air for silence. "Because of Jack Olivier´'s son, my father will not be reborn onto this plane as he had planned. This cannot go unpunished!"

The room erupted once more, calling for the death of Jack Olivier´ and his son.

"My grandfather is not here tonight to join us. For no reason, he was murdered right here on this estate. The man who took his life, who ended over two centuries of his living upon this plane, is, once again, Jack Olivier´. When my grandfather's spirit returned to take his just revenge, he was bound and taken to the dark side to await his turning away from wanting to serve the master."

Gaston looked around, watching as hatred filled the room. The negativity was so strong he felt sick to his stomach.

He backed out of the room, thinking to run when he heard Lawrence call his name. He tried to move, but his legs refused to obey his commands. Terror such as he had never known filled every part of his being.

"Come forth and pledge your soul to the most high, Gaston," Lawrence summoned him.

Almost without being aware of his movements, Gaston walked forth until he stood before the altar and Lawrence's outstretched hand.

Lawrence led him around the podium to stand by his side.

"There is no reason for fear, Gaston. You are making the right choice. I am going to show you what you have in your future if you give your soul to the master."

Gaston stood still then stepped back as a scene began to take form in front of him. He saw himself and Lawrence laughing and sharing their days together in the mansion. Money inside an open safe was withdrawn and put into his hands. People bowed upon hearing his name and smiled when he walked into a room. His heart filled with pride at what he was seeing. No one had ever shown him respect. Now he was overwhelmed with adulation and power.

Abruptly, the scene changed to one of pure love. He was walking through a meadow of flowers and laughing children as they walked beside Gaston toward a man dressed in a long white robe who was holding out his hands to them. Gaston stopped walking and looked behind him to where he could hear people fighting and screaming and withering as their bodies were being charred in burning flames. He could actually smell the burned flesh, and he covered his mouth, trying not to throw up. The scene changed, showing only him and Lawrence and the love he felt for this man. The love welling up inside his chest overpowered anything else he had been shown.

Bobbie tried to get free of the hands stripping off his clothes. "Get your fuckin' hands off me, you perverted sons ah bitches!"

"Hold still, you little prick," Balfur told him, slapping him a hard blow to the back of his head and pulling the white robe into place. "You want to look good for all your friends, don't you? `Course you do. You're gonna be the star attraction." He laughed, yanking the hood over Bobbie's head. "For a while anyway."

"What do you choose, Gaston, a life of ease and respect or a life of hardship and despair?"

Gaston turned toward Lawrence and, taking his face in

both his hands, declared, "I choose to give my soul to the master and to embrace all he has to offer. I choose to be a child of darkness and to live the rest of my life as the master's child. And I choose to live my life by your side, Lawrence."

Overwhelmed, Lawrence pulled Gaston into his arms then stood back as he saw a dark shadow beginning to emerge. "The master has come forth to welcome you into the fold, Gaston. Walk into his waiting arms to receive his gift of immortality."

For a brief moment, Gaston felt his heart leap with fear, then it was gone as he walked forward to embrace the one who would change his life forever.

CHAPTER THIRTEEN

Jack lay back, enjoying the relaxed feelings rolling over his body. He breathed out a deep sigh of utter contentment then cussed aloud into the silence as the shrill ringing of the phone interrupted his moment of tranquility.

"Donavan, what in the fuck do you want now? Can't a man enjoy a night of uninterrupted bliss with his beautiful wife without you having to bother him?" He shook a cigarette out of the pack lying on the end table and was reaching for his lighter when the voice on the other line froze his movements.

"The master awaits the blood of the pure. Very soon, your son will feed this need. Donavan Matthew Olivier"'s days are numbered."

"Who the fuck is this?" Jack yelled into the phone only to hear the steady drone of a dial tone.

"What is going on, Jack?" Seelah sat up in the bed.

"Some son-of-a-bitch just threatened Donny," he told her, turning and pulling the phone onto the bed. "See if you can tell who the hell it was that just called."

Seelah moved over closer and putting her hand on the phone, waiting to see what would come through from the other side.

"Well, who was it?"

"That's strange," she whispered. "I'm not getting anything.

Someone is blocking me."

"Chandra," Jack called out into the darkness. "You need to get your misty ass here right God damn now!"

"Jack," Seelah scolded him. "I think you could ask Chandra to come here a little nicer than that."

"I want to know who the hell just threatened our son, Seelah! I don't have time for pleasantries!"

"I am sure she will come as soon as she can. Spirits aren't idle on the other side. They have a life too."

"I must say, you're takin' this pretty damn good," he told her, reaching once more for the phone.

* * *

Barbara answered on the first ring. "Hey, Jack."

"I need to speak with Donavan, hon. Is he right there handy?"

"He should be just about dried off from his shower. I'll go see. Hold on," she told him, carrying the handheld phone with her. Tapping on the door, she walked inside. "Jack's on the phone for you, sweetheart." She handed the phone to him.

"Yeah, what's up, Jack?"

"Some motherfucker just called threatenin' Donny's life."

"Oh shit!" He braced the phone with his shoulder to finish drying off. "Hold on a minute, Jack, until I slip on a robe," he said, laying the phone down on the sink. He grabbed his robe off the hook on the door, slipped his arms through the sleeves, then picked up the phone. "Okay, now tell me what the hell is going on."

"Like I said, some motherfucker threatened Donny's life tellin' me his days are numbered. It's someone connected with the Hindels. You can bet your ass on that!"

"I would have to agree, but what makes you so sure it is a Hindel involved?"

"Why? I'll tell you why. When I had Seelah try and find out who it was, she said she couldn't because someone was blockin' her. You and I both know this only happens when one of them creepy fuckers are involved."

"I can't believe I am saying this but has she called on Chandra to lend a hand?"

"I don't think she has, but she just went in to take a shower, so she may already be talkin' to her. If not, I'm sure she'll be talkin' to her soon. I do know one thing, though. I'm not steppin' foot out of this house or away from Donny's side until I know who called."

"I don't know, Jack." He pulled the door open to walk out into the hall. "We blow the damn place up to get rid of them, and the asshole just builds another house, *and* I would venture to guess there are more Hindels either on their way here or already here."

"Did you ever run down the cop and the perp? There's a mystery in itself."

"No, and if I wasn't afraid of leaving our families unprotected, I'd suggest I bring mine over to your house, and we go check out the Hindel mansion to see if we can at least find the damn car."

"I'd be all for doin' just that, but we don't even know who the hell to trust to leave on guard. Hell, for all we know, the whole Goddamn police force could be werewolves!"

"Hey, babe." Donavan turned as Barbara brushed past him to go into the bathroom. "So what do you want to do? I can get a couple uniforms over here if you want to bring Seelah and Donny here. Oh, and we don't want to forget Lugar."

"Let me find out what Seelah has been able to learn from Chandra, if anything, and I'll give you a call back."

"Okay," Donavan told him. "I'll be here."

Tapping on the bathroom door, Jack walked into the room to hear a one-way conversation going on behind the glass shower door.

"Just so you know, sweetheart, I am not trying to listen in on your conversation. I am just trying to see if you have heard anything from Chandra on who called to threaten Donny."

Seelah pulled open the shower door to step out. Grabbing

the towel Jack held out to her, she wiped herself off then wrapped it around her, tucking in the top flap.

"Chandra said the one who threatened Donny's life is Rolan Hindel. He is one of the rougarous who was blown up in the Hindel estate, but he has returned to wreak havoc on you and Donavan and your families. He speaks through someone who is still human. She did not say who."

She undid the towel and, turning, hung it up on the shower rod. She smiled as she found Jack holding out her robe as she turned back around.

"So we still don't know who is out to do Donny harm except for a fuckin' spirit who takes over someone else's body."

"I am not worried, Jack. Chandra is going to continue to keep her energy attuned to ours, so if Donny or one of us is in danger, she will be here to protect us."

"Now that makes me feel a lot better. I am going to give Donavan a call back, and we might be going over to his house so we can go and check out something."

"Then I'll hurry and get Donny and myself ready to travel."

When Donavan answered the phone, Jack filled him in on what was going on. "Okay, then we'll let Seelah check out anyone the department sends over and go from there."

"Sounds good."

"I'll bet your left nut the mansion's where we'll find those fuckers. And if I'm right, I don't think our little peepin' tom's likin' what's happenin' to him right about now."

* * *

Gaston felt pain such as he had never experienced in his life. It felt like every cell in his body was being ripped out through his skin. He looked at his hands to see long, sharp nails growing out of his fingers and long, black hairs popping out of his pores. A high-pitched scream tore from his throat, making Bobbie fight all the harder against the hands holding him and forcing him to watch what was happening to Gaston.

"Turn me loose," he screamed, twisting and turning in an

attempt to get free. "This can't be happening."

Gaston raised his head, a long, deep howl erupting from his throat as a strong hunger came over him. A hunger for fresh blood and raw flesh.

"Bring the sacrifice forward," Lawrence demanded.

"That's your cue, Bobbie boy," Officer Balfur told him, grabbing him by the nape of his neck to drag him forward. "I'm savin' the taxpayers a lotta money this day. By my bringin' you here to serve out your sentence 'stead of throwin' your little ass in jail, the parish don't have to feed and house you, and the best part is, I'll bet every cent I have in my pocket this is gonna break your addiction to jerkin' off while watchin' young girls."

While Balfur held Bobbie in a viselike grip, Lawrence said, "Gaston, I offer up your first feast as a child of the master. When you have had your fill, you may share your feast with the rest of the family."

Bobbie screamed and kicked but could not rid himself of the hold Balfur had on him.

As though he had no will of his own, Gaston reached out, yanking the teen forward to sink his teeth into the warm throat of his first victim and at last tasted the sweet red wine he had so hungered for.

Lawrence stood back, watching Gaston as he began the change from a human to that of a rougarou, and closed his ears to Gaston's screams of pain. He knew there was always pain during the change from a human to a wolf. It was the price that must be paid to live the life of a rougarou. With the intoxicating smells filling the air, he could feel his own hunger yearn for fulfillment. Without waiting for Gaston to invite others to join in on the feasting, Lawrence motioned a man standing at the back of the room, holding someone in his arms, to come forward.

Keeping his eyes focused on the long, wide altar ahead of him, he moved steadily forward until he could rid himself of his burden.

She was dressed in a transparent gown of soft, white,

gauzelike material. Her lush curves were exposed to the hungry eyes feasting on her extraordinary beauty. Her long mane of deep auburn hair flowed out around her.

"It is time for you to awaken, my beautiful Christina. Waken and pay for what you wrought on this estate almost a year ago." Lawrence bent over to whisper.

Christina Crawford opened her beautiful green eyes, trying to focus and to think where she was. Then it came to her. A man had come to the door, and when she answered his knock, he had quickly covered her face with a cloth soaked in a strong-smelling liquid before everything went black.

Lawrence helped her to sit up. "Sorry I had to use such devious means to get you here, but I am sure had I called or sent an invitation, you would have declined."

"Lawrence, why are you doing this? I have never done anything to you," she whispered.

"Oh, I do not agree with you, Christina," he told her, laughter sounding in his voice as she stared at him. "Because of you, my grandfather was shot and killed by your old friend Jack Olivier´."

"Rafael struck me. Detective Olivier´ was trying to protect me. No, he did not have to go as far as he did, but that can't be put on me. I didn't tell him to kill Rafael. I loved him. We were to be married."

"Don't lie to me, Christina," he said, slapping her a vicious blow across her face. "I watched you being comforted by Jack Olivier´ after he murdered my grandfather. I saw how you clung to him. You are nothing but trash. You take off your clothes for men to gaze at you! You were not good enough to even *speak* the name of Rafael Hindel, let alone *wear* his name!" His anger was completely out of control now as he stepped out of her line of vision. "Look around you, Christina! See what you have to look forward to! The same thing your precious daughter and her friend had to look forward to after they were caught fornicating on my property."

Christine's frightened gaze scanned the room, and her fear

all but froze the breath in her throat. "Then Jack was telling the truth when he said Tina and Paul were murdered on this estate. Rafael really did kill them."

"Yes, he did, and I watched him kill them," he told her, relishing the sick look in the terrified eyes staring back at him. "This is what *you* would have had to look forward to had you become my grandfather's wife. He could not have allowed you to live as a normal woman. You would have had to become one of us," he told her, taking a perverse pleasure as he watched her frightened eyes staring at those who had already changed from human form.

Lawrence could feel himself beginning to change, and he felt his excitement grow, for he knew that by the time his change was complete, the fear she was feeling would have tinged her flesh with that wild taste he loved, and he knew he could never get enough of. He threw back his head as a deep howl erupted from his throat.

Christina had time for one shrill scream before Lawrence sank sharp fangs into her throat, letting his mouth fill with the sweet, warm blood he so loved.

* * *

Jack turned at the sounds and felt his heart pick up speed. "Uh-oh, that doesn't bode well for somebody," he whispered, crouching low as he continued to check out the different vehicles parked in the driveway.

"A wolf howl followed by the scream of a woman is a sure bet something's not right. I wish we could go find out who needs help, but we both know it would be suicide or worse if we do. I'm sure we'll get a missing person heads up later this morning."

"There's the cop cruiser." Jack pointed up ahead. "That prick brought him right here to the Hindel mansion just as we guessed he would." He stayed low, making his way to the car. He smiled as he pulled open the door to yank the keys out of the ignition. "Let's see how he deals with not having the keys to get the hell outta here later."

"Hell, let's go all the way and make sure he can't get the car out of here without a wrecker," Donavan said, lifting the hood long enough to cut wires.

"I think we need to go, Donavan," Jack said, moving away from the car and back down the driveway to their vehicle. "I don't wanna have to deal with those ugly fuckers until they're back in human form, and we have a fightin' chance."

"Not only that, but if they're turning into wolves, they might be able to smell us out here."

"Ah, shit! I never thought of that." His heart jumped. "We need to beat feet the hell outta here!"

"Right behind you, partner." Donavan broke into a run, thanking God he was back in shape and able to keep up with the younger detective.

Jack turned the key in the ignition, bringing the car to life when he saw movement. "What the fuck was that?" He leaned forward, pulling his .38 from his belt.

"What? I didn't see anything." Donavan craned his neck, trying to see all around the area. "What did it look like?"

"Looked like a person moving under that big oak over there." He pointed off to the left of the car.

"Let's get out of here. There's no telling what the hell might be lurking around here now that Hindel is back."

Jack backed the Jeep out of the grass and was turning to leave when they both saw what looked to be a large wolf caught in the headlights.

"Yeah? Well, here's one that won't be able to wreak havoc for a while." He stomped down hard on the gas pedal to slam straight into the form watching them.

Donavan felt an impact as the machine connected. "I wish we had time to check out what it was, but I have to tell you, I'm almost afraid to chance it."

"Here, take this and go see what it is." He smacked a flashlight into his hand. "I'll keep the motor runnin' case you need to jump back in," Jack told him, glimpsing a why-me look skitter across Donavan's face. "We'd never forgive ourselves if we don't make sure that what we hit ain't a human."

With nerves jumping to the beat of his heart, Donavan got out of the car to walk the few paces off the road and shine the light out over something lying in the grass. What he saw looked to be a man covered in short, thick, black hair. As Donavan moved the light up over the face, the eyes stared out at him. The body was badly mangled and covered in blood. Without taking his eyes off the creature still watching him, he backed his steps until he was even with the car. "It's a rougarou. Let's get the hell out of here before it gets a second breath. It's pretty well fucked up, but given how hard those bastards are to kill, I don't care to stick around and see if it's going to die or stand up and fight!"

"That makes two of us." As soon as Donavan got back into the car, Jack pulled the Jeep back onto the road to head home. "I know we're gonna get a missing person's call sometime today. In fact, we might get three, the woman who screamed, our perp, and the cop. Another thing we need to get is an accident report made out so we can get the front of the Jeep fixed. It looks like hell."

"Not half as bad as what it connected with." Donavan laughed then became serious. "I wish I could feel some sympathy for the little bastard who was looking in at Jenny, but I can't. Granted, he might not have deserved what the hell he got this morning, but one thing's for sure, he won't be watching any more young girls."

Now that they were well away from the mansion, Jack pulled two cigarettes from the pack on the dash. He stuck one in his mouth, tossing the second one to Donavan.

"I just hope the sick little fucker was served up as a meal and not turned into a rougarou. That case, we'll have a rougarou runnin' 'round on all fours peekin' in windows."

Donavan chuckled, relieving some of his tension. "I'd love to see that cop's face when he finds the cruiser he parked at the mansion out of commission. He's going to have to call a wrecker to move it out of there. Which reminds me, I'll need to call all the wrecking places for a head's up if Hindel calls."

"Unless they got rougarous in the wreckin' business, which wouldn't surprise me. Hell, they got'm everywhere else. We should also check and see if someone's been brought into the emergency room from bein' hit by a car."

"Damn good idea, Jack. But getting back to the cruiser, we'll have some uniforms parked off a ways to see who comes and goes from the mansion. But make sure they know they aren't to be there after the sun goes down."

"What I want to do right now is get home and be with my family. As long as I know they're safe and healthy, I can deal with all the rest of the shit."

CHAPTER FOURTEEN

Lawrence and Gaston choose to enjoy their coffee and sweet rolls on the back patio.

"Your life will never be the same now that you have become a rougarou, Gaston," Lawrence told him, still giddy from the night's ritual.

Gaston laid the saucer holding a sweet roll and his cup of coffee down on the patio table before plopping down on a well-padded chair. "I know this will sound as if I am whining, but actually, I'm not."

Lawrence looked over at him, waiting to hear what he had to say.

"Is what happened during the ceremony and the pain I endured becoming a rougarou the worst of it? I mean, do I have more that is going to come forth and bring me pain?"

Lawrence shook his head. "You will always have pain when the change comes over you, just as you will have pain when you change back into human form."

"And those two times are the only times I will feel that pain?" He tried not to sound as though he was whining, but he could already hear it in his voice.

"Are you saying that you don't think the discomfort you feel is worth the life the master has bestowed on you?"

"No disrespect, but since I don't have any comparisons

yet, I can't really say."

"What you are feeling is normal. When you begin to see the difference in your everyday life, you will change the way you look at the gift you have been handed."

"Lawrence, I am sorry to intrude, but I have a problem," Balfur said, walking out onto the patio.

Both Lawrence and Gaston looked over at him. "What kind of problem are you talking about?" Lawrence asked him.

"Someone messed with my police car during the ritual. The keys are missing, and the wires have been cut, making the car unable to be driven."

"That means someone was here. Someone who is not a part of us," Lawrence whispered. Fear quickly followed by anger shot into his mind. "And I would be willing to bet I know who it was who came here." He rubbed an agitated hand across his brow. "Too bad we weren't made aware of their presence. I would love to have offered them up to the master."

"What am I going to do about the car? I can't very well call a tow truck to come to tow it to the station." His voice filled with alarm. "I don't even know how I'm going to explain my failure to transport the teenager I was on my way to have booked into jail." Officer Ronald Balfur was shaking now, for he knew it was not good to call attention to what went on at the Hindel mansion.

"You are making unnecessary problems, Ronald. You know this will not be tolerated by the rest of our family and friends."

"I only wanted to bring the teenager to the ritual as a gift."

"You must admit, Lawrence, the teen *was* needed since we didn't have a sacrifice," Gaston spoke up.

"I am not disputing that fact, Gaston. What *I* am in favor of is Ronald has no answer for why a perfectly good police car is sitting in front of my home, unable to be driven. And the most difficult question that is sure to be asked, why was Officer Balfur at my home in the first place when he was supposed to be transporting a prisoner to jail?" Lawrence stood up to walk into the kitchen. "You are bringing problems that we do not need,

Ronald. We cannot have the sheriff's department coming here asking a lot of unanswerable questions."

Gaston could smell the fear wafting from Ronald as he continued to plead for help, and he felt a sudden surge of excitement as he pushed back his chair to follow after Lawrence.

Ronald knew he was in trouble, and he turned to leave then just as quickly turned back. A deep, guttural growl sprang from his throat as his body started to change.

Lawrence grabbed a thick-bladed butcher knife from the wooden knife holder sitting on the counter and plunged it deep into Ronald's heart. Ronald screamed out in pain and slowly slid to the floor; his transformation from human to wolf stopped in mid-change.

Gaston could only stare as feelings of hunger and lust overpowered him. He dropped to his knees and, pulling the knife loose from Ronald's body, plunged it again and again until he filled his hands with what his voracious appetite cried out for.

Lawrence tried to walk away, knowing how volatile and ugly a situation such as this could turn, but found his own hunger spinning out of control. Grabbing up the warm heart, he quickly cut it in two and dropped one half into Gaston's waiting hands.

As they fed, another stronger hunger overwhelmed them, and they ripped and tore at their blood-soaked clothing until they stood naked in the glare of the early afternoon sunlight. Within moments, Ronald Balfur and the problems he had laid at their feet were forgotten in a lust-filled orgy of sex, blood, and power. At last, Gaston was learning what it meant to be a child of the dark side, and he welcomed his new life with complete surrender

* * *

"I can't shake the feeling that none of us should be alone. I am terrified for our families," Donavan said, uncaring of the fear creeping into his voice at their situation.

"I hear ya. We know there was a party goin' on out at the mansion, and we can just about bet what kinda party it was."

"I'm going to call the station and set up a meeting with the heads of the department. They can bitch and laugh all they want, but I am not about to go through another mess like we had in this parish before."

"I keep goin' back to that scream we heard. Someone is missin' a loved one. We need to find out who."

"Oh, trust me, Jack, if the department doesn't get a handle on this and fast, a lot of loved ones are going to come up missing." Donavan listened as the phone on the other line dialed in.

"Saint Anthony Parish Sheriff's Department, Shelia speaking." The soft and sultry voice perked up his enjoyment of the day.

"Hey, Shelia, how are you doing?"

"I'm great, Detective Hays, and yourself?"

"Fine, thanks. Listen, I need you to patch me through to the chief."

"You have a good day, darlin'," she told him before ringing off.

"Shelia of the purring sexy voice is the dispatcher today."

"I might have to invent an excuse to call the station later. I love hearin' that soft and sexy voice," Jack laughed then cleared his throat as he looked over to see Seelah standing in the room. "Hey, baby, I didn't see you there."

"Obviously." She gave him a stern look then burst out laughing. "You better watch it, old man," — she pointed a finger in his direction — "or I'll be sending your pillow and covers down to the station to let 'her of the soft and sexy voice' tuck you in at night."

Jack leaped off the couch and, before she could run, grabbed her up in a bear hug. "We both know that won't happen. You love what daddy's got to offer too much." He nuzzled her sweet-smelling throat. "You would be down there beggin' me to come back within fifteen minutes, and you know it."

"Uh...if you two don't mind, I'm on the phone here," Donavan told them, laughing as Jack shot him a one-finger salute behind Seelah's back.

Jack slung Seelah over his shoulder, heading out onto the

patio for more privacy, then stopped to breathe a deep sigh as he saw they were being followed by a laughing Barbara and Jenny.

Seelah giggled, squirming as she tried to get loose, then drew in her breath as she saw someone skitter around the corner in an attempt to hide. "Jack, you need to put me down." Her voice told him she was no longer in a playful mood.

Jack quickly stood her on her feet. "I'm sorry, baby. I guess I did get a little carried away with our roughhousing."

"No, it isn't that. Someone is here. I just saw a quick flash as someone ran around the side of the patio."

Jack quickly drew his .38. "All of you in the house, now." He jabbed a thumb in the direction of the sliding glass door. "And take those two police dogs with you," he said, giving each dog a sour look.

"No, Jack, it isn't a person. Brandy and Lugar picked up on that. That's why they aren't upset. It's a spirit. I just need to find out why they feel the need to hide."

"Are you sure?" He brought the hand holding the gun close to his shoulder in an upright position, still reluctant to put the gun away. "A lotta crazy shit's goin' on right now. I don't wanna take any chances."

"You can stay with me while I go find out who it is, but I don't think whoever it is will pose a problem," she told him, walking to the side of the patio. "You don't have to be afraid. No one here is going to hurt you," she called out in a calm voice.

Seelah could see a woman kneeling in the grass, her hands covering her face and crying. Her tortured sobs tore at Seelah, and she reached out, touching the woman's shoulder. The woman looked up at her, screaming in fear and jerking away. In the brief instant, before she turned away, Seelah was able to see that her throat had been torn away, and she was covered in blood. "Oh my God," she whispered. "What happened to you?"

By now, everyone was standing nearby to see who it was Seelah had seen.

"Who is it, baby? Can you tell?" Jack walked closer, putting an arm around Seelah's shoulders.

"Yes, Jack, I'm afraid I can. It's Christina Crawford."

"Oh no," he breathed, pulling Seelah into his arms. "Can she tell you what happened to her?"

Donavan walked over, and with a tremor in his voice, he said, "Ask her if she was murdered on the Hindel estate earlier this morning." He looked over at Jack.

"The scream we heard!" Jack said.

"And we didn't even try and help her."

"If we had, we would probably be in the same shape she is."

"She's very frightened and so confused I can't make out what she is trying to tell me." Seelah held out her arms, trying to get Christina to come to her, but she kept backing away. "Christina, please, don't turn away from me. I am trying to help you. You and I are friends, remember?"

But all of her soft words had no effect on the frightened woman trying her best to understand what was happening to her.

"I want everyone to be very quiet as I get her some help." Taking a few deep breaths to relax her mind, Seelah called on Chandra to bring someone from the light to come and help them.

Within moments, a smile came over Seelah's face as Chandra and a beautiful young girl stood before her. "Thank God you're here, Chandra," Seelah cried, going into her arms.

"I have brought Christina's daughter, Tina, to help her cross over."

"Mama." Tina walked over to hold out her arms, trying to stay strong as she saw her mother covered in blood and so very, very frightened.

"Tina?" Christina took a hesitant step forward. "Is it really you?"

"Yes, Mama, it's really me. I've come to take you home where all your pain and fear will be laid to rest."

Quickly, Donavan stepped closer. "Before she leaves, ask her if it was Lawrence Hindel who killed her and if there are a lot of the Hindel family back on the estate."

"Christina, will you please try and tell me what happened to you?" Seelah said.

But all Christina could do was begin to cry all over again.

"Seelah, she can't talk right now. Once we get her on the other side and she has had a chance to calm down, I will talk with her and perhaps find out what happened," Chandra said. "But it might take a while. When a spirit has been through this much pain, they have to be put into a deep sleep until they can face what happened to them."

"Thank you, Chandra. You are a good friend. Please take her home now. She's been through enough."

Within moments, a brilliant light that glittered and glowed around the surrounding area was gone along with Chandra and Tina and her mother.

"Did she tell you what happened to her?" Donavan asked, afraid to hope.

"No," Seelah told him. "She was too upset. Chandra said maybe after she gets home and has had a chance to calm down, then she can talk with her and try and find out what happened."

"Well, it was worth a shot," Donavan said. "We still need to find out what happened to the officer who took the cruiser to the mansion last night. This reminds me, I need to call around to see if any of the Hindels tried to get a wrecker out there." Donavan pulled his cell phone from its holder.

"Seelah, let's go check on Donny. I want to make sure he's all right," Jack said, taking her by the arm and heading to the door.

"Jack, you are really upset about what happened to Christina, aren't you?"

He remained silent, walking down the hall until they came to Donny's room. He pushed open the door and just stood looking down at his son as he slept, peacefully unaware of all the strange happenings that had just invaded his safe world.

"Jack, come over here and sit down and tell me what is

going on that has you so upset. I know Christina coming here as she did was upsetting, but there is more that you aren't telling me."

Kissing the tips of his fingers, he touched them lightly to Donny's dark head before turning away. Dropping down beside Seelah on the twin bed, he tried to get a hold of his emotions.

"Now tell me what is going on, sweetheart." Seelah pulled him into her arms.

As though a floodgate had suddenly opened, Jack felt himself being racked with sobs. He tried to stop them, but they just kept getting stronger and more forthcoming until, at last, he was drained.

Seelah got off the bed and, lifting up Jack's legs, helped him to stretch out. Pulling a handful of tissues from the box sitting on the small dresser, she placed them in his hand. "You needed to get that emotion out, darling. You know as well as I do what keeping something like that inside can do to a person. Just ask Donavan."

Jack mopped his face then blew his nose, feeling as though a ten-pound weight had been lifted from his heart. "I guess I was more upset than I knew. First, we get a threat against Donny's life from a fuckin' spirit who should be in hell but instead is able to possess someone and talk through them, then Donavan and I hear a woman screaming while we were outside the mansion this morning. Now come to find out the one who was screamin' for help was someone we knew and liked, and neither of us even tried to help her."

"And if you had tried to help, what do you think would have happened? We know how indestructible the Hindels and their kind are when they are in the form of a rougarou. You would have wasted your life, and Donavan would have wasted his, and Barbara and I would be raising two kids alone." She leaned over to drop a quick kiss on his cheek. "This way, you will be able to go and destroy them all again just like you did when it was Jonathan and Rafael and some of their family and friends."

Jack pulled her down beside him on the bed. "God really

smiled on me the day he brought you into my life."

"I feel the same way, my love, even though at the time you took me for one of Jenny's little friends."

Jack smiled, relieving some of his sadness. "Sure didn't take me long to find out that inside that beautiful little body lived a full-grown woman."

CHAPTER FIFTEEN

Donavan hung up the phone. "That was the station. Seems they found the cruiser parked alongside the road."

"Did they say if it was anywhere near the Hindel mansion?" Jack asked.

"Ten miles north of there," Donavan told him, walking out onto the patio. "It's been towed to impound to be processed."

"No mechanic at the house savvy enough to fix it so it could be driven, huh?"

"Naw, it would have been a waste of time to try and solder the wires back together. Too, with the wires cut, it would have shortened out the computer. And thanks again to the computer age, they couldn't hotwire it either."

"Then they had to tow the damn thing. In that case, we can probably find out which wreckin' company they used."

"I don't think they used a wrecker. I think they just pulled it on a trailer, covered it with a tarp so no one could see it was a police car, and hauled it away."

"Wonder who the hell came up with that bright idea, `cause you can bet your ass it wasn't Lawrence."

"We're still going to need to get the K-9s and go to the mansion. I called to see if anyone had been brought to the hospital."

"Yeah, shit, I forgot all about that." Jack grinned.

"You shouldn't have since you're the one who ran his

ass over." Donavan dropped down in a chair then got back up. "I'm in need of something to drink. Do you want something? It can't be anything alcoholic since we're going to be heading to the mansion in a few. We'll just have Blain meet us out there with the dogs. But anyway, no one has shown up at the hospital in need of treatment. So we have at least three people unaccounted for."

"Why do I always feel like déjà vu every time we have to deal with the Hindels? I mean, it's just the same fuckin' thing over and over." Jack raised his voice to be sure he was being heard in the kitchen where Donavan was getting them something to drink.

Donavan pulled a bottle of vodka from the freezer and, twisting off the lid, availed himself of the mind-soothing liquid. He started to twist the lid back on then walked into the living room with the bottle still in his hand.

"Thought you said nothin' alcoholic. Last I heard, vodka was near the top," Jack said, reaching out as Donavan handed him the bottle.

"I know, but then I remembered where we're going. There's a glass of orange juice poured if you need a chaser."

* * *

Lawrence stood in front of a large washer to place, just so, his and Gaston's bloody clothes, and he remembered another time he had washed clothing covered in blood.

It had been when Christina Crawford's teenage daughter, Tina, and her friend, Paul Statler, had had the misfortune of coming onto his property and meeting up with those who were staying on the estate at the time. He had made the mistake of washing their clothing before tossing them around close to the swamp to give the appearance the teens had yanked off their clothing in a frenzy of lust before going for a swim and ended up being eaten by gators.

His grandfather, Rafael, had been very unhappy with him over that mistake. Thankfully, it was his quick thinking that saved them from having to explain how the clothing of two murdered teens wound up on the estate after being washed in the same detergent and softener as the brand found in the Hindel basement.

Lawrence jumped as he felt someone slide their hands around his waist.

"Is there anything I can help you with?" Gaston breathed.

"No, no, I'm just getting our laundry done and out of the way," he said, adding the softener one slight pour at a time instead of pouring a goodly amount all at once. He closed the lid on the washer and tapped three times on the lid.

Gaston laughed. "Why did you tap three times on the lid? Is that supposed to make the clothes get cleaner?"

"I have a mental disorder called Obsessive Compulsive Disorder, Gaston. I have tried to cure it by ignoring it, but I can't.

"Are you serious? I've heard of that before. Never knew anyone who had it, though. Until now, that is," he said, then looked away.

"I think I have had it all my life. At least I can't remember a time when I didn't have it."

"I'll tell you what we can do. Every time you start to repeat your actions, I'll grab you and give you a big hug, making you forget what you were gonna do. How does that sound?"

"I'm willing to try if you are," Lawrence whispered, trying not to get overly emotional.

Knowing they needed to change the subject, Gaston told him, "I took care of burning all the clothes from the bodies. In case we get a visit from the cops."

"Good. That's one less thing to worry about. And yes, you can be sure we will get a visit from the police. I have a feeling that the ones who were here and disabled the police car were Hays and Olivier´. What did you do with the ashes of the clothes?"

"I scattered them in the swamp. It might call attention, but what can they prove? Ashes are ashes."

"I hate that one of our strongest supporters was killed. He probably saw the detectives lurking about, and to shut him up, they ran him over."

"Was he a prominent person in the parish? I mean enough that he will be missed?"

"No, Ralph was just someone who came through the parish every now and then. He was what most would call a bum. But he was one of us. I wished we could have taken him to the hospital and had him treated, but we both know that would have called too much attention to us here. The hospital would have already been alerted to be on the lookout for someone with his injuries being brought in."

"At least his death was quick. He was in so much pain that by the time he had changed back to human form, it only took one shot to the head, and it was all over."

"The gators took care of the rest. I didn't care about the other three whose bodies were thrown into the swamp, but I had a moment of regret for Ralph."

"I don't think we need to worry. They can bring all the cops they want, and they're not going to find anything."

"The only thing that worries me is they will bring the dogs."

"So? If they don't have a body, or in this case, four bodies, then they don't have any evidence that a crime was even committed. Hell, for that matter, they can't prove that the police car was ever here either."

"You make everything sound so easy, Gaston."

"That's because most things are easy, my love. You just make them more difficult than they need to be."

"I hope when they find Christina Crawford has gone missing, they don't come looking for her here. The dogs would be able to pick up her scent and follow it right down to the basement."

"Again, they will need to prove she was here. No body, no crime."

"I hope you're right, Gaston. I just get so upset when the police get involved."

"Let's go upstairs, and I will fix us both some lunch, and

we will eat it out on the patio in the nice fresh air."

They had just walked into the kitchen when the intercom sounded, letting them know someone was at the gate.

"Oh no," Lawrence whispered.

"Calm down. We knew this was to be expected, so there's no reason to get all upset. I'll handle it."

He hit the button then spoke quietly. "Yes?"

"Yeah, who do I have here?" Jack spoke into the intercom.

"You are talkin' to Gaston. What do you need?"

"Hi, Gaston, Detective Olivier´ here, glad to see you're up and about after your wild night entertainin' the furry riffraff," Jack laughed.

"Since I have no idea what the hell you're talkin' about, Olivier´, I guess we can consider this conversation over."

"Gaston, this is Detective Hays. We need to come in. Don't try and ignore me because we have a search warrant and will just crash the gate. I'm sure you've been expecting this visit."

"Since you have a warrant to come on the property, I guess we'll allow it," he said, flipping the switch to open the gate.

"Get the coffee and tea cakes ready. We'll be right up," Jack told him, laughing as he clicked off the intercom.

Donavon swung an arm, motioning the three police vehicles to follow them through the gate as it swung open.

"Here we go with another warrant to search the premises for dead bodies. At least we get to be the ones to christen the new house."

"And neither one of us thought to bring champagne for the momentous occasion," Jack snickered.

Donavan braked in front of the house, switched off the key, and, grabbing his handheld, pushed open his door. The moment his feet hit the cobblestoned driveway, he could feel the coldness begin to creep over him.

"I don't give a fuck how many times we come here. I'll never get used to this evil pile of shit."

"Sure hope it don't take long for us to be able to blow this son-of-a-bitch off the foundation too."

"Won't do no good. They'll just build the motherfucker back up again."

"Yeah, but there's one thing you have to admit. We have gotten rid of well over two hundred years of these creeping fuckers! That has to account for something."

Jack stood by the Land Rover, watching Lawrence and Gaston walk out onto the porch. "Coffee and cakes ready? I'm famished," he told them, his movements jaunty and exaggerated as he walked up the wide stone steps and onto the porch.

Gaston backed up to the door, and with his feet spread wide, and his arms crossed over his chest, he dared Jack to try and enter the house.

Jack stopped walking, placed his hands on his hips, and laughed. "You know what, slick?" He pulled his cell phone from his shirt pocket and took a step back to click off a picture of Gaston as he stood glaring at him. "The way you're standin' here all macho lookin' and shit, if you had one of them Bandoliers stretched across your chest with a big sombrero on your head, I swear to Christ if you wouldn't look a lot like ole Poncho Villa just 'fore he got *his* ass kicked!"

Donavan didn't even try to hold back a snicker. "All right, let's all go inside and get this started. This—" he held up a folded piece of paper—"says I can come in and go all over the grounds. You should be used to this by now, Lawrence."

As Gaston remained standing in front of the door, Jack shot an elbow hard into his rib cage then shoved him out of the way.

Gaston's fist shot out, just missing Jack's jaw, then dropped as Jack leg-swept him to the floor of the porch. Before he could move, Jack stomped a foot on his throat. "I'm only gonna say this once, motherfucker, don't ever come at me again," he warned him, putting pressure on his foot to bring a strangling sound from Gaston. "I know you're a damn rougarou just like your fuck-buddy here." He nodded to Lawrence. "I'm not gonna take a chance on you turnin' one of us into a flesh eatin', blood suckin' pervert. I'll just shoot you."

"He ain't kiddin' either," Donavan told him, stepping over Gaston's laid-out body to enter the house.

"Jack, I think you've made your point." Lawrence touched his shoulder. "You can let him up now."

Jack pushed down on his foot one more time, then moved back to follow Donavan into the house.

"I'll kill that son-of-a-bitch. I swear I will," Gaston whispered, his voice raspy and weak.

"Not now, my love. Our time will come. This I can promise you." Lawrence helped him to stand.

As Blain walked by the two still on the porch, the K9s he had leashed to his side snapped and snarled, their sharp teeth bared and ready to do battle.

"Quiet," Blain demanded, his voice strong and commanding.

The two German Shepherds trembled in their need to be let loose on the two men cowering back against the banister of the porch.

"I swear, every damn time we bring the pets here for a visit, they just get so upset whenever they get anywhere near you furry little critters. Almost like they know you ain't good playmates," Jack chuckled, stepping back out the door to pet the dogs fondly atop their broad heads. "Guess you ain't foolin' them either."

"Could you get on with the search so we can be done with your coarse manners?" Lawrence told him.

"Bet you don't talk like that to little sugar puss here." Jack ruffled the top of Gaston's dark head, letting loose his amusement as he saw a look of pure hatred glaring over at him.

"Okay, come along, Blain. It's time to bring the babies inside and down the basement to see what they can find."

The anxious look passing between Lawrence and Gaston was not missed by either Jack or Blain as they moved to the door.

"You two can stay here outta the way while we conduct our search." Jack stepped to the side as Blain and the K9s walked through the door.

"Are you coming in, Jack?" Donavan stood just inside the front door. "We're ready to begin the search."

"I'm right behind you, partner," Jack said, then stopped. "Did you remember to bring the kit so we can conduct a test for blood? I brought a hairbrush and toothbrush from Christina Crawford's house for later 'case we find any blood here, and the lab needs to do a DNA."

"No. Glad you remembered that. With the kit, we'll be able to tell if any blood found is human blood. I'll go get it right now."

"Yeah, seems Christina Crawford has come up missin'," Jack told the two men huddled together. "I'm sure you remember our beautiful Christina, Lawrence. After all, she almost became your grandma."

"Of course I remember Christina, Jack. It was because of her that you murdered my grandfather."

"Yeah, damn." Jack threw out his hands in his own defense. "He broke bad, and I had to waste his old ass right here on the estate. 'Course he was armed, so it was ruled self-defense in the line of duty."

"You know he wasn't armed. My grandfather never owned a gun in his life. He didn't need to resort to guns to take care of any problems."

"I'll have to agree with ya on that one. He just ripped their throats out then ate'm. But he *was* found with a loaded gun on his person the morning he attacked Christina and forced me to shoot him."

Lawrence could feel his anger rising, and he breathed in deep, trying to gain control over his emotions, knowing how quickly uncontrolled rage could start the transformation into that of a rougarou. Without a word, he left Gaston to walk out into the yard.

Donavan passed him on the way from getting a small black case out of the car. "If we find any blood, we'll be able to check it for DNA from Christina's belongings," Donavan told Jack, noting the sick look crossing Gaston's face.

Lawrence ignored him and kept walking, needing to distance himself from any fear or anger.

Gaston could see how agitated Lawrence was getting, and he left the porch to follow him across the yard. When he caught up to him, he didn't say a word. He simply pulled him into his arms.

"If they determine that the blood around the altar is Christina's, we are in big trouble," Lawrence whispered.

"They ain't gonna find her blood or blood from the other two who were offered up either. I made sure it was all cleaned up and washed away with a strong substance, including bleach," Gaston told him, keeping his voice soft and soothing.

Lawrence leaned back in his arms to stare at him. "Are you sure? All they need is one drop, and they will be able to take me away again. I don't want to go back to the mental hospital." He began to shake, and he didn't bother to wipe away the hot tears falling down his face.

"Stop it!" Gaston's voice was harsh, and he grabbed his shoulders and shook him. "You will not allow these bastards to see you falling apart."

"I can't help it," he cried.

Quickly looking around to make sure they were quite alone, Gaston drew back his hand and slapped Lawrence a sharp rap across his face. "Now you listen to me, Goddamn it! Hays and Olivier´ are responsible for the deaths of two of your most treasured loved ones! They are inside your house touching your personal belongings right now as we speak, and you will not give them the added satisfaction of seeing you break down!" Gaston gave him another shake before pulling him roughly against his chest.

For a moment longer, he remained where he was, then pulled away. "I'm all right now, Gaston," Lawrence told him, smiling as he drew a handkerchief from his back pocket to blow his nose.

* * *

Walking into the basement, Donavan and Jack looked at each other. "He has this set up just like the old one. Same brand washer and dryer. Same shelves against the wall. Except these shelves ain't a front for the hidden room. No reason to hide the room. The secret's already out!" Jack moved over to check out the washer and dryer and drew in his breath as he saw Lawrence's laundry hung up on silk coat hangers on a special clothes rack set up just for that purpose. All facing the same way just like before when they had been in the basement of the old mansion and serving a search warrant.

"O.C.D., remember?" Donavan said.

"Some things never change."

"Dogs pickin' up on anything?" Jack walked through the heavy oak door separating the basement from the spacious room set up like it used to be when Jonathan and Rafael Hindel were still alive and holding rituals.

"They do seem to be fixated on the spot near the bottom of the altar." Blain stooped down on one knee and, pulling his flashlight from his belt, shone the light on the area of interest. "Looks like we got a few spots of blood here, detectives."

Donavan and Jack hurried over to check out what Blain was seeing, and they both smiled.

"We sure as hell do." Donavan turned to pick up the black box he had taken from the vehicle earlier. "Let's see if it really is blood that we have here."

"Somebody did their damndest to clean this place up. You can smell the disinfectant. Looks like they missed a spot or two." Jack watched as Donavan moved two q-tips over the spot then stood up straight. Pulling a small vial from the case, he flipped off the lid and sticking one of the used q-tips in the liquid inside the vial. He waited a few moments, then removed it to hold it up to the light. "Eureka! We have a sample of blood."

"Are you sure? I mean to me, blood is blood," Blain said.

"When I put the q-tip with the blood on it into the solution, as you can see, it changed color. It went to purple. The DNA of an animal is different than that of human DNA."

Lawrence stood inside the basement, and when he heard what Donavan said about the detection of human blood, he walked quickly back up the stairs.

Knowing they weren't going to find anything of importance concerning the missing bodies, Donavan placed the vial back inside the black case, and together they all walked out of the basement.

"I think we have found enough to warrant more investigation into what happened here. You don't find human blood on an altar for no reason," Donavan said.

"Are you sure it was human?" Jack clipped his words as Donavan nudged him to silence.

Knowing that Lawrence and Gaston were nearby in the kitchen, Donavan raised his voice so as to be heard.

"We may not have found any bodies, but we have found blood. Human blood is not something that you find every day. Especially in a brand new house."

"I think the sooner we get this blood sample to the crime lab, the sooner we'll be able to tell who it belongs to," Jack said.

"I'm sure the department will have access to Bulfar's DNA, and of course, we'll be able to check the perp's family for DNA to match his. *And* since we have the toothbrush and hairbrush belonging to Christina Crawford, we will have no problem in checking DNA on her too."

"I still want to take some of the deputies and check out what they've been able to find near the swamp. We know how fond the Hindels have been in gettin' rid of dead bodies by throwing them to the gators to feast on."

"Like Tina Crawford and Paul Statler. Now it looks as though Christina has joined the ranks of the sacrificial lamb."

All Lawrence and Gaston could do was stare at each other. Their hearts picked up speed as their imaginations spun out of control on what the police may or may not have found in their investigation.

Blain changed out the leashes on the two K9s to give them a wider range of movement, walking behind as they headed to the swamp. "I really don't think they're gonna find anything body wise. Gators don't leave much behind when they're feedin'."

"What we're doin' here is for show. I want those two assholes inside to worry that we're going to find something," Donavan told him.

"Ah fuck!" Jack jumped as a crab skittered past him. "I hate it around here. If you don't find a damn snake tryin' to bite your ass in the water, you got gators tryin' to eat you and now Goddamn crabs. Flesh-eatin' motherfuckers!" Jack grabbed up a thick branch and started forward, then stopped. "What the hell's he carryin'? Looks like he's been chewin' on somethin'."

Donavan drew back his foot and kicked the crab up on the bank.

After Jack smashed the branch down hard onto the defenseless crab, they checked it out.

"Ramos," — Donavan handed up his keys to one of the deputies — "run up to my rig and bring back an evidence bag out of the back. Be sure and lock it back up."

"Will do, Detective Hays," Ramos told him, taking the keys and walking away.

"What is it, can you tell?" Jack leaned over to see what Donavan was separating from the face of the crab. "Looks like a small chunk of skin and meat."

"Yeah, now the question is whose skin and whose meat?"

"Oh shit! Do you really think this could be part of a person?"

"Could be. We'll send it on to the lab just to be sure." He reached out, taking the clear plastic bag Ramos was handing out to him.

"You know, I think the next time we blow this son-of-a-bitch away, we should make sure we blow all the land around it away too. There has to be so much evil here it can't be anything but negative."

"And we need to get rid of *all* the Hindels. We both know they're here again. There may not be any vehicles here to let us know for sure they're here, but they are. Not only that, but you can bet your ass there are a lot of people in the parish who are rougarous too."

"We probably never will find Balfur. It's my guess he's right out there in the drink with the perp and Christina and the rougarou I ran down."

"Or this could be part of him I'm sticking in the bag here." Donavan pulled the strip of paper from the top and sealed the opening. Pulling a pen from his shirt pocket, he labeled the bag.

"You know, something has been buggin' me. When we talked with Lawrence and his little friend Gaston, I got the feeling that Gaston was hidin' somethin'. Could be wrong, but I just got that impression. I'm gonna send his picture off to the other parishes and even other states and see if we can find out a little more about him."

"Can't hurt." Donavan got to his feet. "I guess we've done all we can do here. The K9s haven't hit on anything other than the room with the altar, so I would say we can be taking off."

"I think we've dropped all the hints we can to the wolf boys. Always good to keep them on their toes with a little worry."

CHAPTER SIXTEEN

Danny Roberts propped himself up on his elbows in the narrow bed, watching the beautiful black girl with the silky burnt sugar skin, and he motioned her to come forward.

Lifting her long hair, she allowed it to slowly flow through her slender fingers, all the while peering at him with a little girl smile, her light blue eyes teasing and daring.

Wagging one finger back and forth, he beckoned her to come closer, but she only giggled, ignoring him.

Danny jumped off the bed, grabbed her around the waist, and threw her over his shoulder.

"Danny," she squealed, "put me down."

"I intend to," he breathed, walking over to drop her full length on the bed. His dark eyes moved slowly over her, taking in the slender body with the full round breasts tipped with pink nipples aroused and begging to be suckled and nipped.

Without a word, he sat down on the side of the bed and without having to ask, she moved over, taking his swollen member in her small hands to lower her head.

Danny caught his breath as she ran her tongue slowly around the inside groove, then faster until her practiced tongue was actually vibrating she was moving so fast.

Knowing he was about to explode, he grabbed her hair, yanking her off of him, and got off the bed.

Like a hungry cat, she ran her tongue over her full pink mouth, luring him forward.

Danny did not have to be asked twice. Positioning himself in front of her, he grabbed her long legs to drop them over his shoulders and with a snap of his hips, he entered her tight, velvet-smooth vault.

She stared up at him, watching his passion grow right along with her own, and she felt the power she always felt when she had a man in her control.

With a final thrust, Danny felt the hot juices explode from his body to slam against the walls of the beautiful young woman beneath him.

She pulled her legs from his shoulders to wrap them around his slim waist, keeping him imprisoned within her wet and throbbing tightness until she felt her own passions burst forth.

Danny fell forward, and she wrapped slender arms around his shoulders.

She was relaxed and content to be with him again. Sex with Danny was different than it was with the other men who came to see her in her little shack in the bayou. Danny never treated her like the prostitute she was. He always laid some money on her, but he never made her feel like she was trash. Also, he made her laugh, and to a sixteen-year-old who made her living on her back, this was important.

"Leadah, when are you gonna break down and let me make a good girl of you?" Danny gazed down at her, feeling her warm body still attached to his. With her long silky black hair fanned out around her, she had to be one of the most beautiful girls he had ever seen in his life. Her mother was a black hooker, but her daddy had to be white given the thick, sooty lashes framing light blue eyes, a striking contrast against her brown skin. "You know I would like nothin' better than to marry you and take care of you."

"I know this is what you want to do, but you gotta think 'bout what this would mean to your friends. They'd treat you like trash. `Sides, my mama needs me to bring in the money I make. The men don't come callin' on her like they used to. Now they come to me."

The thought of Leadah spreading her legs for other men shot through his chest like an actual attack. "Do you really think I give a fuck about what others think of me?"

Knowing she had hurt him, Leadah pulled his face down to give him a loving kiss then drew back in horror.

"What?" He drew back, staring at her. "You look like you just saw somethin' evil," he murmured, pulling away from her.

"Rougarou! You have the mark of the rougarou on your throat." She was slapping at him and scrambling to get loose from him.

Danny jumped off the bed to go to the oval mirror attached to the small dresser in the corner of the room. Moving closer, he tried to see what she was seeing.

"What the hell are you talkin `bout? I don't see no mark."

"Unless you have the sight, you can't. The mark of the rougarou is an upside-down cross burned into your skin."

"Leadah, Goddamn it, you ain't makin' sense!" He tried to pull her up and into his arms, but she slapped out at him, wanting only to get away.

Running to the door, she threw it open wide, unmindful of people walking by and looking in as she stood in the doorway, naked and yelling for him to leave.

Suddenly, it was as though someone had slammed him in the gut. Crumpling to the floor, he lay in a heap, unable to get dressed and leave.

For a moment, Leadah stood still, watching him, trying to decide if she could trust him, then slowly, she closed the door to come across the floor and pull him to his feet.

"You must come and tell me how you came to be the devil's child, Danny."

He allowed her to lead him over to a chair. When he was seated, she threw the top cover of the bed in his lap.

"A few days ago, I got into a fight with Gaston. He used to be my friend and roommate. But since he moved in with his fuck-buddy, we ain't friends no more."

"Who did he move in with?" she asked him, her voice little more than a whisper.

"Lawrence Hindel."

"Lawrence Hindel? You are telling me he's with Lawrence Hindel in the Hindel mansion? Danny, they are rougarous. Everyone in the bayou knows this. They are evil. They drink the blood of our children!"

"Durin' the fight, Gaston bit me." His eyes grew large. "Now you're tellin' me I'm a fuckin' rougarou!"

She simply nodded. "You ain't changed yet, but unless we get you help, you will, and then it will be too late to stop the change."

"You know someone who can help me?" Danny jumped to his feet.

Leadah was all but dressed now, and after zipping her cutoffs and pulling her top into place, she slipped her feet into her sandals then reached down, grabbing his jeans, t-shirt, and a zip-up hoodie with pockets to toss them to him. "We gotta hurry. After you're dressed, I'll take you to see a lady who might be able to help you."

Danny didn't even take time to rinse himself off in the basin. He simply pulled on his clothes and shoes. "Let's get the hell over there. The sooner we get this taken care of, the sooner I can take a deep breath."

"The woman I'm takin' you to'll want somethin' in return, Danny."

"Oh shit! I don't have a lotta money. Whatever she wants is gonna have to be in labor."

"She don't need money. What she'll ask for might be hard for you to give," she told him, her voice low and filled with fear.

"Leadah, I ain't gotta lotta choice here. Whatever she needs, I'll get it. What the hell is she, a druggy?"

"No, Danny, she's a vampire."

* * *

The woman who answered their knock was a beautiful, voluptuous blond with flashing blue-green eyes that held the power to lure the unsuspecting into giving up without a fight.

"Leadah." The woman stepped back, surprised at seeing her, then motioned them to come inside.

"Jillianna," Leadah whispered, not sure how the woman motioning them into her home was going to feel about her bringing someone to see her unannounced.

Danny stood looking around the great hall, marveling at all the wealth surrounding him. In less than the space of a half-hour, he had traveled from a two-room shack in the bayou to a palatial mansion on the outskirts of Saint Anthony Parish.

"Why are you here, Leadah?" Her dark eyes moved slowly over Danny, and she moistened her full mouth in anticipation as her sharp sense of smell picked up the telltale scent of semen, beckoning her steps forward then freezing them in place as her sharp gaze fell on the side of his throat.

Leadah saw a change come over her face, and she nodded. "I didn't know where else to go, Jillianna."

"It's all right, child," the woman told her, coming to stand near the young man looking around her impressive home. "I see we have work to do," she told him, turning his face to the side and running the side of one long-nailed finger down his neck.

Danny jerked his head away as fear measured his breath. "I don't have any money." The words shot out of his mouth.

"As you can see," — she turned, spreading her hands wide — "I don't need money. What I do need is a warm body whose rich, red blood will keep me looking as I do now."

Danny instinctively stepped back a few steps. "I came here for help, not for more problems." He cast an angry glower at Leadah, who shook her head, warning him to not make trouble.

"Do you expect me to help you for nothing?" Her silky voice glided over him. "The undoing of a curse is not easy. It must be done quickly, and it must be done right, or it will not work."

"I can see this was a mistake." He looked over at Leadah then moved to the door. "Fuck this shit! I'm outta here."

"You will not leave this house, young man. Not until I tell you it is all right for you to leave."

"Fuck you," Danny said over his shoulder.

Leadah's hand flew to her throat. "Danny, no! She can destroy you!"

"Who gives a shit?" He kept walking to the door. "I'm already doomed. What does it matter who finishes me off?"

"You will calm yourself," Jillianna told him, her voice soft and low.

Danny turned to look at her and felt a sleepy, calming feeling move slowly over him. As though he had no will of his own, he moved toward her. When he was in front of her, he stopped.

Jillianna reached out her hand to touch the upside-down cross burned into his neck. "You will both come with me."

Following closely behind, Leadah tried not to think about what she could be getting herself into as they walked down a flight of stairs leading into what looked to be a church.

Without warning, Jillianna stopped. "As I am now unclean, *I* cannot go further, but the two of you can. You will take your friend into the church, where you will find a fount right at the bottom of the stairs filled with holy water. You will wash the mark, then you will bring me the small golden crucifix from the altar. As soon as we have done all we can do here, you will take him immediately to a priest who will administer the body and blood of Christ. You must make sure the priest understands how imperative it is that the sacraments be given tonight."

"I'm not Catholic. I'm not any religion. I'm just a ho," she said. "What if the priest refuses to do this?"

"You will take the gun I will give you, and if he refuses, then you will threaten to kill him."

"I can't kill a priest!" Leadah squealed, whirling around. "The cops'd come and arrest me and put me in jail. Then there would be no one to take care of Mama."

"It is time for your mother to stop behaving like trash and begin to take care of herself. I don't think you will have to actually follow through with the threat. Usually, just showing the gun is enough to get them moving on what they need to do," she said, shooing her the rest of the way down the stairs.

Pulling Danny with her, she led him over to the fount. Moving quickly, in case God decided to strike her down for being in his house and for the life she was leading, she scooped up handfuls of the holy water, rubbing the blessed liquid on Danny's neck the way Jillianna told her she must do. The mark bubbled up, leaving small blisters in the shape of a small upside-down cross.

She left him to make her way up the aisle to the altar, and spying the small golden crucifix, she pulled it up and out of the groove holding it upright.

With the cross held tightly in her hands, she ran back down the aisle. "Come on, Danny, we have to go now," she told him, pulling hard on his arm as she started back up the stairs.

Jillianna was waiting for them, and as soon as they walked through the door, she pulled Leadah to her side.

"You will place the crucifix against the mark on Danny's neck, Leadah," she told her, her hypnotic gaze never leaving that of the man standing before her.

As Leadah did as she was told, the stench of burning flesh filled the air along with the sizzling of liquid from the burst blisters, then a long, agonizing scream.

Danny fell to his knees, his hand covering his neck, trying to stop the pain.

"Get up, Danny. There is still work to do this day," Jillianna commanded him.

No longer in a hypnotic stupor, Danny stood, his hand still covering his neck. "Now what?"

"Now, the two of you will go and visit a priest so he can give you the sacraments. Once the process has begun, we must not tarry."

"I don't know any priests," Danny said. "I haven't been to church since I was little, although I've often thought about going back to church."

"A lot of us have, Danny." Jillianna nodded in agreement. "Now be off with you. We live in Saint Anthony Parish, for Christ's sake, you should be able to find a Catholic Church on every corner."

As the door closed behind them, they ran to the car. In their haste to undo the harm that had been visited upon yet another victim of evil in the parish, they missed seeing the one standing in the shadows watching them.

* * *

"We will go into the first church we see, Danny," Leadah directed him. "God willin' they still leave'm unlocked."

"Hand me the gun. I can put it in my pocket."

She handed over the gun then ran up the wide stone steps of the church. "Lord, don't strike me down. I'm only comin' in so I can help my friend Danny."

"God ain't gonna strike either one of us down." He pulled open the door, motioning her inside. "This is where sinners are supposed to come when they need help. And if ever anyone needed help, it's us."

They looked around, and seeing no one else in the church, they continued walking up the aisle. They were almost to the altar when a man dressed in a black suit and wearing a white collar came through a door at the back of the church.

"Hello," he said, moving toward them, "can I help you?"

"Yeah," Danny spoke up. "I need you to give me the body and blood of Christ. We need you to do it now `cause we're in a hurry."

The priest stopped to stare at them. "I can't administer the sacraments to you. I don't even know if you are of the Catholic faith." A worried frown etched a crease between his brows.

"I was baptized when I was a kid, but I ain't been back for a long time." Danny touched the gun in his pocket.

The handsome middle-aged man standing in front of them followed his movement. "The blood of Christ is not to be given or taken lightly, young man. If you are hungry, I will give you some money so you and your friend can go and get something to eat. But I will not allow you to desecrate the blessed sacraments."

Danny removed the gun and, pointing it straight at the man wasting his time, he said, "You *will* administer the sacraments, Father, and you *will* administer them right now," Danny said, his voice commanding but not disrespectful.

The priest picked up on the tone in Danny's voice and decided to try and reason with the young man.

"If you are in some sort of trouble, we can sit down over here and talk about what is bothering you." He motioned toward the empty pew.

"Father, I'm in big trouble here. I was bitten by a rougarou, and now I'm in danger of becomin' a rougarou myself. I was told by a vampire that if you don't give me the body and blood of Christ and do it fast that no one will be able to help me ever again `cause it'll be too late."

The priest drew a shaky hand through his graying black hair, his dark brown eyes filling with fear. "Are you under the influence of drugs that you would believe what you are telling me?"

"I'm not on drugs. I told you I got bit by a fuckin' rougarou, and I need the blood and body of Christ to keep me from turnin' into one myself! Now get your ass in gear and get the wafers and wine." Danny pulled back the hammer of the gun to let the man know he meant what he said. "After you, Father." He waved him away.

Knowing his life to be in extreme danger, the priest gave up trying to reason with the man who had to be delusional to believe what he was saying. "Follow me," he told them.

In a room in the back of the church, the priest removed a small plate of thin wafers and a carafe of wine.

Leadah grabbed a glass off the sink and held it out. "Danny

can drink the wine out of this," she directed him, knowing they were running out of time.

The priest tipped up the carafe and splashed a small amount into the glass, then handed it over to Danny.

"You need to say the words, Father. I'm not stupid. Get the wafers over here and administer the sacraments like you're supposed to."

The priest, picking up one of the wafers, placed it on Danny's outstretched tongue.

"Wait a minute, have the wafers been consecrated yet? And the wine?"

"Yes." He nodded. "They have."

"Just to be on the safe side, no offense, make the sign of the cross over them," Danny said, unwilling to take any chances.

Adding a small blessing, the priest again administered the sacraments.

"I hope you will go and get some help for your drug problems, son. You don't want to go through life this way."

"I told you, Father, I don't have a drug problem. I have a rougarou problem. Now, thanks to you, though, I may not have it anymore."

The priest remained silent, knowing anything he had to say would fall on deaf ears. He watched the two young people run from the church, and after offering up a prayer for their safety and healing, he busied himself with putting the wafers and wine away. His task finished, he walked through the back door, turning the lock and pulling the door closed behind him. He was on his way to the rectory and to enjoying a few shots of his favorite liquor when someone stepped in this path.

He had but a moment's glimpse of madness before the gun exploded, and everything went dark.

CHAPTER SEVENTEEN

"Hays," Donavan said into the phone.

"Lieutenant Hays, this is Jackson at dispatch. We just received word about a shooting in the back of the Saint Thomas Church at Fifty-two thirty Beacon Street. Ambulance is en route."

"Thanks, Jackson, we're on our way," Donavan said, turning as Jack walked up to him.

"What's up?"

"Got a shooting at the Catholic church on Beacon."

"Give me a moment to tell Seelah we're leavin', and I'll be ready to go with you," Jack called back over his shoulder as he walked down the hall.

Donavan nodded as he picked up the phone. "Yeah, this is Hays. I need a couple of deputies at my residence." He spoke into the phone then waited. "Log it as a family in need of protection." He hung up the phone.

"Okay, I'm ready."

"I just put in a call for a couple of uniforms to come and stay while we're gone."

"With any luck, they'll be human."

* * *

Donavan stopped one of the paramedics to ask what they had found so far.

"Father Austin, the parish priest, was shot in the shoulder.

Guess the assailant was right in front of him, which makes me wonder why he was only shot in the shoulder instead of a more vital area. Almost like the person who did the shooting only wanted to wound him."

"Is Austin able to talk, or was that all the info you were able to get out of him?"

"No, he's coherent. But with a gunshot, as you know, shock can set in pretty fast, so if you want to talk to him, I would do it now."

Climbing into the back of the ambulance, Donavan sat down on a large, closed medical chest across from where the priest was laid out on a stretcher. "I'm Lieutenant Hays of the Saint Anthony Parish Sheriff's Department, Father Austin. Did you get a chance to see who shot you?"

"He had a hood over his head, so I couldn't see his face, but I'm pretty sure it was the same young man who was in the church a short time before."

"Did you get this young man's name?"

"I heard the girl call him Danny," he whispered.

Donavan could see the man was in a lot of pain, and he tried to hurry along his line of questioning. "I'll try to keep it brief, Father, but any information you can offer will help greatly."

The doors to the ambulance closed with a bang with a double slap on the door, letting Donavan know they were ready to leave.

"We're going to be transporting you to the hospital now, Father, so you'll be in good hands before you know it. Did this person say what he was doing in the church this late? Could he have just stopped in to say a prayer?"

"He wanted me to give him the sacraments."

"That was a strange request. Did he say why?"

"Yes, he said he needed me to give him the sacraments to keep him from changing into a rougarou."

"Did you comply with his request?"

"He was holding a gun on me. I didn't argue."

The paramedic who was monitoring the priest leaned

forward to begin checking vitals. "I think the rest of your questioning can wait until later. This man needs to get some rest."

"Yeah, we're almost to the hospital anyway." He looked out the window to see Jack's truck right behind them traveling at the same rate of speed.

Jack veered off into the parking lot as the ambulance drove under the overhanging cover at the front door of the emergency room.

Donavan stood up as the driver opened the doors to the ambulance then stepped to the ground.

"Were you able to get anything useful out of the priest?" Jack asked.

Donavan motioned him away from the door and over to the smoking area. "Who the hell does this sound like to you?" He pulled two cigarettes from the pack in the inside pocket of his suit coat to hand one to Jack. "Father Austin, the man who was shot, said a young man came into his church with a young girl demanding the priest give him the Holy Sacraments. You know, the body and blood of Christ."

"I don't know *who* it sounds like, but I know *what* it sounds like. Sounds like a fuckin' crack head," Jack said, holding the lighter beneath both cigarettes.

Donavan inhaled deeply, drawing the nicotine into his lungs. "The girl called the young man Danny, and the priest said this Danny told him he had been bitten by a rougarou and was in fear of turning into a rougarou himself. I guess receiving the body and blood of Christ is supposed to ward off the change."

"Danny fuckin' Roberts!" Jack whirled, a big grin spreading across his face. "He said Gaston bit him when they were havin' their fight."

"That's who I think it is too. We can find out from his aunt if he still lives over the store."

"Did the good father give him the sacraments like he wanted?"

"Yeah, the man was holding a gun on him."

* * *

When Jillianna answered the knock on her door this time, she was not surprised to see Leadah and her friend standing on the doorstep.

"Come and tell me what has happened since you left my home," she told them, holding out her hand in welcome.

Danny ushered Leadah ahead of him and pulled the door closed behind him.

After they were seated in the spacious living room, a black servant dressed in a white shirt and black slacks held forth a gold tray with three long-stemmed glasses of wine.

Thank you, Baxter," Jillianna told him. "You may leave the bottle, and we will serve ourselves."

"Yes'm." He bowed his way out of the room.

She waited until the man had left the room then leaned forward in her chair. "Now tell me all that happened."

"We went to the first church we came to, which was Saint Thomas on Beacon Street. The priest was already in the church, and he didn't seem too pleased on helpin' us. That is until I showed him the gun," Danny laughed.

"If you had had to use the gun, do you think you could have actually pulled the trigger?" Jillianna refilled their glasses.

"Tell ya the truth, I don't know. I don't think I could have killed a priest, but I don't want to be a rougarou either."

"The priest thought Danny was on some killer drugs," Leadah laughed, sipping her wine and enjoying her surroundings.

"I bet. It's not every day someone runs into a church demanding they be given the Holy Sacraments."

Leadah glanced over at her, noting the sadness in her voice and the tears darkening her oddly-colored eyes. "I bet it's hard on you not bein' able to enter the church now."

"Yeah, how the hell did you wind up bein' a vampire?" Danny spoke up, holding his glass out to be refilled.

At first, his blatant inquisitiveness was like a slap across her face, but as she looked at him, she knew he meant no disrespect. He was simply curious. "I was born and bred in the country of

Romania."

Danny's dark head snapped up. "No shit! Do you know Dracula?" His laughter was loud and invasive. Partly because of the well-aged wine he had thrown down his throat and partly due to his nervousness.

Jillianna reached out, placing one well-manicured hand on his arm. "Danny, with my help, you just escaped a life only a fool would enjoy living. If I choose, I can still turn your life into a living nightmare. There are more ways than one to become the devil's child, Danny. And if that happens, there will be no priest or shaman or voodoo priestess who can lift the curse this time. So you need to choose your words carefully while you are in my presence."

Fear clutched his throat, making it difficult for him to breathe. With a shaking hand, he lifted the replenished wine to his dry mouth. "I meant no disrespect, Jillianna. Sometimes I speak before I think."

"A bad habit that needs to be curbed while you are still able," she warned him, then added, "Now we were on the subject of how I came to be a vampire."

Both Danny and Leadah breathed a deep sigh of relief, knowing they had escaped a harrowing experience.

* * *

As three deputies went around to the back of the house, they tapped on the Roberts door, keeping a hand near their unsnapped holsters.

When there was no response, they tapped two more times. Finally, the door swung open to reveal a scantily-clad Shirley Roberts obviously in her cups. "Why the hell don't you guys call before droppin' in on a lady?" she told them, her words clipped and slurred.

"Oh, come on now, Shirley, you ain't gonna make us believe you ain't happy to see us." Jack slipped an arm around her waist to walk her across the room and drop her gently into a chair. "I thought you and me got to be friends earlier."

She tried to get up out of the chair only to fall back. "Guess I'll stay seated." Her laughter was loud and irritating.

Donavan saw a movement at the top of the stairs, and he quickly nudged Jack, nodding to the stairs.

"Is someone else here with you, Shirley?" Jack asked her, drawing his own .38.

"Hell yes, somebody's here with me. You don't think I'd be runnin' `round the house like this for nothin'."

"Who is it? Is your nephew Danny here?"

"Get outta here!" The silly grin spreading across her face told them all they needed to know. "I ain't into bangin' my own nephew for Christ's sakes."

"Then let me guess." Donavan glanced back at her as he slowly climbed the stairs. "You were in the middle of entertaining a friend when we showed up?"

"Yep." She nodded, giggling like a school girl. "Hope to hell he don't finish without me."

Donavan turned to come back downstairs as he caught sight of a man nearer to Shirley's age. "Shirley, does Danny still live over the store?"

"Yeah, hell, I couldn't just throw his little ass out in the street even though he does owe me money. If I did that with the way my luck's been runnin', he'd wanna move in here with me."

While Jack kept up a constant chatter, Donavan walked into the other room to radio the deputies already in place at the furniture store.

"Be advised, the perp still resides at this address in the apartment overhead." He spoke quietly into the handheld.

A voice quickly responded that they were already in place at the residence.

"All right, Shirley." Donavan walked over to her. "You'll be happy to know we will be getting out of your hair so you can get back to what you were doing."

Jack winked and grinned. "Behave yourself, Shirley."

"Forget that!" she snickered loudly. "I got me a wild one here today and with any luck, all night."

Keeping their thoughts to themselves, they made their way out the door.

* * *

Jillianna settled back in her chair, a glass of red wine in her hand.

Without waiting to be asked, Danny lifted the carafe of wine, pouring a liberal amount into all three glasses.

"I was but a few days shy of being sixteen when my life changed forever," she breathed, allowing her thoughts to reach back into a past of complete sadness...

"Jillianna," called a familiar voice into the gathering dusk.

Her blond head turned. "Karleto," her young voice rang out in answer, "I am here."

Within moments, the sounds of pounding hoofs echoed in the surrounding twilight.

Pulling up on the reins, Karleto leapt from the back of a beautiful black stallion.

"I was afraid you would not meet me after I heard that your father is sending you away from the castle to stay with your grandfather in northern Romania." His words were breathless as he held her against his chest.

"I could not leave without seeing you again," she cried against his shoulder, the pain in her heart growing stronger at his nearness.

Karleto could feel his body respond in heated need as he held her, and a tiny voice warned of the danger of being with her in such an isolated area.

"I don't want to be separated from you, my love." She drew back, gazing at him, her beautiful blue-green eyes feasting on his thick black hair and dark blue, almost black eyes that were always filled with such love for her. Tall and muscular, his dark brown skin always smelling of clean oils that teased the senses. He made her feel small and helpless when in his close embrace. "I want our days together to continue." Jillianna wrapped her slim arms around his trim waist, feeling the thick fabric of his dark blue shirt brush against her face. "Soon, I will reach my sixteenth year, and I will be able to marry."

He gazed down at her, his full mouth holding a brief smile that showed his white, even teeth made even whiter against his dark skin. "Your father would never allow you to marry me. I am but a poor gypsy." His head bowed in shame at his low station in life. "He will marry you off to a rich man of means." He removed her arms from around his waist to walk a short distance away. "I am a poor boy with no hope of ever being rich," he whispered, the hopelessness sounding strong in his voice.

Jillianna looked at him as he stood there dressed in black pants molded to his slim hips, and she felt her heart race with a strange need she had been feeling of late whenever he was near. "We must find a way to be together, Karleto. We must find a way that would force my father to allow me to be your wife."

"There is but one way he could not send you away, and that is if you are carrying my child."

She drew back, staring at him in horror. "You would want me to be like the women who give themselves to a man without the respect of being their wife?"

He could see the pain his words had caused her, and he felt as though a knife had been driven into his already bleeding heart.

"I meant you no disrespect, my beautiful Jillianna. I only meant to find a way for us to be together for the rest of our days. If you carry my child, then no other man will want you, for you will no longer be untouched, and your father will have no choice but to allow us to marry and stay together or be forced to live with the shame his errant daughter has brought down on the family name."

"I will have to think on this, Karleto," she told him, no longer eager to be near him.

"I can tell you no longer wish to be with me, so I will follow you back to the castle at a discreet distance."

She allowed him to hold her for a moment longer, then catching up her long pale blue gown, ran down the path leading to the back of the castle, her heart heavy with the plan he had set forth for them to stay together.

As she ran, she thought upon Karleto's words. She knew that only a woman of the lower class would dare think of doing such a thing to their family name. Fathers had been known to slay their disobedient daughters for lying with a man before she belonged to him. Even a man her father had promised her to. Not until the night of the nuptials would she know what it meant to be totally with the man she loved. Then, too, this night was not always a night to be looked upon with gladness. Many girls found themselves promised to men they had never met before yet were expected to come to the marriage bed with gladness in their heart.

She had been very daring in her leaving the protection of her maid servant when gone from the castle. She knew she was forbidden to stroll the grounds alone, especially at night and especially with a man not her husband. Her doing so not only put her own life in danger but that of the girl who had been given to her to see to her needs.

"Jillianna, your bath is ready, and I have chosen the yellow gown with the white flowers embroidered on the hem and around the neck for you this day."

Jillianna sat up in her bed, yawning in the early morning hour. "Why are you calling me from my bed so early, Renna?"

"Your father has summoned you to join him in breaking the morning fast, Jillianna." Renna smiled over at her.

Jillianna looked at her, noting the beauty of her face and body, and she smiled back. Dressed in a light orange gown of thin gossamer material, she all but floated across the room to pull back the covers from her mistress. Barely into her fifteenth year herself, Renna was someone Jillianna enjoyed being with since she had no female siblings to be close to and share her thoughts with.

Later, sitting at the end of the long table, she waited until the man servant had left before turning her attention to the man sitting at the other end of the table.

"I am very happy you requested my presence this morning, Father. Being with you always makes me smile," she told him, waiting for the look of pleasure her words never failed to bring to his handsome middle-aged face.

Not yet reaching his fiftieth year, his black hair showed only a hint of gray but was more pronounced in the close-cropped beard. His black eyes always lit up at the sight of his beguiling and only daughter, whom he loved with all his being.

"Your beautiful face will begin my day on a happy note, Jillianna," Nicholas told her. Drawing up the sleeves of his deep blue tunic, he picked up a piece of the thick toasted bread covered in butter and jam made from his favorite fruit, the pomegranate.

Taking a sip from the silver-rimmed goblet filled with the juice from the orange, she asked him, "Was there a reason you wanted to see me at this early hour, Father?"

"Yes, daughter, since you will be celebrating your sixteenth year soon, I have taken the liberty of choosing a husband befitting the station this family holds here."

Busy with enjoying his meal, Nicholas missed the shocked look covering her face.

"I know it is your right as my father and the head of our family to choose the man who will be my husband, but I had hopped with our closeness that you would allow me to choose the man I will spend the rest of my life with."

Nicholas stopped what he was doing to stare over at her. "The choosing of a husband for one's daughter is the right and responsibility of the father. He must make sure she will be well taken care of and that all the children she bears him will be from her husband's seed. You have been well protected and guarded, so I have no worry that you are unchaste. The man I have chosen for you comes from a very wealthy and well-respected family. His father is much loved among those he governs."

"Is this man much older than me?" she whispered, her stomach doing an involuntary roll as she pushed away her plate.

"No." Her father shook his dark head. "Rolan Hindel is but a dozen years older than you. He is at the time in his life where he needs sons. Most of the sons his older brothers have sired have been killed off in the fighting between those of his people and those who wish to take over his father's empire. You are young. You will give him many strong and healthy sons, daughter."

Unable to hear anymore, Jillianna excused herself from the table.

Knowing that his news had to be unsettling to a young girl of Jillianna's tender years, Nicholas allowed her to leave the room.

When she reached her room, Jillianna threw herself on her bed, wanting only to block out the terrible words of her father. Unable to stay in the confining room, she ran down the hallway and out the heavy oak door.

"Jillianna, wait, I will go with you," Renna called out, trying to catch up with her, knowing she would be held responsible if anything happened to the young girl running ahead of her. Within moments, she knew it was useless to try and catch up. Unwilling to go back to the castle without Jillianna, she dropped down on the thick grass to wait.

Finally, out of breath, Jillianna stopped running and sat down with her back against a tall tree. How could her father, who never missed telling her how much he loved her, want to destroy her? What would Karleto do when she told him? As these thoughts continued to race through her mind, she heard the sounds of a horse nearby. Hardly daring to hope, she stood to see who rode towards\ her so early in the day.

"Karleto." She whispered his name, her breath catching in her throat as he dismounted to walk toward her. "How did you know I would be here?"

Without answering her, he pulled her roughly into his strong arms to cover her full mouth with his. When the kiss ended, they were both left wanting. "I know everything there is to know about you, my beloved Jillianna. I keep watch on who comes and goes from the castle," he murmured against her throat.

"You must not stay here, Karleto. Someone will see you and tell my father."

Bounding onto his horse, he held out his arms to her. Without giving herself time to think about what she was about to do, she took hold of his hands, allowing him to lift her up in front of him.

The horse broke into an all-out run, and all she could do was laugh as she leaned into the arms of the man she loved, trusting him to keep her safe as they rode into the densely wooded forest.

After helping her to her feet, he dropped to the ground beside her. Without a word, he guided them deeper into the forest. Tethering his horse, he undid the saddle, lying it down on the forest floor, then pulled *a brightly-hued blanket from the horse's back to lay it on a thick bed of pine needles.*

"We should not be doing this, Karleto, but I cannot face what is happening in my life without feeling the touch of the man I love."

"I will not allow you to belong to any man except me, Jillianna. I will die before I let you go." He pushed her to the blanket and, without another word, began removing her gown.

She did not stop him. Instead, she lifted her hips to help him remove the last of her clothing. Being sure to keep her garments neat and clean, he hung them on a nearby branch.

Karleto took a moment to enjoy the sight of her thick, blond hair fanned out around her, then slowly disrobed, all the while holding her blue-green stare with his own.

Beside her now, he pulled her into his arms, enjoying the velvet smoothness of her soft, warm skin.

"You are beautiful, my Jillianna. Just as I knew you would be," he murmured, taking one full breast into his hungry mouth, flicking the already hardening nipple with his tongue and bringing a deep moan from her throat. Karleto smiled, knowing the great pleasure she was feeling. Knowing there would be pain when he took her for the first time, he continued to ready her young body for what lay ahead in their coming together.

Jillianna savored their closeness, her eyes shut tight as Karleto taught her body to respond to his gentle touch.

"Open your eyes, my sweet one. See the love I have for you shining in mine." He drew a finger across her brow, willing her to look at him. When she did, he drew in his breath at the passion he saw reflected there.

"I have never felt like this. I feel as though a liquid fire is covering my body and all I can do is let it burn brighter."

His hot mouth moved down her body until he reached the core of her passion. Lifting her slim hips to his mouth, he savored the taste and the strong womanly scent bathing his senses. His tongue glided into her golden curls, searching for the tiny nub hiding in the velvet folds, and he flicked it gently, eliciting a long, drawn-out moan.

Without warning, Jillianna grabbed his thick black hair in her small fists, pushing his face and searching tongue against her pulsating womanhood, a small scream leaving her throat as Karleto jabbed his strong tongue back and forth within her hot tightness.

As the first chills racked her body, she ground her hips against his mouth until she felt herself shiver with out of control passion.

Karleto moved over her still shivering body and, with a sharp flick of his slim hips, ripped through the thin sheath guarding the entrance to her virgin womb. He felt her body tense, but he had gone beyond being able to call a halt to his needs. To his surprise, Jillianna moved her hips beneath him, urging him on until his body exploded, releasing the tiny seeds stored within his well-endowed manhood. With a groan, he slumped forward to feel her warm arms surrounding him.

Knowing his weight was too much for her to bear, he rolled his body to the side.

"I belong to you now, Karleto. My father will have to listen when I tell him I am no longer untouched."

The wondrous moments they had just shared came to an abrupt end as Karleto got to his feet to begin pulling on his clothing.

"Karleto," she whispered, her heart fluttering in alarm at the look on his handsome face. "What is wrong?"

"You must not tell your father what has happened between us. We must keep our meetings a secret until we know you carry our child. When we are sure the seed within your body has ripened, then we will flee this place and go far away."

"I have no choice but to tell my father about us, my love. He is sending me away soon to be married to a man far away from here."

"This cannot be true, Jillianna. You must have heard his words wrong. I cannot allow you to belong to another man after what happened between us." He was on his knees now, gathering her small body up in his arms.

"It is true, Karleto. My father told me of his plans to marry me to a man whose father has requested I be given to his son in marriage. He is in need of sons to replenish his father's empire."

"We must leave here soon then. You will meet me two nights from now. We will flee to my family far away from here where your *father will not find us."*

"I thought you and your family camped down by the water's edge. Are you telling me you have other family?"

"Yes, we have been visiting my mother's band. She has been very homesick for her people."

"How will your mother accept me when she finds out we are fleeing from my father? I know you will not want to leave without telling her where you are going and why."

"She will not have any say about what I do. She is a woman, and she will have to accept that as her son, I hold the upper hand in what happens in our family."

Although she did not like his words, she knew they were true. A man would always have the last say where a woman was concerned.

Later, when he let her leave him to go back to the castle, she was startled to find Renna waiting for her.

"Renna, you scared the life out of me appearing like that."

"Your father is looking for you, Jillianna. He has men out searching the grounds for you. Why were you with that gypsy?" Her full mouth curled into a sneer. "Gypsies are evil. They delve into witchcraft."

"Oh, do hush with your silliness, Renna!" Jillianna turned on her in anger. "How do you know my father is looking for me?"

"He sent word that the man you are to marry is on his way here to claim you. He will be here on the morrow."

Without waiting to hear more, Jillianna took off running in the direction of the castle, where she hoped to hide from her father for a while longer.

Reaching her room, she grabbed Renna's hand to pull them both inside. With real trepidation in her heart. She threw herself across her wide bed.

Renna stood, one hand pressed to her mouth, the other pressed against her churning stomach. "Do I have reason to fear where you have been for so long?" she asked, her voice little more than a whisper in the quiet room.

"Only if my secret is found out before we can flee from here."

Almost the same in age, the two girls were more like sisters than mistress and servant. "What have you done that you feel you must flee from home and family?"

"I allowed Karleto to make me his woman," she murmured, her face aglow at sharing such a delicate matter with another.

Renna ran across the room to kneel down in front of her mistress. "You must be telling me an untruth. You know you have been promised to another."

"I could never allow another man to put his hands on me after Karleto. I would rather die."

"You may get your wish if your father finds out what you have done. Do you not know a man can tell if another has already entered your body? It is a husband's right to know his seed is the only one to grow inside your body. If he is not, then he has the right to end your life or return you to your father in disgrace."

Jillianna leapt off the bed, going to the high window to stare out into the gathering darkness of an approaching storm. "You will have to come with us when we leave here," she told Renna. "My father will blame you for not watching over me close enough."

"I will come with you. I would only worry myself sick if I did not know what was happening to you."

"Do you think you can get a message to Karleto for me? He must know what is happening." She turned to look at her as she sat on the edge of the bed.

"Yes, I will send a friend whom I trust with my very life to deliver the message. He knows the band that Karleto belongs to."

"Tell him to meet me later this night where I wait for him to come to me and to bring an extra horse." She tried to quiet the rapid beating of her heart. "I know when I tell him that I will be leaving, he will take me with him, and he cannot take me without taking you too."

Standing in the dark, she waited for a man who could cause her the loss of her life and bring shame to her family's name. At last, she heard the sounds of a horse blowing and snorting nearby in the overgrown trees.

He came to her slowly, wrapping her in his strong arms. "I have not been able to think of anything but you, my love. When I am away *from you, it is as though a part of me is missing," he whispered against the hollow of her throat.*

"I had to see you one more time before I leave."

He drew back, looking at her. "I thought you were not to leave until later. When did your father say you are to leave?"

"The man I am being forced to marry is coming here on the morrow."

Without a word, he picked her up in his arms to carry her to his horse.

"No, we cannot leave without Renna. My father will have her killed if she stays here."

"This is why I was asked to bring along an extra horse." He smiled over at her. "Renna," Karleto called out quietly, "you will come with us."

Within moments, Karleto and the young women were racing across the grounds to what they hoped would be a place of refuge from Jillianna's father and the man who was traveling a great distance to make her his wife and the mother of his sons.

* * *

"How could you be so stupid, Karleto, as to bring the daughter of Nicholas Romanitti here to our campsite?" The older woman, dressed in a long dress of brightly hued colors, crossed her weighty arms in front of her. "Do you not know that her presence brings death to all who are here?"

"She is to be my wife, Mother. Her father has promised her to another who travels through this night to claim her. She could not remain in the home of her father. She must stay here where she and her servant will be safe."

"Bah! She cannot stay here," she hissed at him, shaking a finger in his face. "When we leave here to join your father, she must not be with us."

"It is already too late, Mother. Jillianna and I have lain together. The man who would take her as his bride would be able to tell that she is not pure. He would kill her."

"It is no more than she deserves! She is unclean. The children she would bear you would be unclean. Nicholas Romanitti is a very

powerful man. He will destroy you and all your family over what you have done."

"Then I will take her and leave here. There is no reason for his wrath to come down on our people."

"Who is the man her father has promised her to in marriage?"

"He is not from here. He lives far to the north. His name is Rolan Hindel."

As the breath rushed from her lungs, she grabbed his arm to spin him around. "Have you not heard the rumors of the Hindel family? Have you not listened to what others say about them?"

"I do not have time for idle gossip. They are only silly superstitions."

"Go to Luna, let her tell you about the Hindels and their dark secrets," she told him, nodding to give strength to her words.

"Luna is a witch. She believes anyone whose veins are not filled with the blood of the gypsy is unworthy to breathe the air."

"And she is right. However, she is also a seer. She can tell you of the darkness surrounding the Hindel family."

Knowing there would be no peace for him until he did as his mother suggested, he agreed to speak with Luna.

Seated around the campfire with Jillianna and Renna beside him, he waited for Luna to begin telling him all the evil curses that would befall him if he did not return Jillianna to her father this very night.

Luna reached out her hand. "Give me your hands, child. I must see what the future holds for you."

When Jillianna did as she was told, she tried not to show her fear before this ancient woman dressed in a long and flowing gown of green and gold with a matching swatch of cloth wound around her stringy white hair.

"You already carry the seed of Karleto. This does not bode well for him or his family or any of us who belong to this band."

Karleto ignored her words to leap to his feet. Swinging Jillianna up in his arms, he planted a hot kiss on her full mouth. "You have already been blessed with my child, my love."

"No, Karleto, you have not been blessed with the seed growing

in the womb of this child you have brought to me. You have both been cursed."

Shaking the thoughts from her mind, Jillianna picked up the carafe of wine to refill her glass.

"Well, don't stop now, Jillianna." Danny sat forward in his chair, "we want to know how you became a vampire."

Leadah nudged him sharply in his ribs. "Hush, Danny. Jillianna will tell us the rest of her story when she is ready. I think it is time we left here."

"The hour grows late, Danny, and you have yet to pay your debt to me." Jillianna rose from her chair to stand before him. She reached out, pulling him to his feet, and smiled. "You have escaped one life of darkness only to be threatened with another. Your debt to me is to bring me a young female who will keep my sexual juices flowing and whose blood will keep me young and alive and looking the way I look now."

"You're a dyke?" A wide grin crossed his face. "The way you're stacked and the story you just delivered," —his brows lifted —"I'd never have guessed it." At the angry scowl covering her face, he quickly became serious. "Anyway, I don't know where the hell to find a woman to bring to you."

"I must feed, Danny, and when one is a part of the dark side, needs and tastes change." Her dark eyes slid slowly over Leadah, then returned to rest on him. "You have two choices. Either you will find a young woman who will feed my needs, or I will simply feed upon the beautiful young woman standing before me."

Danny threw up his hands, stepping in front of Leadah. "No, I'll find a woman. It might take me most of the night, but I'll find one," he promised.

"I will be waiting for you to keep your word, Danny. You can accompany him on his search, Leadah. A woman will be more trusting if they see another woman."

"Come on, Leadah, let's get the fuck outta here while we still can."

Sliding across the seat, Danny turned the key, bringing the

car to life. "That was close. Now we can go home and forget all this evil shit."

"No, Danny." Leadah touched his hand. "You'll keep your word to Jillianna, or she'll come find us. She's not one you want to anger, 'cause if you do, she'll turn our lives into a livin' hell."

Chapter Eighteen

Hays and Olivier´ sat outside the furniture store waiting for Danny to make a showing.

"I still don't understand why Roberts would want a priest to give him the Holy Sacraments. And at the point of a gun? What the hell's up with that?"

"Who knows?" Donavan blew a stream of smoke out the car window. "Maybe someone told him that taking the Holy Sacraments can keep him from being a rougarou."

Jack thought about what Donavan had just said, then breathed, "Odd as that may sound, you could have found the answer. I mean, think about it, where do we go when we're in trouble?"

Donavan glanced over at him then nodded. "Maybe." He opened the door and stepped to the curb.

"Where you goin´? I'll come with you."

"No need," he laughed. "I got it handled."

Jack pulled the door to as he heard the sounds of urine hitting asphalt.

* * *

"Where the hell are we gonna find a woman? She should be able to find her own snacks for Christ's sake." He turned onto the main drag, looking to spot a hooker working the street. "You fightin' with anyone you'd like to see gone?"

Leadah laughed, trying to chase away the sick feeling in

her stomach. "None that I would want to see murdered."

"I don't know if I can do this. I've never hurt anyone in my life."

"If we don't find a woman so she can feed, she'll come after us."

"Hell, we can't even go to the police with this. They'd just haul our asses off to the nut ward."

"Danny, stop!" she told him. "I saw a woman walking by herself back there." She nodded behind them.

"Did she look young?"

"It's dark. I couldn't see how old she was," she said, her voice taking on an angry tone.

"No need to get pissy." He went to the end of the block to turn around.

"I don't want to do this. She's probably just tryin' to live like me."

"Calm down," he told her, rubbing a gentle hand up and down her back. "Okay, I see her. I think our search is over."

He pulled over to the curb and, rolling down the window, called out softly to the pretty young girl making her way toward him.

* * *

Donavan keyed the mike. "Simmons, Olivier´ and I are going to be out of vehicle for about ten minutes."

"Ten-four, detective, we'll be here when you get back."

"Yeah, no shit." Jack grinned at Simmons' reply. "We'll pick them up something to munch on too."

"I wish that little prick would get home. I really didn't think we were going to have to spend the night sitting in a car watching a furniture store."

As they pulled up in front of the little market, they spied a young girl who looked to be about seventeen or eighteen dressed in a very short skirt, a pullover top, and sandals leaning into an open car window.

"I don't know 'bout you, but I don't feel like doin' extra

paperwork tonight," Jack said.

"She could be talking to someone she knows or just...let's go get what we came for."

Grabbing a buggy, Jack walked up one aisle and down another, throwing chips and dip and chocolate cupcakes inside.

"What the hell...do you have a tapeworm?" Donavan looked at all the snacks he was accumulating. "I watched you eat dinner."

"You know I always eat when I'm uptight. Bein' on a stakeout makes me edgy."

"Hmmm, never noticed you getting hungry on a stakeout before."

"That's because most of the stakeouts we went on were spent out in a fuckin' swamp. How the hell can anyone muster up an appetite with the smell of gator shit surroundin' them?"

As the man at the checkout began ringing up their purchases, Jack pointed to a cooker filled with plump sausages. "Better give us two of those too."

"If one of those is meant for me, I'll have mustard and onions on mine."

As the two walked outside with their goodies, Jack stopped in his tracks. "Holy shit! Did you see that?"

"See what?" Donavan looked around, trying to find what Jack was seeing.

"That hooker standin' up the sidewalk just got into that vehicle."

"We call them Johns. Let's get back to the stakeout."

Rushing to the Jeep, Jack all but threw the sack into the backseat. "Hurry up, Goddamn it," he growled. "I think we just found our man."

"Are you sure?"

"I got a good look at the driver when he flipped around to go back the way we just came."

Donavan grabbed his handheld. "Simmons, get a couple of the deputies around in front of the store. We think the perp may be headed your way. Our ETA is approximately five minutes,"

Donavan said.

"Will do, detective."

"He should be gettin' to his place right about now." Jack stepped on the gas, making the Jeep shoot forward. "One of the perks of bein' a cop, you get to speed and not have to pay a fine."

"Slow down, so you don't draw attention to our being after him. He knows what he did, so he'll be expecting the police."

"What the fuck? Where the hell is he?"

"Simmons," Donavan spoke into the mike, "see if anyone just pulled up out back."

"Nothing here. We would have seen them if anyone pulled up," Simmons came back to him.

"Keep driving. We'll see if we can get a sighting," Donavan said.

"If he just picked up a hooker, why the hell wouldn't he take her to his place?"

"Who knows? Maybe he has a rodeo fetish, and he's taking her out near a farm so he can whoop and holler and pretend he's hung like a stud horse."

Jack looked over at him then nodded to the backseat. "Speakin' of which, why don't you see what shape those sausages are in? I forgot about them when I threw the bag in the back," Jack said, then slammed on the brakes, making Donavan lurch forward.

"Goddamn it! I wish you would announce when you're going to stop!"

"There's his vehicle over there in front of that mansion."

* * *

Danny, along with the two females, made their way up the long walk leading to Jillianna's home. As he reached out to bang the heavy knocker, he found the door being pulled open.

Jillianna held out her hand to motion them inside, her dark eyes moving over the young woman following behind Danny. The bright gleam in her eyes told him she approved his choice.

"Sorry it took so long," Danny apologized, his voice

humble with none of the foolhardiness of before.

"You have done well, Danny," she told him, walking over closer to the young girl who was watching her with a look of uncertainty in her long-lashed black eyes. Jillianna felt her heart beat a stronger rhythm as she gazed at the beautiful girl before her noting the long, black, satin-soft hair hanging all the way down the girl's slender back; full pink full mouth that begged to be kissed and tasted; full hard breasts straining against the cheap fabric of her pullover top. She felt her breath rush from her lungs in anticipation of what lay ahead for the two of them.

"Danny, Leadah, the two of you may leave now. I will not be needing your services anymore this evening. My new friend and I wish to be alone." Jillianna placed her arm around the girl's shoulders to draw her near.

"Don't need to ask us twice," Danny breathed, taking Leadah's hand and moving toward the door.

The heavy knocker sounded, and before anyone could move, the man who had served them earlier walked ahead of them to answer the door.

An angry scowl slid across Jillianna's face at the unannounced intrusion.

"Two detectives are here to see you, madam. Shall I show them in?"

Her curiosity piqued, she nodded. "Yes, Baxter, please show them in."

The man turned, motioning the men inside.

"Sorry for the intrusion, madam. We'll try to be brief," Donavan told her, holding out his badge. "I'm Detective Donavan Hays, and this is my partner Detective Jack Olivier´."

Without a word, Jack moved forward and, grabbing both of Danny's wrists behind his back, slapped a pair of handcuffs into place. "Danny Roberts, you're under arrest for the attempted murder of Father Austin earlier this evening. You have the right to remain silent. Anything you say can and will be used against you in a court of law."

"What the fuck you talkin' 'bout? I never tried to murder

anyone!" He tried to yank away.

"Shut the hell up `til I'm through readin' you your rights." Jack pulled his cuffed wrists up high, bringing a squeal of pain from the man glaring at him.

"You can read him the rest of his rights in the car, Detective Olivier´," Donavan spoke up as two deputies walked through the open door.

Leadah moved forward. "Danny never tried to kill anyone. I've been with him all evenin'. Are you talkin' `bout the priest at Saint Thomas church?"

"That's the one. He said someone fitting the description of our man here pulled a gun on him earlier and then shot him twice as he was on his way to the Rectory."

"All right, I did show him a gun when we were inside the church, but I only did that to scare him."

"Why would you want to scare a priest?" Donavan asked.

"I had my reasons." Danny tried to sound tough but couldn't quite pull it off.

"You're in some pretty serious trouble here, Danny, my boy. You might want to stop playin' games and come clean about what you and your friend here" — Jack nodded to Leadah — "were up to this evenin'."

"You fuckers wouldn't believe me, so why waste my time?"

Moving forward, Jillianna spoke up. "I don't know what this is all about, detectives, but as you can see, I have a guest, so if you don't mind, I will bid you all a good evening."

"If you're referring to the young lady here, I would like to ask what those plans are. My partner and I saw these two" — he gestured toward Danny and Leadah — "pick her up off the streets not fifteen minutes ago."

"My plans are of no concern of yours, Detective Hays. You are in my home, not out on a public street."

"How old are you, girl?" Jack turned her around to face him.

"Seventeen." Her voice trembled as she spoke.

"Got any ID on you?"

"No, sir."

"Seen by two police officers bein' picked up off a public street without any ID and in the presence of two suspects in an attempted murder places you in a precarious situation, miss. I think you better come along with us," Jack told her, giving Jillianna a smug grin.

"This girl has every right to be in my home. She hasn't broken any law." An angry Jillianna shot forward to place an arm around the young girl's shoulder.

At the extreme fear in the girl's face at Jillianna's touch, Jack pulled the girl away. "Sorry, but this girl is suspected of being involved in prostitution. Are you sayin' that you have purchased this girl's services?"

"I have requested that this girl stay and keep me company. I did not say I want her to do anything except offer her presence to a lonely woman."

Jack looked at her then grinned. "Uh huh. Well, seems like this just ain't your night, Ms. Lonely." Still grinning, he guided the girl out the door behind a handcuffed and scared Danny Roberts.

After putting the young girl in the backseat of one of the cruisers, he walked over to the driver's side window. "You don't need to run her in. I just want to get her away from here. She can tell you where she wants to be let out," Jack told the deputy.

The girl leaned forward to place a hand on Jack's arm. "Thank you, detective, I `preciate it."

Jack nodded and, with a wave of his hand, walked away.

Jillianna watched from the window as the police left, her anger at having to ignore her hunger growing steadily worse. She had already dropped the curtain back into place when she snatched it back from the window. Instantly, her hunger dulled as she stood looking at a man standing beside a large maple. He was dressed in jeans and a hooded sweatshirt with the hood pulled up to hide his face.

"You son-of-a-bitch!" she screamed aloud as she ran to the front door.

He stood watching her run down the steps and straight up to him. "Hello, Jillianna." He whispered her name. "I hope you don't mind my dropping by to see you."

"Rolan." She tried to hold onto her anger as she saw him smile. "Why aren't you in hell where you belong?"

"I have too much work to do to leave this plane."

"It was you, wasn't it? It was you who shot the priest, knowing that Danny Roberts would get the blame for it."

"He should have accepted the life of a rougarou, Jillianna. We don't help your victims to reverse the curse once you have had *your* fill. You should have known there would be a price to pay for his returning to normal."

"You're a dark spirit. How is it you could harm a man of God?" She tried to quiet the fear creeping over her.

Walking closer, Rolan lifted his head and, sniffing the air, grinned over at her. "I can smell your fear, Jillianna. You should never have pitted your strength against ours." He reached out, taking her by the shoulders. "But you asked how I could harm a man of God. The priest has allowed his weakness for alcohol to dull his senses, and as you know, when the senses are weak, it is so easy for the dark side to move in and dominate. As for how I actually shot the priest, I simply entered the body of Gaston Roberts, the one Lawrence Hindel holds dear and near at the mansion. The priest will live. I only wounded him."

"You wanted Danny to get the blame and be made to suffer. Your evilness knows no bounds, Rolan. But then you have been this way for centuries, so why would you change now?" Taking a step back, she shrugged his hands from her shoulders, wanting only to be away from him, then turned back as she heard his demonic laughter.

"Always the pious one, right, Jillianna? That is until you have a beautiful young girl spread out before you with her veins filled with the rich, red blood you need to fill every cell in that beautiful body of yours."

"Spare me, Rolan." She gazed up at him. "I never found you sexually appealing when you were alive. I certainly don't find you appealing now."

"No, you preferred to wallow with gypsy trash even though you had been promised to me. It gave you great pleasure to pull the name of Hindel into the muck while you allowed your gypsy lover to take what belonged to me."

"How many centuries must pass before you let go of what happened in another lifetime?" She gazed at him, unable to believe he could still be harboring so much bitterness over what had happened when she was but an innocent young girl.

"Some things never go away, Jillianna. To be made to look the fool by someone who was not good enough to tend my horses is not easy to let go of."

"You would do well to try, Rolan. Grow up! It has been almost two entire centuries."

"Do you ever mourn the child you lost all those years ago, Jillianna?"

His question, coming as it did without warning, shot to the very core of her being.

The look on her face told him all he needed to know.

Without a word, she walked into the house to take a seat in front of the softly glowing hearth. With shaking hands, she poured a tall glass of her best red wine and motioning Baxter to leave her. She sat back in her chair, trying to relax her mind enough to blot out the images Rolan's words had brought forth.

Accepting she could not blot out the past, she allowed the images to grow stronger until she, at last, returned to a time that continued to haunt her all these many years later…

Jillianna struggled to free herself from Karleto's suffocating embrace. "Put me down, Karleto. I want to hear what Luna is trying to tell us."

Stung at her harsh words, Karleto drew back, then stood her on her feet. "Luna is an old woman who thinks to fill you with fear so you will wish to be returned to your father," he told her, unwilling to be made a fool before the men looking at them now with mistrust and more than a little fear.

"Your words are harsh, Karleto. I am not one to tell you a falsehood. This child has brought the hand of evil upon all here by allowing you to place your seed within her body." Luna drew back her hand, slapping him across his handsome face. "That is for bringing death to us who love you and especially to Morganna, your mother, whose safety and well-being your father entrusted to you."

Jillianna stood, one hand covering her mouth, trying to silence her tears.

"Whore!" Karleto's mother screamed, coming down the steps of her wagon. "You will leave here. I will not allow you to bring death and destruction to all here with your slatternly ways."

"Mother!" Karleto whirled, staring over the heads of the people as his mother's steps hastened in his direction. "How dare you speak such filth to Jillianna. You will take your words back and beg her forgiveness."

"Never!" Morganna ran forward. "I will tell you of this girl!" She refused to be silenced. "She is the daughter of Nicholas Romanitti, who lives in the castle. The man who looks upon us as the filthy gypsies who pitch their tents and allow the wheels of their wagons to make deep cuts in the land. The filthy gypsies who steal babies and sell them to other bands. We know these are untruths. But this is not why I say this girl must leave here, especially now that she carries the seed of my son. She must leave here because she has been promised in marriage to a man who is right now on his way to claim her. This man will bring death and destruction to each and every one of us, for he bears the name and carries the same tainted blood of Rafael Hindel!"

"Rougarou." The word spread amongst the crowd, gaining in strength as it was repeated. "Rougarou!"

"What are they saying, Karleto?" Jillianna screamed. "What is a rougarou?"

"A rougarou is a werewolf," he whispered, pulling her away from the campfire and the crowd.

"Oh my God. Why would they be calling Rolan a werewolf?

There is no such thing."

At the familiar usage of the other man's name, Karleto drew back, staring at her. "Why does the name of a man you have never met flow so easily from your tongue, Jillianna?"

The controlling tone in his voice and the anger in his eyes had Jillianna backing away from him. "I do not wish to quarrel with you, Karleto. I simply find it ridiculous that people who should know better choose to believe in superstition."

Forgetting his own dismissal of superstitious beliefs, his hands shot out, grabbing her by her slender shoulders and yanking her forward. "How dare you scoff at our beliefs!" The fear in her eyes strengthened the male dominance raging through his veins.

Renna jumped to her feet to run forward. "You will take your hands off her this instant!"

Without thinking, his hand shot out, slapping her away from him. "You low-life bitch! Never put your hands on your betters!"

Renna got to her feet, the anger still strong in her heart for the man who dared manhandle her mistress. Going to Jillianna, she pulled her into her arms. "Do you see what you have put our lives in danger for, Jillianna? He thinks only to treat you like his property, not like the noble lady you are."

"If you are going to talk, then speak up so I can hear your words," Karleto snarled, unable as yet to halt the terrible anger raging inside him.

"I was telling my lady she has put our lives in danger for nothing. You live up to the things people say about the gypsies. You are nothing but trash!"

Karleto grabbed the young girl by the throat and squeezed until she went limp. When he allowed her body to slump to the ground, he looked up to see Jillianna staring at him, the horror in her eyes saying it all.

"Those who do not know their place do not deserve to live."

Jillianna whirled to run blindly away. The hot tears stinging her eyes were making it difficult to see where she was going, but she knew she must not stop. The man she thought she loved no longer existed. In his place was a man who could kill another simply because they spoke *their feelings.*

When at last she could go no further, she dropped down on the damp grass to get a sense of where she was. To her great relief, she could see the castle off in the distance. Almost afraid to move from the cover of trees, she listened to see if she could hear the sounds of a horse. When all remained quiet, she moved off in the direction of home.

She had gone but a short distance when her heart jumped in her throat. The sounds of many horses came to her, and before she could dart into the cover of trees once more, she found herself surrounded by guards from the castle.

As one of the guards lifted her tired body onto his horse, she caught a glimpse of someone watching them from a short distance away.

Without a word, Karleto kicked his horse into an all-out run straight toward the guards and the girl who was being taken from him.

Swords drawn in defense of Nicholas Romanitti's most prized possession, they quickly ended the life of the one who sought to do them harm.

Jillianna felt hot tears welling up in her eyes and, swallowing hard, pushed her face against the man holding her in his arms to hide her reaction to the one lying on the ground, his life's blood staining the grass all around him.

"You're safe, my lady," the man holding her told her. "I'll take you to your father, who is waiting for you."

* * *

At the sight of his young daughter being led into the castle, Nicholas moved forward to take her in his arms.

Jillianna could only sob out her fear as her father held her closely.

"I will not pretend I am not very put out with you, Jillianna. You had your mother and me worried out of our minds when we could not find you."

"Renna and I went to see the gypsies who are camped down by the water's edge, Father," she lied. "I did not mean to frighten you."

"And Renna? You have not said where she is." His voice was gentle yet authoritative.

"The man who was chasing me killed her. The guards stabbed

him with their swords. He is dead." *She fell into a fit of weeping that only grew worse as her mother ran into the room to pull her into her arms.*

"Oh, Jillianna, you had us worried sick," *her mother, Johanna, cried.* "Why were you such a silly girl? You know better than to leave the castle without many guards to protect you."

"Yes, I do know, and now because of me, my sweet Renna is dead."

"Oh no," *her mother whispered. Then her stricken eyes fell upon her daughter.* "Jillianna, were you harmed in any way while you were gone from here?"

"No, the man who chased after me and who had already killed Renna did not reach me before the guards killed him."

"Thank God in his heaven." *She crossed herself to add strength to her gratitude for her daughter's safe return.*

"Jillianna," *her father spoke up,* "the man who is to be your husband is on his way here to claim you. He will arrive late this night. You are not to tell him of your absence from the castle without the protection of many guards or of being chased by a man who ended the life of your servant."

"So many secrets," *she whispered, then seeing alarm enter into her father's gaze, she spoke aloud her grief.* "Her name was Renna, Father, and she was more than my servant. She was also my dear friend."

"Yes…well…be that as it may, you are not to say a word about any of this to anyone. Do I make myself clear, Jillianna?"

"Yes, Father," *she breathed.*

"Good." *Nicholas rose to his feet.* "From what you have said about what happened, the man who killed Renna did not do anything to you. Is this correct, Jillianna?"

"He did not do anything to me." *She turned away.*

"Then there is no reason for me to have our family physician check you to make sure you are still chaste and pure."

Knowing he would be waiting to see if she could look him in the eye while giving her answer, she turned to face him. "There is no reason to have me checked. The only thing I suffer from is sadness for the death of my Renna, and for that, there is no remedy."

"Yes, I must agree, Jillianna. Renna was a good girl who will be missed. And now that you have lost her, you will need to choose another to tend to your needs," her mother told her, her voice devoid of feeling.

"You will go to your chambers now and bathe so you will be ready to meet the man who will be your husband. You don't want him to see you looking as you do now. He might withdraw his offer for you." He chuckled, thankful his worries over a possible defilement of his only daughter were all for naught.

"What of Renna, Father? Will her body be returned here for burial?"

"I will send some of the guards to retrieve her body. Also, I will have the body of the gypsy who murdered her returned to his family. I want them to know why he was killed. Perhaps this will put an end to their continuance to camp on Romanitti land."

Jillianna's heart jumped in her chest. What if they told the guards about her being in their camp with Karleto? Even worse, what if his mother, in her anger and now grief over the death of her son, were to repeat the words of Luna about her carrying the seed of Karleto?

"Jillianna." Her mother touched her hand. "Are you all right? You have grown quite pale."

"Yes, Mother, I am only tired and sad. I think I will go and have my bath and then lay down for a while."

"I think that is best. I will have a girl sent to you." She placed a warm kiss on her daughter's cold cheek, her worried eyes following behind as Jillianna left the room.

After her bath, Jillianna was stretched out across her bed, trying to relax, when a light tap sounded on her door. Genene, the girl who was now taking Renna's place as her servant, went to see who dared to bother her new mistress's time of rest. When she saw Jillianna's mother standing in the hallway, she pulled the door open wide and, bowing her head, motioned her inside.

"You will leave us, Genene. I wish to be alone with my daughter."

Genene hastened to obey, touching both sides of her flowing gown of silver interwoven with light green threads in a light curtsey before bounding out the door.

Moving her daughter's slender legs out of the way, she seated herself on the bed. "I know you are not asleep, Jillianna. I have come to talk with you. The fear in my stomach tells me you are holding something back from your father and me. If I am to help you, I must know what this something is."

"If I tell you, you will no longer want me for your daughter."

"There isn't anything you could say that would make me not love you, daughter." She reached out and rubbed a gentle hand over Jillianna's back.

"I lied to Father about not being untouched."

"I know. I saw it in your face. Now we must form a plan so that only you and I know you lied."

"Karleto was not a stranger who chased Renna and me. He was my lover. And according to a gypsy witch who lives in the band of Karleto's mother, I am already carrying Karleto's seed in my womb."

"How long has Karleto been your lover?" Johanna whispered.

"We made love but one time, only a short time ago."

Johanna breathed a deep sigh of relief. "Then here is what you will do. On the night of your wedding, you will make sure your new husband drinks many glasses of wine. After he takes you for the first time and after he falls asleep, you will cut your finger with a knife. You must be sure the cut on your finger is very slight but deep enough so as to bring forth the blood you will need to rub between your legs and into the opening of your womanhood. Do not allow your girl to clean you before your husband sees the blood between your legs. This will make him believe he was the first to enter your body."

"I do not want this marriage with a man other than Karleto. And even though I do not hold the same feelings for him as I did before he murdered Renna, I am happy that I will have a man to give my child a name."

"Your gypsy lover thought only of his own wants. He cared nothing for you or what shame this would bring down on us."

"I know your words are true, Mother, but I loved him."

"We must never speak of this again. This will be our secret," Johanna told her, placing a quick kiss on her forehead. "I will pray that the child you bear will not have the look of the gypsy but instead have

the soft look of his mother."

Suddenly, all of Jillianna's worries seemed to be over as she turned onto her side and allowed her tired body the rest it needed to get her through the night that was to come.

* * *

"I done told you, I didn't shoot any priest! You got no reason to hold me in this fuckin' jail!" Danny Roberts yelled out his frustration.

"Settle down, Roberts," Jack told him.

"Settle down my ass! You ain't the one fixin' to be put in a Goddamn cage! I can't stand bein' locked up! I got that phobia shit!"

"It's called bein' claustrophobic. You should have thought of that before you tangled with your ole roommate Gaston and shot a priest."

"I told you, Goddamn it! I never shot no priest. And if I hadn't been fightin' with Gaston, I wouldn't need to be talkin' to a priest in the first place!"

"All right, Roberts, why don't you just come clean and tell us why you thought you had to hold a gun on a priest. You would be surprised what I might believe."

Reaching a foot to the chair on the other side of the table, Danny pulled the chair forward to prop his feet up. "Okay, you think you have heard all there is to hear in this fucked up world? Try this on for size."

Both Jack and Donavan pulled out a cigarette and, after offering over one to Danny, lit up.

"As you know, I got into a fight with my ex-roommate Gaston. In the course of the fight, the prick bit me. Okay, now here's where shit gets strange. I was visitin' my girlfriend, and after we got it on, she noticed this mark on my neck, which just happened to be where Gaston bit me. She said it was the mark of a rougarou."

"Wait a minute. You're tellin' us you had a mark on your neck big enough for her to see, but you couldn't?"

"Not just anyone can see it," he murmured, giving Jack a sheepish grin. "My girl has what the people in her family call The Sight. It's…" His voice trailed off as Jack waved his explanation away.

"Yeah, we know what it is, Roberts. Just get on with the story."

Jack glanced over at Donavan, who shook his head, warning him to stop interrupting.

"Then what happened?" Donavan asked.

"She said since I hadn't changed yet, there was still time for me to get help."

"She said you could get help to keep from changin' into a rougarou? How the fuck did she figure that?" Jack leaned forward in his chair.

"She said she knew a woman who could reverse the curse. That's how I happened to be with Jillianna, the woman whose house me and my girlfriend was at when you arrested me."

"What is she, a voodoo woman?" Jack laughed.

"No, she ain't a voodoo woman. She's a vampire."

"Oh, Christ! And I thought I'd heard it all." Jack threw up his hands in frustration. "A vampire."

"Yes, Goddamn it, a vampire. I didn't believe it at first either. But by the time we was through doin' what she said needed to be done, I believed all she had to say. And if you need further proof, check out my fuckin' throat." He turned his face to the side.

"Damn, that's quite a burn. How'd you get it?"

"That's where that bitch Gaston bit me." His voice rose in his excitement. "My girl Leadah had to boil out the spot with Holy Water then hold a crucifix against it to literally burn away the sign."

"What sign?"

"The upside-down cross, the sign of the rougarou."

As the three of them sat in the interrogation room at the jail, Danny told them all that had happened from the first time he laid eyes on Jillianna until they arrested him at her home earlier.

"And you swear you didn't shoot the priest. Even though you and the man Father Austin said shot him were dressed exactly the same."

"I don't know anything about that, but you can check out the gun I was carryin'. I still had it on me when you two arrested me. The cops took it when I was brought in here."

"Go see what kind of gun it was, Jack. We can compare the two with what Austin was shot with. Also, check to see what the powder residue tests showed. The results of the two should tell us if this man needs to be held any longer," Donavan said.

"Check it out, man. You'll find I'm tellin' you the truth. But until you get the word, do you think I could stay here 'stead of bein' locked in the cell?"

"Yeah, we could do that. I'll have one of the uniforms sit in here with you. It shouldn't take long to find out what we need to know," Donavan told him as Jack left to find out if Robert's story would hold up.

* * *

After the wedding ceremony that tied her to a man who would dictate her every move for the rest of her life, Jillianna tried to settle into her new life. Although her new husband was a very good-looking man with his dark red hair and beard and dark blue eyes, he was not the man who still claimed her heart.

"Your body grows large with my child." Rolan seated himself in one of the chairs placed on the well-manicured grounds. "My father is well pleased that your body accepted my seed so quickly."

Jillianna simply nodded, preferring to keep him happy instead of having to listen to his anger if something did not please him.

"Soon, this child of your womb will be making his entrance into the world. You have done well, my wife," he told her, touching her hand gently in a rare moment of giving. "Not every man gets to enjoy both beauty and fertility in his woman."

"I am happy that I please you, Rolan. You are a man who holds great respect among your people. I would never wish to bring shame on the Hindel name."

"Yes." He lifted the glass of wine to his lips, enjoying the sweetness flowing over his tongue as he looked out over the vast grounds lined with large trees and abundant flower gardens.

Jillianna allowed his hand to linger on hers a moment longer before getting to her feet. Pulling her long gown of green and white to the side, she took a few steps away from him.

Rolan watched her, trying to understand why she always moved away when he tried to be close to her. Perhaps her youth was to blame. A more mature woman wise in the feelings between a man and a woman would be more understanding of his carnal needs.

Jillianna turned now, gazing at him as he stood staring out over his lands, taking in his wide shoulders hidden beneath his long-sleeved shirt of white and his lean hips beneath his dark pants. She told herself she should be happy she was married to a man so near her own age who was both pleasing of face and body instead of a man many years her senior who thought only of his own pleasures when he came to her in their marriage bed.

"Do you feel any love in your heart for me, Jillianna?"

The question, coming as it did with no warning, made her breath catch in her throat. "Why would you ask me this question, Rolan? You and I have married, so I can bring forth sons to carry on your bloodline. I doubt your heart holds anymore love for me than mine does for you," she answered him honestly.

"Is there someone who does hold your heart, Jillianna?"

The way he stood with his back turned to her, and his asking if she loved another was beginning to make her feel very uneasy. "Why are you asking me such questions, Rolan? Do you doubt you are the only man I have ever known?"

He turned to look at her. "No, I saw the blood staining your legs and the bed sheets the morning after our wedding telling me I was the first man to enter your body." He walked toward her and, taking her firmly by the shoulders, forced her to look at him. "I was told a strange story by one of my guards on the morning your father's men went to retrieve the body of your servant girl from the band of gypsies."

Jillianna could feel her fear growing until she was afraid it would strangle her as she waited for him to continue.

"He told me of an old woman in the camp who was screaming out her rage over the death of a young man in the band." He waited for her to respond to his words, and when she remained quiet, looking up at him, he continued. "According to him, this woman said a very strange thing. She claimed the young man was killed because he dared to father a child with the daughter of Nicholas Romanitti."

It took every bit of her strength to remain staring up at him.

"Do you have any idea why she would say something like that? Given you are the only daughter of Nicholas Romanitti, she had to be talking about you."

"I would say this woman is someone prone to fantasy. My father had threatened to have them beaten if they continue to camp on Romanitti land, but still, they would come. He should have followed through with his threat. Perhaps then they would stay away."

For a long moment, he remained quietly looking at her, then releasing her, he whispered, "Even though I saw with my own eyes the proof of your virtue staining the marriage bed, if it turns out this child does not have the look of a Hindel, I will end its life myself."

At that moment, the child inside her womb jumped as if it feared for its very life. Jillianna rubbed a comforting hand over her extended stomach, trying to let the child know she would not let any harm come to the small life growing within her body.

"You will have no reason to doubt this child of your loins, my husband. You are a man of wealth and respect. You should not allow the ravings of a crazy woman to bring fear into your heart."

With a deep sigh, he pulled her tight against his chest. "Your words bring peace to my heart, my wife. I should never have doubted you."

Jillianna wrapped her arms around his trim waist while her unborn child kicked and fought to be released from the confines of her body.

That night, her screams of labor could be heard by all who dwelled on the estate.

While his wife labored to bring the son he needed into the world, Rolan, along with his father Rafael, celebrated the upcoming birth with *glass after glass of strong ale.*

When at last her screams had quieted, telling them the birth was at long last successful, father and son walked into Jillianna's bedchamber to welcome the newest Hindel.

Reclining back amongst the plump pillows, Jillianna was just reaching for her newborn when her husband and his father walked into her room.

"We have come to welcome the heir to the Hindel estate upon his first breath," Rafael Hindel told her.

Jillianna held the child against her chest in an effort to protect the newborn from harm.

"Your lady has given you a beautiful baby daughter, sire. Would you like to hold her?"

"I would like to be the first to hold my granddaughter," Rafael spoke up, moving to stand beside the bed.

Jillianna pulled the child away for a brief moment to look into her innocent face, her stricken eyes noting the child's black hair, dark skin, and black eyes that looked so much like the man who had sired her.

"Give me the child, Jillianna," Rafael told her, holding out his arms.

Knowing she had no choice, she handed him her child, breathing a prayer for her safety.

The look passing between the two men as they gazed upon this child she had just brought into the world was not missed by Jillianna or the nursemaid who stood watching.

"You have not been truthful about when this child was conceived or by whom, Jillianna," her husband said, his anger at having been fooled by a mere woman barely under control.

"Do you wish to tell us the name of the one who sired this child?" Rafael snatched the babe from his son's hands to hold her upside down by her tiny heels.

The baby cried out her anger at being held in such a way.

"Don't hurt her!" Jillianna screamed, jumping up and coming across the floor. "Give her to me!" She tried to lift the child from Rafael's large hands, only to be slapped with brutal force across the floor.

The nursemaid, seeing what was going on, ran to help the young mother. *"You need to get back in bed, my lady,"* she told her, helping her to her feet.

"Girl! Come here!" Rolan demanded.

When the young nursemaid stood before him, Rolan handed the child into her outstretched arms. *"Take her to her mother. I will return later for her. You are not to speak of this child's birth to anyone."*

"No, my lord." She dropped a slight curtsey before moving away.

Jillianna pulled the babe against her, raining kisses over her dark head and whispering words of love.

Alone now, she motioned the young girl to come closer. *"You must help us to leave here. If we don't get away, my child will be killed."*

"My lady, I dare not help you. If I do, they will kill me too," she cried, wringing her hands.

"They cannot allow you to live now that you know the wife of Rolan Hindel has given birth to a child not sired by him."

"Please do not say this. It cannot be true. I would not tell what has gone on here. I would give them my word."

"Your life is in as much danger as mine and my child's are. How can we get away from here safely?"

The frightened girl stood, trying to decide what she should do. Then, her mind made up, she came forward. *"I will take you to my grandmother. We are of the same blood as the one who fathered your child."*

"Will she protect my child? This is all I ask."

The girl simply nodded, unwilling to tell her all she could expect.

Knowing their only chance to get away was to leave right then, they did not even take any extra clothing.

Jillianna tried to keep up with the younger girl, but her body was weak from the long and rigorous labor she had suffered through earlier that day.

"We must hurry. Soon the sun will be gone, and the night will call forth the ones who seek to destroy us."

"I can't go any further." Jillianna dropped to the ground, her energy completely gone. *"You must take my child and get her to safety. I don't care what happens to me. I only care about my child."*

The girl came kneeling down to take the child Jillianna held out to her. "Are you sure, my lady? You know if I take her, you will never see her again."

"I know." Her breath caught in her throat, making her words come forth in a mere whisper. "Let me look upon her sweet face one more time, then you must go."

Pulling the blanket away from the small face, Jillianna placed a gentle kiss on her daughter's soft cheek. "Go."

With the child wrapped safely in her arms, the young girl ran as though all the demons of hell were out to trap her.

Jillianna leaned back against a large tree to wait. She knew he would come after her. The Hindel name was too important to allow it to be tarnished by a mere woman. Rolan Hindel could not allow her to escape her punishment.

While she waited, her tired body took advantage of the quiet to glean some much needed rest.

When she woke much later, the full moon cast a glow out over the surrounding area, showing the faces of many people gathered around her. Startled completely awake now, she tried to get to her feet, but her legs were numb from her being in the same position too long, and she fell back.

"So good of you to wait for us, Jillianna." Rolan came forward. "Now we can begin the ceremony."

Jillianna laughed aloud as he yanked her to her feet. "You cannot hurt me now, Rolan. For the only one I care about is far away from here where you and your family cannot touch her."

"We will continue to search for her, and perhaps someday we will find her. In the meantime, we have you, my wife. And for now, you are enough."

Gathering up her strength, she glared at him, letting him know she was not afraid of him.

"You have thought to make me a fool before those who depend on me and my family. The Hindel name goes back many centuries. We are a proud people, and we will allow no one to defile our good name. You knew the child you carried in your womb was not of my seed, yet when I came to you and told you what I had been told, you did not come forth

with the truth."

"Did you expect me to admit the child I carried was not yours? You would have slain us both on the spot. Are my words not true, my husband?"

"You are never to call me your husband again. To me, you are worth less than the filthy women who walk the streets for their living. And yes, I would have slit the throat of you and your bastard child had she survived."

"And now you will slit only my throat. Is this what you are telling me I can expect?" She did not back up but instead moved closer to him.

"No, Jillianna, I have something else in mind for you." He watched her to get her reaction to his words. When she failed to cower before him, he pushed harder. "Jillianna, have you ever heard any stories concerning the Hindel name and the dark secrets we are said to keep hidden?"

"No, I have heard no secrets. I do not listen to idle gossip, Rolan," she told him, wondering where he was going with his silly chatter and wishing he would get what he was going to do to her over with so she would not have to listen to him anymore.

Rolan tried to keep his anger at her indifference to him at bay but knew he was losing the battle. "Do you know what a rougarou is?"

"No."

"It is a French word for werewolf."

"All right, and what does this have to do with me?"

"It has nothing to do with you, Jillianna. However, it has everything to do with me and my family."

"Are you telling me that you and the rest of those in your family are werewolves?"

"Yes, I am."

Instead of the complete terror and backing away he expected, she showed him only laughter.

His anger at her indifference to him and all he was telling her boiled over into a killing rage. He reached out, grabbing her by her shoulders to roughly shake her back and forth. "You cheap, filthy cow!

You think to laugh at me? I am Rolan Hindel! You will show me the respect I deserve!"

"And if I don't, what are you going to do? Turn me into a werewolf?" Her disgust for the man standing before her was so strong it gave her courage she otherwise would not have had.

"No, Jillianna, as I told you, I have something far more sinister in mind for you. You are not good enough to be a werewolf, or as we prefer to call ourselves, a rougarou."

"Okay, so what do I get to be, one of the filthy women who walks the streets to earn her living?"

"Do you actually think I would allow you to be a woman who sleeps with complete strangers? As much as I hate to admit it, you are still my wife! People who live here know you carry the name of Hindel!" His hand lashed out, slapping her across the face and knocking her to her knees.

She lay on the ground, trying not to let him see her pain. After a moment, she got to her feet to stand in front of him. "You can beat me all you want, Rolan, but it does not change what I am. I am your wife, and as you said, everyone knows this. They will talk, Rolan. They will see how you treat me, and they will lose respect for you as a man they can count on. And the child I carried? Did she disappear, or did she simply die? It does not matter what you tell those who look up to you."

She knew she was inviting his wrath by standing up to him, but she could not seem to stop herself.

Without a word, he turned and, holding out his hand, motioned someone to come forth.

The woman who walked forward was beautiful with her long auburn hair falling like a soft onyx jewel down her slender back. Her dark green eyes lit up as they fell on Jillianna. Her glittering green gown fit her body like a second skin, and the scooped-out neckline showed off her full, firm breasts to perfection. She stopped a mere arm's length away, and holding out her hand, she beckoned Jillianna to come forward.

Jillianna felt as though she no longer had control of her movements as she reached out and took the hand being offered to her.

"My name is Madalina," she said, her soft and sultry voice flowing into the quiet.

"This is my wife, Jillianna," Rolan told her.

"She is very beautiful, and now she will be able to remain beautiful." Madalina drew near and, taking Jillianna into her arms, pulled her close.

Jillianna could smell the bath oils the other woman had rubbed into her skin, wafting up to her. The smell was that of jasmine blossoms mixed with the oils of the almond. The scent was very pleasing to her senses.

"From this night on, Jillianna, your life will never be the same. As the years go by, I want you to remember you brought this on yourself by trying to make a fool of a man who wished only to love and protect you throughout your years on this earth."

At his words, Jillianna turned to look at him. "How quickly your love turns to hate, my husband. I choose to welcome your hatred rather than allow you to put your hands on an innocent child who was fathered by a man I will never stop loving."

Rolan lunged, trying to get his hands around the throat of the woman who dared speak such words to him in front of his family.

"No, Rolan!" Madalina pulled Jillianna to the side out of his reach. "You promised this woman to me. I will not allow you to go back on your word."

Jillianna tried to control her breathing and her fear as Madalina stood her before her.

"I will ask you this one time, Jillianna. If you can protect the life of the child you bore from the seed of a man other than your husband, what will you give in return for this protection?"

"How can you offer this protection when you have no idea where my child is or even who she is with?"

"Your child is at this moment with your nursemaid as she travels to another land far away where she will be safe and not have to fear a life worse than death at the hand of Rolan Hindel and his family."

Jillianna could only stare at the woman speaking to her without words for the others to hear as Madalina allowed her thoughts to drift through Jillianna's mind. "For this, I am willing to give up my life."

Madalina pulled Jillianna once more into her arms, and before

Jillianna knew what was happening, Madalina sank her teeth into Jillianna's throat to taste at last the sweet, red blood she so desired.

The scream began low in her belly and traveled upward until it reached the air around them.

Madalina drew back, her mouth covered in blood. "Now you will have life eternal, my beautiful Jillianna. Now no one will be able to hurt you. The creatures of the night will be your protectors, and you will remain young and beautiful for centuries."

With Jillianna held close to her side, she guided them from the clearing, talking with her all the while so as to keep her from seeing what was happening with Rolan and his family as they began to change into the creatures they had traded their souls to become...

Pushing the memories from her mind, Jillianna drank the last of her wine and, getting to her feet, walked across the room to the opened glass doors, allowing the sweet smell of rain to surround her. Leaving the sanctuary of her home, she walked out into the night.

CHAPTER NINETEEN

"What did you find out about the gun and tests?" Donavan asked, turning in his chair as Jack walked through the door of his office.

"Negative on the powder residue, and he's tellin' the truth 'bout not havin' the gun that shot the priest. Whole different caliber."

"Now the question is, who the hell did shoot Austin?"

"Maybe our lady vampire knows. Can't hurt to go ask her."

"I think we can forget that one. We already have our hands full with fighting rougarous. I don't care to start tangling with fucking vampires."

"Our little parish is startin' to attract some real undesirables."

"Which reminds me, did you ever hear back about that check you were going to do on Gaston?"

"He's clean. Guess he just came off as a lowlife that might be wanted for shit in another state."

"Either that or Seelah is starting to rub off on you, and you picked up that he was going to turn into a worse piece of shit," Donavan laughed. When Jack remained quiet, Donavan nudged his leg. "What is it? You look too serious."

"When you mentioned Gaston bein' a lowlife, I

remembered the phone call I got about Donny."

"I felt as though someone had punched me in the gut when you called me and told me that."

"I still feel like someone kicked me in the gut."

"I feel a lot better though, knowin' Chandra's got our backs."

"It just blows my mind how spirits and ghosts can come and go on this earth without any of us even bein' aware of them. I mean, fuck, Rolan Hindel, or Lybbert Hindel, or whatever the hell he called himself, was a piece of shit when he was alive, and now we find out he's just as big a prick dead!"

Donavan laughed. "I have a friend named Dave who has a saying that I sure can identify with. He believes if you're an asshole in life, you're an asshole in death."

"Yeah, for real. Holy jumpin' up Christ! I just had a thought!"

"And that thought is?" Donavan looked at him, waiting to hear what he had to share.

"If the spirit of Rolan Hindel's able to possess someone to make a threat as he did on Donny's life, why the hell couldn't he possess someone to commit attempted murder? Granted, he only shot the priest in the shoulder when he could have aimed for the heart, but who knows what can happen in the long run? A person sufferin' from a gunshot wound can go into shock and bring on a heart attack, and if that happens, the one who shot him is lookin' at murder one."

"Except no one is gonna be able to pin a murder one charge on a spirit. And the question still remains, why did he dress up like Danny Roberts and try and get him arrested for attempted murder?"

"Still think we don't need to go back and talk with the lady vampire? It's a whole new day; maybe she can give us some new information."

Donavan didn't say a word, just got to his feet, pulled open the desk drawer, and stuffed his loaded Forty-four in his holster to walk out the door.

"Guess that's an affirmative."

* * *

Baxter ushered them into the house and after they were seated, left to inform his mistress she had company.

"This is one helluva house. I guess bein' a vampire has its perks," Jack snickered, getting to his feet to walk around the room.

"Maybe you should come sit down. Our hostess might not like having strangers roaming around her house."

"I ain't hurtin' nothin'. I just wanna check out these cool oil paintin's. The way these people are dressed, these portraits have to go back at least a hundred years or more. Wonder if she has any rougarou portraits?"

"No, I don't. But then why would I?" Jillianna asked, walking into the room.

"Oh hell, I don't know," Jack laughed, turning to look at her. "Accordin' to our buddy Danny Roberts, you're a vampire, so I just thought one bloodsucker probably knows the other bloodsuckers in town."

"Do you believe everything you hear, Detective Olivier'?" Her voice was smooth and warm as it flowed over him.

"I don't believe everything, but I do believe Roberts. I think he was set up to take the blame for a shootin' he didn't commit."

"And why do you think that is, Detective?"

"I don't know, Jillianna, but I bet you do."

"Madam...what is your last name?" Donavan entered into the conversation.

She turned, smiling. "My name is Romanitti. However, you can call me Jillianna."

Donavan took out his pad and pen. "Romanitti?"

"R-O-M-A-N-I-T-T-I." Jillianna sat herself in the chair closest to the hearth. "If you wish to research the name, you will find it is a Romanian name. My father's name was Nicholas Romanitti."

"So tell me, Jillianna, how long have you been a vampire?" Jack took the chair next to hers.

"Over two centuries now," she told him.

"It doesn't bother you to admit you are a vampire?" Donavan spoke up.

"No." She grinned over at him. "How many people do you think will believe you if you tell them you have been sitting with a vampire, having a conversation?"

"After what this parish has been through with our fight against the Hindels and their family of rougarous? More than you may imagine, Jillianna," Donavan told her.

"I'd venture to guess you ain't always lived in Saint Anthony Parish. 'Cause if you had, the department would have been gettin' calls 'bout missin' females. Am I right?" Jack stared straight into her blue-green eyes.

Rising to her feet, she walked over to the small portable bar set up in the corner of the vast living room. "I am going to have a glass of wine. You gentlemen can have whatever you like to drink."

Donavan was the first to speak up. "I'll have a Vodka Sour. Jack?" He turned to get his take on drinking on the job with a possible killer.

"I'll have the same. I want you to know, though, we don't make it a habit of drinking on the job, but I guess havin' just one can't hurt none."

She mixed the drinks, handed the detectives theirs, and with her glass of wine in hand, sat back down in her chair. "I have lived in this parish for almost six months now. Before then, I lived in New Orleans. Where, by the way, many of the Hindels live."

"Are you a close friend of the Hindels?" Donavan watched her to get her reaction to such a leading question.

"No." Her voice took on a harsh tone.

Jack took a sip of his drink, watching her over the rim of the glass. "Why the change in tone all of a sudden? You sound as though it would give you great pleasure to cut out their hearts with a dull blade."

"It isn't important for me to go into what I feel. Suffice it to say you will not find I have any involvement with missing females."

"I think you would have been singin' a different tune if we hadn't removed the young black girl who was in your home the night we arrested Danny Roberts." Jack glanced up at Donavan, who nodded for him to continue. "I think Roberts and his girl brought her here for you. Am I right?"

The look flowing over Jack as Jillianna leaned forward in her chair had Jack reaching for his .38.

"Do you see a dick hanging between my legs, Detective Olivier´?"

"Not at the moment, but I hear it doesn't take long to strap one on."

Jillianna was all the way on her feet now and moving toward Jack in her anger.

Jack pulled his .38 the rest of the way out of the back of his belt and cocked the hammer. "I won't hesitate to blow your fuckin' head off your shoulders if you come any closer. I don't intend to become a bloodsuckin' rougarou or a bloodsuckin' vampire, so you best calm down and think `bout what the hell you intend to do."

Jillianna stopped a mere arm's length away. "You will not disrespect me in my own home, detective. I gave you no reason to take that tone with me."

"Do you deny you had plans for the young black girl we removed from your home?" Donavan stepped forward, his own weapon drawn.

"Sometimes I need companionship," Jillianna lied. "Is that a crime?"

"I've never heard of anyone hirin' a hooker for the night just for companionship, but I guess we can go with it."

"This is probably a dumb question." Donavan moved a little closer. "But, have you ever tried to stop being a vampire?

I mean…you helped Roberts to stop being a rougarou. Maybe there's something out there that can reverse your being a vampire."

Jillianna sat back down, knowing she would only make matters worse if she continued with her anger. "There is nothing to be done about what I am," she whispered, the sadness surrounding her words bearing witness to the fruitless situation. "I have been this way for close to two centuries."

"Get the fuck outta here!" Jack breathed. Then he nodded as he recalled how long Chandra had been alive. "Okay, let's say what you're tellin' us is true, then you have to admit that in all those years, you have had to have taken the life of at least a couple thousand girls so you can go on livin'."

Jillianna glared at him. "Where are you getting your information about the life of a vampire?"

"The same place I *was* getting it on the life of a rougarou… folklore." Jack grinned, then became serious. "Do you deny you need the blood of another livin' creature to live?"

"I disagree with your thinking that in *present-day*, I need to kill someone to get what I need. There are people for a price who will let me take their blood. It is called feeding."

"And just how do you go about this…feedin'?"

She stood up from her chair to hold out her hand. "If you give me your glasses, I will freshen up your drinks. I think it goes without saying we need a little relaxing of the nerves at the moment."

Jack was the first to comply.

Jillianna sat her glass of wine down on the small table beside her chair before walking back to the bar. Opening a small drawer, she withdrew a folded leather bag then returned to her chair.

Donavan and Jack walked over to stand in front of her, watching as she opened the bag to show a thin, razor-sharp dagger along with a small bottle of rubbing alcohol and some cotton balls.

"Observe, detectives. These are the tools of the new age

vampire."

"So…where do you suck from?" Jack leaned forward.

"Wherever I make a cut. Usually on the wrist. I am always careful not to take too much, thus leaving my donor weak and unable to function." She smiled up at them.

"Haven't you heard of the AIDS epidemic?" Donavan asked her in all seriousness.

"The diseases of this plane do not frighten me. Remember, my body has had centuries in which to build up an immunity."

Jack sat back down in his chair, finding the conversation all of a sudden very interesting. Rolling his filled glass back and forth in his hands, he told her, "This reminds me of a conversation I had one day when Donavan and I were at the Hindel mansion talkin' with Jonathan Hindel."

"That had to be interesting," she quipped.

"Scary as hell was more like it. I had asked him how a person becomes a rougarou, and he proceeded to enlighten me on all the ins and outs, includin' freely givin' the soul to the dark side."

"He was telling you the truth, Jack…uh…do you mind if I call you Jack?"

"No, not at all, my wife calls me Jack all the time," he told her, grinning as he held up his hand to show her his ring.

"Touché." She bowed her head slightly.

"Jillianna, I think we need to come to the reason we are here," Donavan spoke up, leaning forward in his chair. "We've been told by a very good source that the one who tried to kill Father Austin wasn't Danny Roberts but a spirit by the name of Rolan Hindel. Do you know anything about this?"

For a long moment, she remained silent, thinking about his question and how telling the truth could affect her. "First, can I ask how you came by this information?"

"We were told by someone named Chandra," Jack told her.

"Ah yes, our beautiful voodoo priestess Chandra. How I

miss her," Jillianna whispered.

"I guess bein' a vampire and livin' in the parish, you would have to know the local voodoo queen," Jack said, taking a sip of his drink.

"Yes."

"So, is our info correct on another Hindel killer?"

"Yes, it is, Jack. Chandra does not lie."

"Okay, now can you tell me how since he is a spirit, he was able to hold and fire a gun?"

"He possessed someone who *is* able to hold and fire a gun."

"And that someone is?" Donavan asked.

"His name is Gaston. He is the man Lawrence Hindel is enamored with at the present time."

"Must be Gaston's way of getting back at Danny for the fight they had," Donavan said, starting to get to his feet.

"You would do well to stay here for a while, Donavan. There are those who wish to do you harm, and they await your departure from my home," Jillianna told him.

Jack turned, looking out the floor-to-ceiling window directly behind him. "I don't see anyone out there, `course they could be hidin' behind the trees."

"They are hiding. They are the kind who come from behind, not to your face. I have no respect for the weak, and anyone who cannot look you in the eye and say what they have to say is weak."

Donavan nodded in agreement, his respect for her growing. "Since you put it that way, I guess we will be your houseguests for a while longer. Besides, you were saying it was Rolan Hindel who possessed Gaston's body so he could hold a gun and shoot the priest?"

"Yes."

"We have had run-ins with our friend Rolan before. In fact, it's thanks to Donavan and me that ole Rolan is no longer a livin', breathin' contributor to our fair society."

"Rolan is not one you will want to anger. He holds a grudge

for a long time. I should know; he has held a grudge against me for almost two centuries now."

"Are you serious?" Jack breathed the words. "What the hell'd you do, cheat on him?"

"Yes, but I cheated on him before we were married." She then proceeded to tell them all that had happened to her all those many years ago, including how she herself became a vampire.

Jack came forward, stooped down in front of her, and in a surprising move, took her small hand in his. "I'm sorry you lost your child like that, Jillianna. That had to break your heart."

Both she and Donavan looked at him, amazed at the feelings sounding in his voice for a complete stranger.

"I have a young son, and if anything were to happen to him, I don't think I would want to go on livin'."

Jillianna continued to allow her hand to rest in his, feeling oddly comforted by his energy.

"Someone a few nights ago called and threatened my son's life."

Her heart jumped in her chest. "What were the exact words this person said to you, and what was the sex of the person calling?"

"A man called saying 'the master awaits the blood of the pure. Very soon, your son will feed this need. Donavan Matthew Olivier''s days are numbered.'"

"Rolan Hindel is your caller, Jack. He always speaks in an archaic manner. I think he has more anger against you than from you simply being the cause of his death. I find it odd he would want to harm your son since your son could not have caused him pain."

"He's going after Donny because it was Donny's soul Jonathan Hindel was trying to push aside so he could enter his body to be reborn back onto this earth," Donavan spoke up.

"That would be enough for Rolan to seek revenge. Too, I am sure Lawrence has a lot to do with this vendetta against your son since Jonathan was his father." Jillianna pulled her hand from the warmth of Jack's touch, feeling uneasy all of a sudden.

"That's it!" Jack stood up, slamming a fist into his hand. "He's a dead son-of-a-bitch! I already warned Lawrence and the rest of those creepy fuckers if they messed with our families, they might as well lay down `cause they're as good as dead."

"Jack, you and Donavan do not want to go up against the Hindels alone." Jillianna got to her feet. "They have been on this earth for hundreds of years. Their strength is very powerful. And…they would like nothing more than to destroy all of you."

"I'm not about to stand by and let someone threaten the safety of my son."

"Our children can touch a place in our hearts no one else can," she told him, brushing his dark hair back from his forehead. At that moment, a picture drifted into her mind of her standing in a gypsy camp with the man she loved while the child of his seed grew in her womb. "Jack, I know you are anxious to confront the Hindels, but would you come sit down for a few moments? There is something I would like to try."

"I'm not into a bunch of voodoo shit, and I already told you, I'm married, so I'm not into any other kinda shit either." He turned, headed to the door, then stopped as a feeling of complete relaxation flowed over him.

"I am not going to harm him, Donavan, but there is something I need to know, and it won't take long for me to find it out."

"All right, and since it looks like we don't have a choice, I'll just sit over here and observe. I warn you, though, Jack Olivier´ is not only my partner, he is also my best friend."

"I can already see that, Donavan. And if what I suspect *is* true, he and his family will also become close friends of mine."

CHAPTER TWENTY

"Why the hell are we standin' outside when we need to be inside where our prey is?" Gaston asked, the taste for the rich, sweet blood he coveted so much tormenting him.

"Jillianna would not take kindly to our satisfying our hunger on the bodies of her houseguests," Lawrence said.

"Then we will just add her to the feast too."

"You need to calm down, my love." Lawrence pulled Gaston over to him. "If you keep on like this, you will change before it is time, and then we will have to leave before we have had our fill of the two we covet most."

"I would rather be in the home of Jack Olivier´. His child must be made to pay for cheating your father out of returning to this plane, Lawrence." Rolan breathed the words, the hatred in his voice cutting like a shard of ice into the silence while his spirit emerged beside them. "His father is seated at this moment inside the home of Jillianna. We can take the boy and be gone while his mother sleeps the sleep of the ignorant."

"Do you wish to dwell in darkness for all eternity, Rolan? Or would you prefer to come and go on this plane as you wish?" Lawrence stepped forward. "You did not tell us the names of the ones inside this house. Jack Olivier´ and Donavan Hays have the protection of the Light. My father and grandfather dwell in the darkness of the other side all because they tried to do harm to the detectives and their families."

"We still have a vendetta to settle, Lawrence. I cannot and will not forget the shame Jillianna brought to me and my family. The two of you need to remember what they did to Jonathan and Rafael. There has to be a way to destroy *them* without destroying ourselves."

"That time is not here yet. When we can be sure the destruction of our enemies will not cause us the destruction of our own souls, then we will move forward with all the rightful vengeance allotted to the children of Satan. But for now, we will leave this place."

As they made their way from the estate of Jillianna Romanitti, Gaston felt something all too familiar about the house and the surrounding area. "Standing on these grounds reminds me of a strange dream I had the other night," Gaston spoke up.

Wanting to divert Gaston away from his growing hunger, Lawrence walked with him, speaking quietly so as not to be overheard by Rolan. "What was the dream about?" He draped an arm over the other man's shoulders. "Try and be as detailed as possible as it will help you in determining what the dream meant."

"It was odd. I dreamed I was standing right here on this estate. I was alone even though I could feel the presence of someone else standing right beside me. Then the next thing I remember is standing in the back of a large church. I could feel the wind on my face, and I was dressed in a pair of jeans and a sweatshirt with a hood. The hood was pulled over my head and covered part of my face. I had the feeling I was trying to hide who I was for some reason."

"Then what happened?"

"Someone came out of the back door of the church and started walking toward me. I lifted my hand that was holding a gun, and I shot him. I think he was a priest."

Lawrence stopped walking to gaze at him. "That *is* odd. Do you remember what led up to you having such a strange dream?"

"The only thing I remember before that is going to sleep beside you, and then the next thing I knew, I was dressed and standing in the back of a church shooting a priest. It was so real, not all over the place like most dreams."

"Don't let it worry you. We all have strange dreams now and then."

"Yeah, except the pullover I was wearin' in the dream was on the floor beside the bed when I woke up. I don't own a sweatshirt with a hood, Lawrence."

Lawrence was beginning to feel very uneasy but refused to admit it. "That does seem strange. It was probably just a very realistic dream. Put it out of your mind."

"But how do you account for the hooded sweatshirt on the floor?"

"I don't know, maybe you were sleepwalking and pulled something out of the closet that you forgot you had."

"Maybe, but for some reason, I don't think so."

A guttural laugh nearby made them both turn.

"You were not dreaming, Gaston. What you saw as you stood behind the church was real. You did shoot the priest as he was walking to the rectory."

Gaston looked to the ghost of Rolan Hindel then over to the shocked face of Lawrence. "What the hell are you sayin'? I didn't shoot anyone!"

"I hate to disagree, but you did. I needed a body to hold the gun, so I possessed *your* body. Sorry." He laughed, letting them know he wasn't sorry at all for what he did.

"You dared to involve Gaston in a murder?"

"The priest still lives. I only wounded him. I wanted to teach Jillianna a lesson."

"Why, all of a sudden, would you wish to teach *her* a lesson?"

"She intervened in Danny Roberts becoming a rougarou. She helped him remove the curse before his first change."

Gaston could feel his anger rise at having his former

roommate involved in a shooting through no fault of his own. "You don't care about people, do you?"

Rolan turned his dark eyes, gazing at the one who dared to reprove him. "You would do well to think about your words before you speak them, Gaston. And to your questioning of my feelings for others, the answer is…no."

"You must not take offense, Rolan," Lawrence told him, moving forward. "Gaston is not used to dealing with spirits and has been touched by the dark side but a short time."

"Then if he wishes to remain on this plane, you would do well to teach him respect for his betters."

Lawrence felt Gaston move, and he immediately tightened the arm he had around his shoulder.

"Gaston meant no disrespect, Rolan. He knows you have been on this plane a lot longer than he has, and from now on, he will afford you the respect you deserve."

Rolan, pleased that Lawrence had put Gaston in his place, simply nodded. "Jillianna would do well to show the same respect. She knows better than to undo a curse once it has been placed on a mortal."

"My grandfather told me the story of what happened between you and Jillianna all those many years ago. Women are not to be trusted. They are nothing but users."

"Women have but one purpose in life, and that is to satisfy a man. That and bring forth the sons he needs to keep his name from dying."

"From the bits and pieces I'm pickin' up here, sounds like you got cuckolded," Gaston told him, not bothering to keep the laughter from his voice.

The scream of anger erupting from Rolan's throat filled the space around them.

Lawrence quickly spun Gaston behind him, throwing out his arms. "He did not mean his words, Rolan! You and I are both Hindels. You know the love I hold in my heart for this man!"

Bone-chilling coldness numbed him as Rolan's vaporous spirit filled every cell in Lawrence's body.

Gaston stepped back, feeling all of a sudden that something was terribly wrong. "Lawrence, speak to me. Tell me what is happening."

"Lawrence can no longer hear you, Gaston. I am in control now. You should not have made light of my earlier life. A man's sons should always come from his seed alone. When a woman tries to trick her husband into believing the child who wears his name is of his blood when that child was sired by another, she deserves to suffer throughout eternity."

Gaston could only nod, his fear of the moment so strong no words could come forth.

"Jillianna is an evil woman. She will live the life of a vampire the rest of her days on this plane."

At last, Gaston found his voice; trying to call on as much strength as possible, he faced the one threatening his life and the life of the man he loved. "I regret my words to you earlier, Rolan. I shouldn't have said what I did. I'm sorry. I'm askin' you not to hurt Lawrence. Like he said, you two are family, and I always heard families are supposed to stand together. So what can I do to make it up to you?"

"Kill the son of Jack Olivier´."

* * *

After Jack was seated in the chair he had vacated, Jillianna pulled another chair over in front of him.

"Jack, I want you to listen to my voice. You are in no danger and will do only that which you would ordinarily do. You are in control of your body and your mind. I am simply going to take you back in time to a past life."

When she knew Jack to be completely relaxed, she began to turn back the years until she came to the time posing a question in her mind.

"I want you to look down your body and tell me the color of your skin and describe the clothing you are wearing."

His voice was slow, as though speaking in a dream. "My skin is dark brown, and I am dressed in a pair of black pants of a rough fabric, a white shirt with full sleeves, and a long swath of brightly colored material is tied around my waist. I think I'm a fuckin' gypsy."

Jillianna tried to hold back her laughter at Jack's description of himself. "Now, I want you to tell me your name."

"My name is Karleto. And yes, I am a gypsy."

"I want you to look around and see your surroundings. Are you in a house, or are you outside?"

"I am outside. My black horse is tied to a tree branch."

"Are you fat or slim?"

"Karleto would never be grasime!" He jumped to his feet to stand straight before her. "Karleto is frumos and a great dragoste for beautiful women!"

Jillianna cast a quick glance to where Donavan sat, enjoying the scene he was witnessing. "He says he was never fat. He says he is handsome with a great love for beautiful women. Karleto, was there ever one woman whose love captured your heart?" she asked.

A look of pure love moved into his dark eyes, and without warning, tears dampened his face. "Her name was Jillianna Romanitti." His eyes closed as he whispered her name. "She was the only woman to capture the heart of Karleto. In her body grew my precious copil. Our fiica would have grown to be a beautiful woman."

By now, hot tears were covering her own face, and for a moment, she grew silent, unable to continue asking Jack the questions she needed to know. "Yes, our baby daughter would have grown to be a beautiful woman."

"Why is my body covered in blood?" His voice rose in terror, and he clutched his heart.

The fear in his voice shook Jillianna from her memories of that long ago time. She knew it was time to bring Jack out of his regression.

With a gentle hand, she eased him back into the chair then slowly led him back through the many years until he reached the present. Before bringing him all the way back, she told him the past life he had been living would still be fresh in his mind, but without fear or sadness.

Jack rubbed a hand over his face then looked around. "Is all this I just saw and talked about for real?"

"Yes, Jack. The past life you went back to and relived was all very real."

"Then that means you and me" — he pointed first to her then himself — "had a thing goin' back then."

Donavan rose to his feet to walk over to the portable bar and fix them all a much-needed drink. When he handed them around, Jack threw his down his throat and held out his glass for a refill.

Donavan glanced at Jillianna, who smiled. "I think he has earned a couple of drinks. And he is not the only one. Thank you, Donavan."

"Now, I will tell you all about what happened back two centuries that involved both of us. I will say this before I tell you everything. You are the only man I have ever loved, Jack."

"You mean the only man you ever loved was Karleto. I am not Karleto." He sat down in the chair closest to hers.

"In a real sense, you are both...Jack and Karleto. You see, when it comes our time to leave this plane, it is only our body that dies. Our soul lives on in lifetime after lifetime. The soul is never erased. Unless you are regressed into a past life, it is doubtful you will remember those lives or the time you spend on the other side, but you still lived them."

"I'm starting to notice a pattern here, partner. You seem to have a knack for attracting women of the older persuasion. First Chandra, and now we find out you were also the love of Jillianna in a past life. And both of these women were or are almost two centuries old," Donavan told him.

For the first time, Jack laughed. "I don't know why you're surprised. Women of all ages find *me* appealing. Once you've had the best, you don't settle for the rest."

"We can add egotistical in there too." Donavan joined him

in making light of the situation.

Jillianna got up from her chair and walked over to the window. "It looks as though the ones who would like to do you both harm have moved on for the night," she told them, trying to keep her eyes from lingering on Jack, who resembled Karleto so much she was finding it difficult not to put him in a trance and ravish him on the spot.

She was so wrapped up in keeping her needs at bay, she failed to pick up on the dark energy standing in the room watching and listening, the burning rage he had carried while searching tirelessly for the one who had shamed him, building, for now, he knew the soul he had been searching for and the one who had caused his own blood to be banished to the dark side were one and the same.

CHAPTER TWENTY-ONE

Seelah moved back and forth with a crying Donny snuggled close. She had already rubbed the medication over his swollen gums to numb his pain.

"My brave young man, I know it hurts. When those old teeth start coming through, it isn't pleasant. I wish there was something more Mama could do, but I don't know what it would be," she crooned to him as he fell into another fit of crying.

"There is something I can do, Seelah. Carry him over to the twin bed," Chandra told her.

Doing as Chandra asked, Seelah moved out of the way to give Chandra a place to sit beside her son, turning a deaf ear to his howls of pain mixed now with anger at being away from the safe arms of his mother.

"Chandra would never hurt you, Donny," Chandra whispered in his ear, her voice low and hypnotic.

Donny stopped struggling when she rubbed a hand over his back. With the utmost, gentleness she smiled as he looked up at her, his large dark eyes glazed with the light sleep she had placed him in.

"I rubbed his gums with the medication I bought from the pharmacy, but he is cutting three teeth at the same time."

Chandra simply nodded as she rubbed the palms of her hands together then reached out, placing one hand behind

Donny's head. The other hand was placed on his forehead. Closing her eyes, she repeated in her mind the words to deaden the child's pain and heal his sore gums.

Donny's eyes were closed, and he turned onto his side, smiling as his mother pulled the coverlet up over him.

"He will sleep through the night," Chandra said, then told Seelah the herbs she would need to gather to keep Donny free of pain while going through the teething process. She reached out, running a hand over Donny's dark head and immediately tuned into the danger suddenly surrounding him.

"Chandra, what is it? What's wrong?" Seelah leaned forward at the look of distress covering Chandra's beautiful face.

"Donny is in extreme danger. Someone is coming forth to do him great harm," she whispered.

"Yes, remember I told you about the phone call Jack received telling him Donny's days are numbered? You couldn't see who it was. Since nothing has come of the threat, I was in hopes someone could have been playing a cruel prank."

"No, it was not an idle threat, and the threat is going to be fulfilled very soon. One thing we can be sure of, a Hindel has something to do with this threat. They hate all of you and will stop at nothing to see you destroyed. I wish I could break through this block!" She was getting angry.

Seelah motioned her away from Donny, who was sleeping peacefully in his crib now. "How is it you are blocked? You are the strongest voodoo priestess I have ever known. I know the dark side is nowhere near as strong as The Holy Light of Home."

"The dark side will never be as powerful as the Light. However, since I turned my soul back to our Holy Father, I am not as in tune with the dark side. My soul is surrounded at all times with the Holy Light. No darkness can penetrate this wall. But since I keep my energy attuned to all of you, I will know when there is danger, and right now, Donny is in extreme danger."

Car doors slammed out front, telling her the men were home.

"I want Jack and Donavan to hear about this," she said,

turning and heading out of the room.

Jack caught her as soon as he moved through the door. "God, woman, I needed to feel you in my arms." He pulled her tight against his chest and simply held her, inhaling her scent into his mind.

Seelah felt his fear and knew something bad had happened. Glancing over at Donavan, she tried to read *his* energy rather than wait for Jack to calm down enough to read his, but he was already off in search of Barbara and Jenny.

"Darling, I can tell something has happened. Come sit down and tell me what is going on." She walked with him over to the couch, trying to keep her own worry over Donny out of her voice so as not to upset him more than he already was.

"I just went through some really heavy shit. The most important of which, I now know who threatened Donny's life and why."

"Oh my God, Jack. Chandra is here, and she said it would have to be a Hindel involved since she is being blocked from seeing who it is. She came to help Donny get over his pain from cutting so many teeth at one time, and when she patted him to soothe him, she picked up on the danger he is in."

"You don't know the half of it. I just finished talking with Jillianna Romanitti, the vampire I told you about, and after we talked for a while, she asked if she could do a regression on me to take me back into another life."

"That had to be interesting," Seelah said, the jealousy she was feeling over another woman's interest in her husband creeping into her voice. "What brought that about?"

"She had the feeling that we had a thing goin' in a past life."

The jealousy dug in a little deeper.

"Yeah." He tousled her dark hair at seeing the look of anger stealing into her black eyes. "She was convinced I'm the man she was in love with and the man who fathered her daughter."

"Were you?" The anger she was feeling was no longer

being hidden.

"Yeah, believe it or not, I was. After going back into the past in my life as a handsome and suave Gypsy lover, I was the man she thought I was. Not only that, she had already been promised to a man by the name of Rolan Hindel who was not too pleased when she gave birth to a baby with all the dark looks of a gypsy 'stead of the lighter skin and red hair and beard of a Hindel."

"Rolan Hindel was Jenny's teacher, right?"

"*Was* is the keyword since he's one more piece of vermin crawlin' 'round in the spirit world."

"I want to hear more about you and the vampire. You said you and she had a child together in a past life?"

Jack explained what all had happened in his regression and filled in what Jillianna had told him about Rolan Hindel.

"I now know that it was Rolan Hindel who possessed a living, breathing man to make the threat against Donny. The son-of-a-bitch!"

"And he did this because this woman Jillianna Romanitti gave birth to a child fathered by you when she was married to Rolan Hindel."

"You make it sound like I went out and had an affair behind your back, Seelah. This all happened in a past life. I sure as hell can't be held responsible for something that happened in another lifetime."

Without warning, Seelah reached out, pulling Jack into her arms and covering his full mouth with hers. When at last she drew back to stare at him, she whispered, "You are my man, and I don't care if it *was* a past life. I don't want to know about another woman enjoying what is mine."

"Trust me, baby, no other woman will get even a taste of what belongs to you alone."

"I don't mean to interrupt, but I agree on who it is threatening Donny's life," Chandra spoke into the silence.

Without thinking, Seelah pulled away. "Chandra is here with us, Jack."

"Ah, another woman from the past of Jack is heard from," Donavan said in passing.

Jack shot a sour look his way as Donavan walked past his chair on his way to the kitchen.

"All right, now that we are all in agreement on who it is that is out to get my son, what the hell are we plannin' on doin' 'bout it?"

"Rolan Hindel is a very evil man," Chandra told them, making herself visible to all in the room. "He will come from behind when he comes to destroy Donny. He will possess a living soul and dictate that person's movements."

"How do we stop him, Chandra?" Seelah whispered, one hand clutching her throat in her fear.

"I think the one he will choose to do his bidding is the same one he used to shoot the priest. We will keep our senses attuned to his energy, Seelah," Chandra told her.

"I have a question," Jack spoke up.

"What is it, Jack?" Chandra turned to him, her eyes drinking in the sight of him, then glanced away as she caught the look Seelah was aiming her way.

"If, say…we happen to shoot the one who is possessed… oh hell, let's just cut to the chase and say…if we shoot Gaston while he's possessed by Rolan Hindel, what will that do to Hindel's soul?"

"It will do nothing to Rolan Hindel's soul. He will simply leave Gaston's body. But when Hindel's soul vacates the body he is possessing, we can have White Spirits waiting to take his evil soul to the dark side just as we have done with other of the Hindels."

Jack's face broke out in a wide grin. "That'll work. Let's go get Gaston and figure out an excuse to shoot him."

"You can't shoot Gaston just because we suspect he is the one who is going to do Hindel's bidding. Besides, if Gaston is the one chosen to harm Donny, then we want to keep an eye on him. If we kill him before Hindel possesses his body, Hindel will simply choose someone else. Maybe someone we don't know about."

"You married a smart lady, Jack. Consider yourself a fortunate man," Donavan told him, seating himself on the couch across the room and pulling Barb and Jenny down on each side of him. "I think we both lucked out when it comes to getting a smart wife."

Both Seelah and Barb winked at one another. Chandra turned her face, trying to keep the memories of another time at bay.

Trying to turn the conversation to something other than Donny and the danger stalking him, Donavan brought up a subject he had forgotten about until now.

"Did you ever hear if we got the results back on the chunk of meat and fat the crab was chewin' on at the Hindel estate awhile back?"

"Why in the world would you send something off that a crab had been chewin' on, Dad?" Jenny spoke up.

"It's not important, baby girl. Just police business." Donavan tried to divert her attention away from the grisly subject.

"I'm not a kid, you know. If a crab was chewing on something from the Hindel estate, it was probably part of a dead body."

"All right, Jenny." Her mother broke into the conversation. "You don't need to get into police business. And I don't care to hear about it."

"The results came back negative for human remains. Probably some poor dog got too close to a gator sunnin' itself on the banks," Jack said.

"Well, hell, we never got anything on the perp that we can be sure was out there when he met his end. Nothing on the rougarou we did in, and never any DNA on Christina either."

"Gators don't leave much evidence."

"Chandra, were you ever able to talk with Christina about what happened to her?"

"Christina is still in a twilight sleep that all entities are placed in when they have suffered a death they are unable to face."

"Thanks, Chandra. I guess when she is able to tell what happened to her, you will let us know what she said," Jack said, a smile broadening his mouth as he looked at her.

"I am going to go check on Donny. I don't like leaving him alone now that we know what danger he is in. Chandra," —she reached out a hand to her— "would you like to accompany me?"

"Good idea, sweetheart. I'm sure she would get a heads up if anyone was here, though."

Alone in the room with just a sleeping Donny and Chandra, Seelah turned to her. "I want you to tell me the truth, Chandra. Is Jack's and my son going to be safe from the evil that is coming for him?"

"The man that wishes ill on your son is a very evil man. He not only wants to destroy Donny because he is the son of the man who shamed him in a past life, but Donny is also the one who was supposed to be pushed aside to allow the rebirth of Jonathan Hindel."

"I wish we could destroy all the Hindels. Then they could no longer spread their hate and destruction on the innocent."

"The Hindels are very clannish, and their souls are steeped in centuries of darkness. They will not be easy to destroy."

Seelah stood and, with slow steps, walked over to stand, looking at Donny as he slept, peacefully unaware of the fear and disquiet he was causing his mother.

Chandra placed a comforting hand on Seelah's shoulder. "You must trust in The Holy Ones to see you through at this time in your life. I will do all I can to protect this child of your heart."

Jack walked into the room and, without a word, pulled Seelah into his arms. "No one is going to hurt our son, Seelah. If I have to kill every Hindel on this earth to see to it, I will."

With a deep sob, she turned, throwing her slender arms around his neck, crying against his chest.

Chandra stood back, watching the man she still loved

trying his best to comfort his wife and the mother of his son. "I will do what I can to see this child stays safe."

At that moment, an entity dressed in a long, white robe entered the room to stand at the head of Donny's crib. In silence, her wings folded to lay flat against her slender back.

"You have only to call out, and you will be surrounded with White Entities from the Holy Light of Home," Chandra told the one whose beauty and radiance could be equaled only by those touched by the hand of The Holy Father.

CHAPTER TWENTY-TWO

Lawrence and Gaston huddled together in the darkness outside the home of Jack Olivier´, trying to keep the deep fear they were both feeling from forcing them to turn and leave.

"I can't kill a baby," Gaston whispered into the night. "It's one thing to feed off someone who's evil, but an innocent kid, `specially a baby, don't deserve to be touched by darkness."

"I can see it is going to take you longer than most to give over your feelings to the dark side. This child is the cause of my father Jonathan and my grandfather Rafael not being here on this plane where they deserve to be." He drew back, anger at Gaston's refusal to be brought around creeping into his voice.

Gaston's anger matched that of Lawrence. "And for this... not steppin' aside to make room for someone who has been crawlin' the earth for hundreds of years, this little kid has to be taken out! You are startin' to really piss me off, Lawrence!"

Lawrence stepped back, unable to believe he was hearing such words of anger from the man he loved and who he thought loved him.

"You need to think about what you are saying here, Gaston. The son of Jack Olivier´ must be killed." Lawrence put both his hands on the sides of Gaston's face, gazing into his eyes for a long moment. "His life is the price called for to appease the spirit of Rolan Hindel. Do you want *me* to be destroyed? Because if you don't do what you promised Rolan you would do, I am the one he will come after."

"'Stead of destroyin' the kid, why don't we destroy Rolan Hindel instead? It shouldn't be that difficult since he's already dead."

"How do you purpose to carry out this destruction of my soul, Gaston?" A deep and rasping voice erupted into the surrounding darkness.

Gaston jumped, then turned. "I really don't know how I'm gonna go about it, Rolan. But I do know I'm not gonna waste a kid just because you got cuckolded in a life that should have been over and done with centuries ago." Gaston knew he was tempting his own fate at the hands of someone he could not hope to best, but he couldn't seem to stop his words or the anger he was feeling at the moment.

"Gaston!" Lawrence moved to stand in front of him. "Think about what you are saying. I was of the opinion you hold the same love in your heart for me as I feel for you. Have I been wrong about you?"

"It looks as though we have both been made to look the fool, Lawrence." Rolan laughed before slipping unhindered into Gaston's body.

Lawrence cried out, rushing forward to pull Gaston into his arms, then drew back as the man he loved stood, a blank stare covering his face.

"Don't do this, Rolan. Enter my body for anything you need done." Lawrence grabbed Gaston and shook him, trying to get a response. "Gaston has only been touched by the dark side for a short time. Let him get used to his new life before asking him to do your bidding."

"Your words fall on one who cannot hear you, Lawrence. My name is Gaston, and it is through my own choosing I dare to destroy the mind of the reincarnated soul of Karleto Besnika by ending the life of his only son."

Lawrence watched Gaston as the words fell from his lips. He knew the feelings in the words belonged to Rolan, but since he was the only one to know this, he also knew that the one who would get the blame for the murder of Jack Olivier''s son would be Gaston.

"For the first time in your life, you have no one to come forward to decide your actions, Lawrence. What are you going to do to stop this murder from happening and your lover from taking the blame?"

Without a word, Lawrence turned, moving up the walk, and without stopping to think about what he was doing, pushed his finger on the doorbell.

It was a surprised Donavan Hays who answered the door.

"Lawrence? What the hell are you doing here?" Donavan spread his feet to deny the man standing on the doorstep entrance into the house.

"Who is it, Donavan?" Jack asked, coming forward.

Upon seeing Lawrence Hindel, Jack rushed forward.

"What the bloody hell are you doin' comin' to my house, you cocky son-of-a-bitch?"

"I have come to warn you that your son is in grave danger."

Donavan threw out his hands, stopping Jack from getting out the door.

"Let's give Mr. Hindel a chance to tell us what he is talking about, Jack. It had to take a lot of nerve for him to come here like this."

"I warn you, Lawrence, you better not be comin' here to harm my son because if you are, you're as good as dead," Jack told him, stepping to the side.

Chandra watched her son walk into the house, and she smiled, enjoying the sight of him.

"We have an unexpected visitor," Jack told those present in the room. "Lawrence Hindel came here, he says, to warn us about the danger Donny is in."

Seelah moved forward, throwing out her hand and directing Lawrence to be seated in the chair closest to the couch. "You can sit here, Mr. Hindel, while you tell us what you have come here to share with us."

"And don't try feedin' us a bunch of bullshit about how you've had a change of heart and want to turn your soul over to the Lord either because I'd believe that about as fast as I'd believe you ain't a fuckin' rougarou."

"Jack, I know how imperative it is for you to be in control of a conversation, but now isn't the time. Now is the time for you to shut up and listen to what I have to tell you and your wife about your son and the extreme danger he is in," Lawrence told him, surprised at how calm he felt in the midst of his worry over Gaston.

"Jack." Seelah held up her hand. "Perhaps we need to hear what Mr. Hindel has to say. After all, Donny's welfare is at stake here, and if there is something we can learn that will protect him more, I want to know what that something is."

"Donny's life is in danger because of a man named Rolan Hindel." Lawrence then proceeded to tell them about the life Rolan had had with Jillianna and how that life included Jack. When he was finished, he sat back in the chair to await their disbelief and was surprised when it was not forthcoming.

"We know all about Jillianna Romanitti and her lover Karleto Besnika, who, by the way, was me in a past life," Jack spoke up.

"Do you also know that Jillianna is a vampire?" Lawrence told him, watching him closely for his reaction.

"Oh yeah, she told us all about how she became a vampire after ol' Rolan found out she was carryin' her lover Karleto's baby."

"Then you will not find it surprising when I tell you this is part of the reason your son's life is in danger, and the one who waits to end his life is at this moment standing outside your house in possession of the body of my friend Gaston."

Donavan and Jack jumped to their feet at the same time and, drawing their guns, headed into the hallway. Throwing open the front door, they bounded down the steps toward the body of a man lying in their yard.

"Is he alive, Donavan?" Jack asked, standing beside the body as Donavan checked for a pulse.

"No, he's gone," Donavan said, getting to his feet. "I'll be anxious to hear what the medical examiner has to say for the cause of death."

"Oh my God, no!" Lawrence cried, dropping to the ground to take Gaston into his arms. "What happened to him?"

"We don't know. None of us heard a shot or a scream, so we just don't know, Lawrence." Donavan pulled his cell phone from his shirt pocket. "This is Hays. I need the coroner at Olivier's house for a white male. Cause of death unknown."

The scene going on at their feet was a little more than either of the detectives could stomach.

Lawrence had Gaston gathered in his arms, rocking him back and forth as though he held an injured child in need of comfort instead of a grown man whose body was already growing cold to the touch.

Between the two, they lifted Lawrence to his feet.

"I think you'll be more comfortable seated in one of the chairs on the patio, Lawrence. I've already called the coroner. He should be here directly," Donavan told him, standing in front of him and blocking his view of Gaston's body.

"Rolan is an evil son-of-a-bitch. He didn't need to kill Gaston." He withdrew a handkerchief from his pants pocket and blew his nose. "I can't believe he carries the blood of a Hindel. He had to know how much this would hurt me. He did it because I warned you about what was about to happen to your son, Jack."

Jack came forward and, holding out his hand, placed it on Lawrence's shoulder. "I appreciate your coming forward with this information too, Lawrence. I know we've had our differences, but today you helped save the life of my son, and I can tell you now, I won't forget you for it."

Chandra moved out onto the patio to stand beside Lawrence's chair. Wanting to ease the pain her son was suffering, she leaned down and wrapped Lawrence in her arms.

JUDITH ANN MCDOWELL

Lawrence felt her touch, and the warmth was so comforting he remained still, allowing himself to be made over. Her essence brought back a memory of all those years ago when he was a child and being held in the arms of the beautiful lady who always took him into her arms and sang to him.

Donavan and Jack looked over at Lawrence and caught the look of pure love covering his face.

"Lawrence, can you see the one who is holding you in her arms?" Seelah asked him, coming forward.

"No," he whispered, "but I remember her touch from when I was a small child."

Seelah walked the rest of the way over to the patio and, pulling a chair alongside the one Lawrence was sitting in, sat down close to him.

"Have you ever heard the name Chandra mentioned while you have lived at the Hindel estate?"

"Vaguely. My grandfather Rafael said she was a ghost. But he never said a lot about her."

Seelah looked at Chandra, waiting for her to say it was all right to tell Lawrence who held him so lovingly in her arms. When Chandra nodded her head, Seelah took hold of one of Lawrence's hands to hold in her own.

"Chandra was not only a great and beautiful voodoo priestess in the parish. She was also your mother."

Lawrence looked at her and then got to his feet. "My mother was a black woman of the bayou?"

"Yes, Lawrence, Chandra was a black woman."

"Why would my father, Jonathan Hindel, who could have had the love of any woman in the parish, waste his time on a black woman?"

All eyes except those of Lawrence turned to look at Chandra as she drew back, the sheer pain covering her face easy to see.

Jack was the first to step forward. "I'll be a son-of-a-bitch if you ain't pissin' me off just as bad as you always have. I appreciate your comin' forward and warnin' us 'bout Donny, but I'm not gonna stand here and allow you to make slurs on a woman I once loved with all my heart."

At Jack's words, Chandra twined her arms around her slender body just as she always had when she was upset.

The extreme pain slicing him unmercifully over the death of Gaston and the killing rage he was feeling for Rolan merged into an all-out show of thoughtless hostility. "Choosing to wallow in filth with a sow is one thing, but to have one for your mother is more than the human mind can tolerate!"

"You evil motherfucker!" Jack swung, catching Lawrence on the chin and knocking him to the ground. "Chandra was more of a lady than you have ever known, and she sure as hell didn't deserve to give birth to a worthless piece of shit like you!"

For the first time in his life, Lawrence refused to stay down. Bounding to his feet, he ran headlong right into Jack's stomach, sending him reeling backwards, his head just missing hitting the patio floor.

In an instant, Jack was on his feet and coming forward. "Come on, you gender-flawed little ass stretcher! You've had this comin' for a long time!" Jack grabbed him by the front of his shirt to plow a fist into his mouth.

Chandra screamed, running toward them. "You will stop! Now! You will stop!"

Jack turned, catching Lawrence around his skinny waist to drop him on the ground. "Enough, Lawrence. We're upsetting your mother, and she doesn't deserve this."

"Fuck that cow! As far as I am concerned, I have no mother!" He stood, dusting the dirt from his clothes.

"Then you won't be upset to hear you have no father either. At least not the one you thought you had, you miserable little piece of puke!"

Chandra stood, both hands pressed to her mouth, but she did nothing to stop Jack from doing what she knew he was going to do.

"What are you trying to say, Olivier'? You know my father

was Jonathan Hindel. Are you and Hays still jealous over the fact that the Hindel name is the most respected and feared name in the parish? Still, after all these many years?"

"I hate to burst your bubble there, sunny buck, but your daddy was not Jonathan Hindel. Fact is, you ain't even a Hindel."

"I didn't think I hit you that hard, Jack, but I must have since it is apparent you have lost your senses. You and everyone in this parish knows I am the son of Jonathan Hindel and the grandson of Rafael Hindel." Lawrence stood up straight as though to remind them of his importance in the community.

"You may need to sit down, Lawrence, as this news is going to rock you," Donavan told him.

Suddenly, Lawrence began to feel uneasy, but he refused to sit down. "Tell me what you need to, Hays. I won't believe what you have to say, but go ahead and say it anyway."

"It is true that your mother was a voodoo priestess named Chandra, and yes, she was a black woman. In fact, she was a beautiful black woman."

"I don't have all day, Hays, so if you would get to the point, I would appreciate it."

"All right, you little bastard, since you are in such an all-fired fuckin' hurry, we'll just cut to the chase. Your daddy wasn't the all-powerful parish eatin' piece of shit Jonathan Hindel. Your daddy was Quigley. You know, the little groundskeeper and the Hindel go-for?"

"You are a liar!" Lawrence lunged only to be leg swept to the ground by a snickering Jack.

"Yep, it's true. Your daddy was ole Quigly, the sweat stinkin', snot slurpin', 'fraid of his own shadow Quigly. Pretty funny, don't you think? And all this time, the Hindels paraded you around like a little puppy dog because they thought you were one of them."

"I don't believe you." But this time, his anger was quieted by the fear filling up every cell in his body.

"Looks like ole Rolan wasn't the only Hindel to get cuckolded, Jack laughed.

Without warning, a scream of such violence erupted into the surrounding silence that all there turned to see who was in such pain. What they saw made them doubt their own eyes.

Lawrence was being lifted high into the air then slammed into the ground with killing force. As they watched, his limbs were ripped one by one from his body.

"What the fuck?" Jack ran forward as blood flew into the air to land on all present.

"Oh my God, Donavan, do something. He is being ripped apart before our very eyes!" Barbara screamed.

"I can't even see what is attacking him! His body is being destroyed while all we can do is watch," Donavan said.

At last, the attack ended with Lawrence's bloody body lying in a heap on the ground.

"Chandra, I am so sorry you had to witness all of this with your own son," Seelah told her, rushing forward to surround her in her outstretched arms.

"Rolan Hindel is the one who has done this. And now he will pay for what he has done." Raising her arms, she called out to the Holy Angels, who answered her call immediately to surround a black mist moving on the ground beside Lawrence's body.

Once more, screams could be heard echoing into the surrounding area until, at last, all was silent, and the black mist no longer crawled along the ground.

"Oh my God! Donny!" Seelah called out as both she and Jack ran into the house.

At the sight meeting their eyes, they both stopped.

A woman dressed in a shimmering robe of white held Donny in her arms with her soft white wings moving steadily and silently behind her. She looked over at them and, with her arms outstretched, held out their son.

Almost afraid to breathe, Jack lifted his son from her arms and, as he did, felt Donny move and open his eyes.

They both began showering him with kisses and hugs

until Chandra stepped forward to take him from their arms.

"Please indulge me for a brief moment while I hold his small body close to my heart."

Donny looked up and smiled at the beautiful lady holding him close. Then without a word, she handed him back into the arms of his father before leaving them alone.

"I feel so terrible that Chandra had to witness what happened to Lawrence since he was her only son," Seelah whispered as she walked beside Jack outside to find Donavan and Barbara and Jenny.

Donny was in a receiving mode as he patiently allowed everyone to kiss and make over him, including Lugar and Brandy and all their newborn babies.

"I guess we already know what the autopsy will show on Gaston. From the looks of Lawrence, we can already guess Hindel just destroyed every organ in Gaston's body. It will be one for the medical books, that's for damn sure," Donavan said.

"Once again, the Hindel mansion is empty. But for how long?"

"That's right, for how long? Who knows, maybe Jillianna Romanitti will fulfill your prophecy of years back and be the vampire to move in."

As dusk darkened, a lone woman stood off in the shadows watching the happy couple as they held their child safely in their arms and her heart cried out for her own child lost to her these many years. As she stood watching, she fought to quiet her growing passion for her gypsy lover, whom she now knew lived within the body of Jack Olivier´.

See where it all began...

About the Author

Judith Ann McDowell is a novelist with four finished books. When not working on a manuscript, Judith, along with her husband like to travel to different cities such as New Orleans to talk with people about voodoo and to talk with those who have experienced firsthand, true hauntings.

Judith is the mother of five grown sons Guy and David and Rhett and Nick and William Michael, and lives in the Pacific Northwest with her husband Darrell and their two Pekingese Chi and Tai and three cats Isis and Lacy and Keefer.
Judith is at present working on her next novel.